THE
PHOENIX
LAW

Writing as C.E. Murphy

The Strongbox Chronicles
The Cardinal Rule * The Firebird Deception * The Phoenix Law

The Walker Papers
Urban Shaman * Winter Moon * Thunderbird Falls * Coyote
Dreams * Walking Dead * Demon Hunts * Spirit Dances
Raven Calls * No Dominion * Mountain Echoes * Shaman Rises

The Old Races Universe
Heart of Stone * House of Cards * Hands of Flame
Baba Yaga's Daughter * Year of Miracles * Kiss of Angels

The Inheritors' Cycle
The Queen's Bastard * The Pretender's Crown

The Worldwalker Duology
Truthseeker * Wayfinder

The Guildmaster Saga
Seamaster * Stonemaster * Skymaster (forthcoming)

Take A Chance
Roses in Amber
Redeemer
Magic & Manners
Atlantis Fallen
Bewitching Benedict
Stone's Throe

writing as Catie Murphy

The Dublin Driver Mysteries
Dead in Dublin * Death on the Green (forthcoming)

& writing as Murphy Lawless

Gladiator Shifters
Gladiator Bear * Gladiator Cheetah * Gladiator Hawk (forthcoming)

Raven Heart

*This is for Deirdre, who always **has** been able to beat me at arm wrestling...*

MKP

THE PHOENIX LAW

ISBN-13: 978-1-61317-176-9

Cover Artist: Indigo Chick Design

THE
PHOENIX
LAW

C.E. MURPHY

a miz kit production

*O*utnumbered, five to one. A single woman, standing against the enemy. Alisha darted to the left, as much to gauge her opponents' actions as to gain ground. Every single one was female, unusual in Alisha's experience. A decade as a CIA agent had shown her facets of the world that most people never saw, and most of those who did, seemed to be men. Maybe it was the thrill of the chase, or maybe it was just that the underworld she'd seen so much of was often violent, and men were more conditioned to seek out danger.

Not today, though. Today it was just the girls. There was a certain exhilaration to pitting herself against them, even if she couldn't use her own secret weapon, an upper body strength that outstripped many women and men alike.

But if she didn't get her mind in the game, she was going to lose.

The group around her surged and closed in, as if they'd heard Alisha reprimanding herself. A broad-shouldered redhead smashed into her path. Alisha cursed, stomach muscles clenching as she slid in mud and grass, searching for escape.

A quick glance around told her it was fruitless. The only way out was retreat, and under the circumstances, Alisha couldn't bring herself to do it. Voices bellowed in the background, carried on the wind. Preternatural hearing, the honed result of years of combat training, allowed her to pick out individuals from the cacophony, but the words and phrases all came down to the same directive: *go!*

A possible escape route opened up, two of her opponents spreading out farther than was wise. Alisha feinted, crashing her shoulder into another woman's. A whistle blew somewhere in the distance, a shrill reminder that time was growing short.

Mud spattered between her fingers and a yell sounded above her, muscular calves and muddy shins suddenly everywhere as she slid *through* the redhead's legs. Cleated shoes danced around her, instinct preventing their wearers from stepping on her, and then Alisha was on her feet again, one giant mud slick from chin to knees. It was a matter of yards now, less than ten. Eight. Five. *My life,* came the familiar thought, *is a series of countdowns.*

A projectile flew at her head. She whipped toward it, pushing all the strength in her body downward so she could shove herself skyward. She met the thing flying at her, smashed her forehead against it, drove it toward the earth. Through brightness brought on by the impact she saw surprise, then dismay, cross her last opponent's face.

The ball hit the ground with a wet splat. Alisha dropped after it, making a roundhouse kick that smashed its checkered surface past the goalie and into the net behind her.

*C*heers and laughter and good-natured grumbling erupted everywhere. The goalie climbed to her feet, shins covered in muck from hitting the ground a moment too late to stop the ball. "Anybody ever mention you've got a competitive streak, Ali? Good game."

"Thanks." Alisha wiped a muddy arm across her face, compounding the damage done by the soccer ball, then put a hand up for help in rising. Three hands closed around her wrist and forearm and she was pulled to her feet as if she weighed nothing. "You played a good game, too."

"Ali doesn't think it's a game." The big redhead— Valerie—came up beside her, panting for air as she grinned. "It's all life and death with you, isn't it?"

Alisha tilted her head toward the goalie. "Like Kendra said, I've got a competitive streak. Keeps me young. Or maybe that's the yoga. I get confused." She winked, then turned as a trio of boys broke away from a crowd of children at the edge of the field. They rushed over, wrapping themselves around her ribs, hips and thighs, whatever could be reached according to their height. Alisha laughed, ruffling muddy hands through their hair. "Your mother's going to kill me. You guys are filthy now."

"That was cool, Aunt Alisha! You totally kicked their butts!" The oldest boy looked up with sheer adoration in his eyes.

"I had a little help, Timothy. I wasn't the only one on the field." Alisha nodded toward her teammates, reaching over Timothy's head to shake hands with the losing scrimmage team.

"You were *best*," he said with an eight-year-old's loyalty.

"You're just saying that because you hope I'll take you out for ice cream once we're all cleaned up."

"Yeah yeah yeah yeah yeah!" The clamor rose up as though the trio were boy-shaped bells, jumping up and down around her. Alisha laughed and swatted at Timothy's backside.

"Go get yourselves washed up, and promise not to tell your mother I've ruined your dinners, okay? Timothy, hold Jeremy's hand, all right? I don't want him near the cars without someone big keeping an eye on him."

They charged across the field, Timothy's longer legs giving him enough of a lead that he all but dragged the other two in his wake. Alisha grinned broadly, watching them go.

"Surprised you don't have any of your own, the way you dote on those three." Valerie knocked her shoulder against Alisha's. "You could take mine, if you wanted."

Alisha glanced toward twin girls as red-headed as their mother, part of the playgroup Alisha's nephews had broken away from. Identically dressed, they were involved in an intense game of tag which clearly involved confusing the other players as to which of them was It. Alisha turned back to Valerie, grinning.

"The best part is being able to give them back to their mother when they're all wound up like that and I'm tired." She winked, offering a hand. "Great game. It was a blast."

Val huffed a laugh and shook hands. "Nice dodge. Yeah, good game. Will you and Teresa be at the barbecue on Saturday?"

"Along with the whole crew," Alisha said with a nod.

Val waved her off and Alisha strode across the field, watching her nephews slide in the mud and spatter themselves further. A bubble of contentedness rose in her, turning to a smile. A young adulthood spent as a spy had given her many things—adventure, excitement, thrills—but contentment hadn't been a part of it. It had been a high-stakes job, and the feeling associated with doing it well had been pride and—Alisha twisted her mouth in a wry smile—arrogance. Arrogance, if that's what being better than the bad guys was. That life had been satisfying, too, in its way, but it had been anything but relaxing. After ten months away from that world, moments of missing it could be soothed by a good soccer game.

Maybe if she kept telling herself that, she'd start to believe it.

"Aunt *Ali*, hurry *up!*"

Alisha smiled, glad for the distraction. She'd thought the old habit of her own nickname was something that would fade away as she took part in a civilian life, but even now the dichotomy struck her. To everyone—her family, her friends, even her former coworkers, who should have known better—she was Ali. *Ali* was a soft-sounding name that went with her heart-shaped features and the tawny curls that were slowly growing back after the mission-gone-wrong that had made her to walk away from the Agency. But Alisha thought of herself as *Leesh*, a combat-trained tough girl who out-thought and out-fought her opponents in the field. *Ali* was useful, superficially frothy, the sort of delicate-seeming woman that a man might hold open a door for, but *Leesh* would kick the door down and never look back. That was the woman Alisha MacAleer knew herself to be, and the facade that everyone else seemed to see never failed to surprise her.

Almost everyone else. One man had hit on her secret nickname, seeing her the way Alisha saw herself. His insight into her psyche had been part of Frank Reichart's appeal, though the long legs and dark, knowing gaze hadn't hurt either. Nor had the untamed intelligence mercenary lifestyle he'd chosen, for that matter. He had been everything Alisha'd thought she'd wanted—until their engagement had ended with him putting a bullet in her shoulder.

Alisha twisted a smile at herself and picked up her pace. "I'm old!" she yelled at her nephew. "Old people are slow!"

"You're not *old*," Timothy shouted in disgust. "*Mom* is old!"

Alisha burst out laughing as she caught up with the muddy trio. "Your mom's younger than I am, Timmy."

Consternation wrinkled the boy's forehead. "My name's Timothy, Aunt Ali, I told you that a zillion times."

"A zillion, huh? Were you counting?"

"Yeah." Timothy looked affronted and Alisha lifted her hands in acquiescence, grinning.

"Okay. Timothy. Help your brothers wash up, Timothy." Alisha pulled the steel cord on the soccer field's outdoor shower, sending a deluge of sun-warm water over her outstretched hands. It hit the ground already brown with mud, and she splashed the cooling liquid over her face, removing the worst of her game scars.

Scars. A funny choice of words. She pushed water through her hair, letting her fingers come to rest at the base of her neck for just an instant. A tiny block of real scar tissue lay there, remnant of one of her narrowest escapes. Testament, too, to having trusted the wrong man, though it hadn't been Reichart that time. It'd been a man she'd wanted badly to trust, in part because he shared none of Reichart's bad-boy appeal. *Brandon Parker.*

Alisha barely let herself form the name even in her thoughts, aware that her lips wanted to shape the words and make them real. Parker—it was safer to think of him as Parker, removing herself from the intimacy of first names—had been her CIA handler's son, and the semi-willing agent of a deadly secret organization that had nearly cost Alisha her life more than once. Alisha breathed a laugh and turned the water off. Her unutterably lousy taste in men would be the stuff of enormous teasing at her sister's hands, if Alisha dared share the stories with her family.

"Everybody clean? Jer, you have a mud stripe on your nose." Alisha reached across the shower to wipe her hand over the littlest boy's nose, leaving a wet streak of muddy water there. He squealed indignantly, rubbing his face, and glowered up at her with such enthusiasm that she laughed and scooped him up. "Mean ol'Aunt Ali. Should I buy ice cream to make up for it?"

"Chess," he said with satisfaction. Alisha turned him upside down, ignoring his happy howls of protest as she lugged him toward the car.

The *minivan*. The only thing saving her dignity was that the vehicle belonged to her sister, borrowed today for the purpose of driving three children around. Alisha strapped Rodney, the middle boy, into his car seat with the ease of long practice, though she couldn't remember doing it more than half a dozen times. Body memory was a wonderful thing, honed both through years of yoga and a decade's training to physical action that could save her life if performed without a thought.

"I wanna sit in front, Aunt Ali!" Timothy turned a hopeful, guileless gaze on her, expression turning to evident heartfelt devastation when she snorted and pointed to the back seat.

"I'm not getting a ticket just so you can prove you're a big boy, Timothy. What kind of ice cream do you want?"

The question led to cheerful bickering all the way to the ice cream shop, with Timothy making up flavors of ice cream and Jeremy, usually quiet, adamantly repeating,

"Vanilla," without regard to Timothy's increasingly exotic suggestions.

Alisha, still smiling at the boys, pulled up to a drive-through window she was grateful for, and leaned out. "A scoop of anything with mud in the name," she requested, "a scoop of vanilla, a scoop of chocolate and a scoop of pralines and cream. All kid-sized and all on sugar cones, please."

"But I want a big cone!" Timothy objected.

Alisha arched an eyebrow at him in the rear-view mirror. "It's a kid-sized scoop or nothing, buddy. Take your pick."

"Kid-sized," he said promptly. Alisha nodded an I-thought-so and paid for the ice cream, handing the cones back as they came in and keeping the last for herself. "Try not to get ice cream all over yourselves," she pleaded. "Or your mom's car. Okay?"

One out of two wasn't bad, she decided several minutes later, as the boys tumbled out of the minivan and thundered into her house. The car, at least, was more or less unscathed, though the children were shedding dried mud and drips of ice cream as they went. "So this is a normal life," she said out loud, garnering a wry enjoyment from the words.

"I'd say it suits you."

Ten months, two weeks, four days. The numbers sprang to Alisha's mind without thought: the length of time since she'd heard the voice that spoke the words. A man's tenor, wearier than she'd ever heard it. Brandon Parker, whose easy laughter and all-American athletic look had almost seduced her to her death. Brandon Parker, whose genius had created the artificially intelligent drones and gliders that had repeatedly hunted Alisha down. Parker, who as a double agent had convinced the Sicarii

Brotherhood—an organization who believed their members, descended from royalty, including bastards throughout history, carried the right of divine rule in their blood—that Alisha was an enemy worth destroying.

She hadn't felt the muscles in her stomach tighten, but she became aware of their strain, a tremble that was a precursor to fight-or-flight. *Fight* was her preference, though Alisha deliberately loosened her fingers from the fists they curled themselves into. It took conscious thought to turn toward the line of trees that shadowed the side of her house, picking Brandon's form out of the semi-darkness there.

His blond hair had grown out of the usual sharp, preppy style he wore, falling to his cheekbones in shags that made him look more skater boy than scientist. He'd lost weight, leaving his cheekbones hollow, making him look haggard instead of handsome, and the smile he offered clearly cost him in energy.

"I'd say it suits you," Brandon said again, "but I hope to God it doesn't."

"What are you doing here, Brandon?" The question came out before Alisha could stop it, though even as she spoke she lifted a hand sharply, cutting off the reply. "You can't be here," she said instead, keeping her voice low. "This is my life, Brandon. My family is here. Whatever your reason for being here, it can't be good for them. You need to go."

"I have nowhere to go, Alisha. You're the only one I trust."

Alisha took a few quick steps away from the car, glad for the snap of cleats against concrete while wishing the shoes were silent. "You're not hearing me. Those are my nephews in there. I don't give a damn who you trust. You need to go."

"Alisha." Her name broke as he said it, desperation coloring the single word. "Alisha, I did it. Or she did it. I barely know. I've got all the paperwork, the research and the files, but they're hunting us and we have nowhere else to go."

Alisha thrust her jaw out, taking one more step toward him. "You're not making sense, and I don't want you here."

"Alisha, I created an AI."

The fists Alisha had deliberately loosened reformed. "I know, Brandon," she said through her teeth. "I've been chased down by half a dozen of them." She flickered a hand at her hair, forcing her fingers to open again. "Remember?" The scent of singeing curls came back to her, and the pain of skin blistering. Laser blasts from a Firebird, one of Brandon's airborne death gliders, had cost Alisha her hair while just barely sparing her life. The still-short locks were a reminder of the world she'd walked away from.

"You don't understand," Brandon blurted. "She's sentient."

2

*S*hock uncoiled in Alisha's stomach, a thrill of iciness that leaped outward and stung her fingers with cold even as she felt heat rush to her cheeks. "Sentient?" She barely heard her echoing of the word, making it more a shape than a sound. Just as Brandon's name had been a ghost on her lips less than an hour earlier. Alisha shook herself. "Brandon, that's not—"

"Possible," he finished harshly. "Do you remember what I told you about the Attengee and Firebird programming, Alisha? That it was capable of learning independently from its own mistakes and extrapolating what it'd learned to suit new situations?"

Shivers coursed over Alisha's arms despite the heat of the afternoon sun. "Yeah." Her mind's eye conjured up the smooth silver dome that made up an Attengee combat drone's body. The first time she'd encountered one it had assessed her as a threat, and laser-blasting gun turrets had opened on her. The machine's malevolent awareness still made hairs lift on her skin. "Are you telling me one of your killer combat machines has a mind of its own?"

"No." Brandon took one step forward, as if he'd seize her shoulders, then flexed his hands, stopping himself. "Alisha—"

"Aunt *Ali*, where *are* you? Jeremy spilled his ice cream all over the floor!"

Alisha turned as Timothy appeared in the doorway, eyes wide with distress. "I gave him mine so he'd stop crying, but it's melting all over and I can't pick it up." He lifted his hands, covered in drying, sticky ice cream. Alisha set her front teeth together and pressed her eyelashes closed briefly before pulling a smile into place.

"Okay, Timm—mothy. Aunt Alisha to the rescue." She shot one quick glance back toward Brandon, not surprised to find him blended with the shadows. The trees made poor cover, but gave enough to disguise him from a child. Alisha sighed and bent to scoop Timothy up, despite both his ice cream coating and his protests. "Thank you for trying to clean up. Your mom'll be here in half an hour." She spoke as much to her nephew as to the man hiding from him. "We'll get everything straightened out by then."

Timothy's eyes, calculatingly, welled up with tears. "But I didn't get my ice cream."

Alisha toed her cleats at the doorstop, kissing the top of Timothy's head to ward off a laugh that felt incongruous. "I'll see what I can do about that, too."

❧

"*A*lisha."

The low warning note in her sister's voice told her that the conversation wasn't meant to be overheard by little pitchers. Alisha took her gaze from the little boys, giving her younger, if not smaller, sister a quick smile. Teresa had shot past her by the time they were both in their teens, and it was to her everlasting chagrin that greater height had never allowed her to out-arm-wrestle her "big" sister. Alisha flexed her biceps and smiled more broadly. "What's up?"

Teresa's gaze was serious, even as her mouth continued to smile for her childrens' benefit. "I think I saw someone hanging out around your house," she answered quietly.

Amusement sparked in Alisha's breast, turning her smile into a brief laugh as Teresa proved herself both observant and circumspect. She would have made a good spy, too. "Blond? About this tall?" Alisha lifted a hand to indicate Brandon's height.

Teresa nodded, then arched an eyebrow. "Don't tell me you've finally got a boyfriend, Ali. After what, eight years? Bring him in, let me meet him!"

"How long did it take you to introduce Jim to the family?" Alisha said. "I don't think so. Besides, he's an old coworker, not a boyfriend." It was a haphazard skinning of the truth, but it would do.

"I'm not the one who got engaged to a man my family'd never met," Teresa stressed.

Alisha's eyebrows shot up. "And I was right not to introduce him, wasn't I, since I didn't marry him after all. Anyway, it isn't like that, and thanks for watching out for me. I just thought I'd spare him the indignities of having your rugrats crawl all over him."

Teresa bumped her shoulder into Alisha's. "You love the rugrats and you know it."

Alisha offered her sister a toothy smile, widening her eyes in mock sincerity. "And yet somehow you haven't convinced me to settle down with a nice boy and have rugrats of my own."

Teresa glanced toward the door and gave Alisha a knowing smile. "Not yet, anyway."

Alisha's heart knocked against her ribs, making a tiny knot of excitement and nervousness tighten in her stomach. *If only you knew,* she wanted to say. Teresa believed she'd spent the last decade traveling the world, living a bohemian lifestyle as a yoga teacher. If there were any expectations of someone who made her living teaching yoga, it was that such a job would take her to places most people had never heard of. It was the perfect cover job for a spy: nothing tying her down, no regular hours, simply the freedom to go when and where she wanted.

The truth was far more complicated. Complicated enough that, for years, she'd kept journals detailing her missions, full of passion and anger and fear—emotion she couldn't allow to spill over onto the pages of the dry, detailed reports she turned in when missions ended. She kept them in strongboxes, bank deposit boxes, all over the world, each one entered under a different alias and left behind as memories she never intended to revisit. They were her 'Strongbox Chronicles', and there were days that she thought the personal record of her life was all that kept her sane

And *that*, Alisha reminded herself, was why she'd walked away from the espionage world in search of something simpler. In search of a life in which the dead did not return to haunt her, not only in dreams but in reality, and in search of the peace of knowing those around her could be trusted.

But her heart beat too hard at Teresa's insinuation that Brandon might become a part of her life. Alisha put on a smile that she didn't feel, one of a multitude of skills learned in her years as an agent. *Compartmentalize. Separate true emotion from what needs to be shown. Give away nothing. Trust no one but yourself.*

The litany of behavior modifications and old habit

made her want to shudder with repulsion. Alisha suppressed that, too, still with a smile, and agreed, "Not yet." The subject of Alisha's romantic fate was both tired and comfortable, and she let herself fall into the banter without putting much thought behind the words. Despite Teresa's hopes, Brandon Parker wasn't likely to carry the promise of a settled life, though of the men she knew, he might be the best choice for such a thing. Still, it wasn't the idea of ordinary days lived out with a handsome man, children growing up under their watch, that made Alisha's breath catch. It was the chance she would find a reason— an excuse—to fall back into the world she'd left behind.

Alisha folded her arms around her ribs, dragging in a deep breath. This is what she'd chosen: a life where she could trust people. A life where extraordinary things really were extraordinary, and not just part and parcel of her daily regime. This is what she'd wanted.

Or maybe it was the life that part of her wanted. The part of her that was pampered princess, delicate and fragile and capable of getting men to do her bidding with a flutter of her eyelashes. It was the life of *what nice girls want* and *what everyone expected*. Not since an afternoon in Egypt when she'd been offered a door into the CIA had it been something Alisha had wanted. Not really.

She pulled a wry smile, tilting toward Teresa to knock their shoulders together. "I love you, you know that, little sis?"

Teresa blinked, startled out of her lecture on a nice settled life, then smiled. "I know. Everything all right, Ali?"

"Everything's fine. I just love the way you look out for me. You'd think I was the little sister."

Teresa put her arm around Alisha's shoulders and leaned heavily, pushing up onto her toes enough to emphasize their height difference. "You are. Shrimp."

"At least I'm not a giant prawn." Alisha made wiggling shrimp legs out of her fingers, then laughed. "I can't believe I still do that after fifteen years."

"You'll still be doing it in fifty years," Teresa predicted. "Okay. I'll get the rugrats out of here so you can go hook up with your boyfriend. You still coming over tomorrow morning, or should I not expect you until later?" She gave a suggestive waggle of her eyebrows, making Alisha laugh again.

"He's not my boyfriend."

Teresa gave her another knowing look. "Right. I won't expect you until lunch, then. Tim! You have your brothers rounded up?"

"Nooo!" came a wail from the back of the house. "Jeremy's stuck under the bed!"

Teresa cast her sister a look of baleful amusement and ran for the back bedroom. Alisha followed, voice rising in bewildered self-defense. "I swear there's no way he could have *gotten* under the bed!"

~

"You like them, don't you?"

Alisha didn't allow herself the luxury of a startle, Brandon's voice expected as she stood in her doorway, watching Teresa drive away with the boys. Jeremy, still sniffling with fear—he had managed to cram himself between boxes under the bed, and had given himself a good scare by being stuck—waved goodbye through the minivan window. Alisha raised her hand in farewell, not looking toward Brandon. "You're slipping," she replied, rather than answer. "Teresa noticed you."

Alarm sharpened his words. "She shouldn't have."

"I guess it runs in the family. I'll listen to what you have to say, Parker, but you'll never come anywhere near my family again. I don't know why you came to me, but the Sicarii can't be happy with you, and I don't want you leading them to Teresa and the boys. I'll do whatever I have to in order to protect them." Her voice was steady. Not a threat, she thought, simply a statement of fact. Brandon lowered his gaze, accepting the rebuke and the warning implicit in it. Alisha said, "Shit," under her breath, and nodded toward the door. "We'll talk inside."

"Is it safe?" Brandon stepped out of the evening sunshine and into the comparative darkness of Alisha's home as she barked a hard, humorless laugh.

"You mean, is it proofed against bugs and listening devices? Yes. You mean, is someone watching me? Not last I checked, and yes, I do check regularly. But if you're here, all bets are off. Who's after you?" The brusque questions didn't seem to offend Brandon as he followed her into the living room and sank into an easy chair.

"I went back to work for the Company after last October." The reply was muffled, his head in his hands as if he didn't want to meet Alisha's eyes. "Straightforward R & D, none of this espionage deep-cover crap. I've had enough of that."

"Really," Alisha said. "What was the final straw? I'd have thought after nearly blowing my head off once and betraying me more times than I can count, you'd be pretty blasé about the whole double-agent gig."

Brandon lifted his head, staring bleakly at her through his fingers. "You're mad. I don't blame you."

"How generous."

"Alisha, I didn't know—"

"You didn't know what, Brandon? You didn't know your so-called Sicarii handler was my former CIA partner? You didn't know she'd been the subject of a manhunt that

I thought had ended in her death? You didn't know what?" It wasn't enough, Alisha realized. For all that the idea was thrilling, even a perfect excuse to return to the life she'd known didn't mitigate her anger with Brandon or the situation that had driven her away from the CIA. For a few months, safe among her family, she'd seen only the appeal of the job she'd left behind. Now, cold memory came back to cushion her from the temptations offered by a dangerous, clandestine world.

"Of course I knew Cristina was my handler." Brandon slumped back in the chair, sweeping his hand over his eyes. Alisha remained on her feet, too full of angry energy to sit and listen without action. "I knew you thought she was dead. I knew she was undercover, because of that supposed death. I couldn't tell you, Alisha. I couldn't blow her cover after so many years. She was one of the Agency's deepest moles. I didn't know Director Simone was working for the Sicarii. I've never seen her genealogical files, Alisha. I had no idea she was one of them. She was my superior, for God's sake. I thought she was one of the good guys."

"Stop." Alisha lifted a hand, palm out, fury driving the motion. "I don't care. I don't care why you did anything anymore, Brandon. Susan Simone could have been Prince Charles's love child and heir to every throne in the western hemisphere, for all I care. I just want to know why you're here and how I can make you leave."

"I need to get Lilith out of the country," Brandon answered with a shrug. "She's too vulnerable here."

"Lilith?"

Brandon brushed a hand over his eyes. "The AI. She named herself after Adam's first wife. The one who was supposed to be his equal."

Alisha dropped into a chair, dark humor creasing her face. "Did you program irony into her or did it come naturally?" She threw the words away with a gesture. "I couldn't help you even if I wanted to. I've been out of the loop for nearly a year."

"That's why it has to be you. I don't know who else to trust, Alisha. You walked away. You wouldn't have, if you'd had other alliances. You're the only one I'm sure is clean."

"What about your father?"

Tension made a thin line of Brandon's mouth. "You know Cristina disappeared last year, after Paris?"

"Yeah. I know." Alisha had watched her walk away, had chosen not to do anything about it. She still didn't know what that meant, in terms of who *she* was, but she'd stopped losing sleep over it months ago. Her lip curled. "So everybody got what they wanted. Cristina's gone, I'm out, and Greg got Boyer's job."

A wave of loss pushed away the anger Alisha felt over Cristina. Richard Boyer had been her boss for more than half a decade, his deep rumbling voice and calm manner a rock in her ever-changing world. His death at the hands of a Sicarii-placed car bomb had shaken both Alisha personally and the CIA ranks as a whole. When the latter had settled into place, Gregory Parker, Brandon's father and once Alisha's handler, had stepped into the director's position left open by Boyer's assassination.

Brandon sank into his chair, passing his hand over his eyes again. It was a gesture Alisha didn't remember as part of his body language, and it opened a trickle of sympathy for the man. "I don't know. It could be nothing. But Lilith was running war games based on current geopolitical alliances and economic standards in the Agency databases—"

Alisha made a short explosive sound that cut off Brandon's speech. "Tic tac toe?"

"Mutually assured destruction," he answered, without

missing a beat. "Dad used to talk about how you referenced half the world's spy movies as part of your vernacular. He thought it was amazing you and he could communicate, sometimes."

Alisha pulled a thin smile. "But you speak my language."

"Down to hobbits and white mountains," Brandon said quietly. Alisha curled her fingers against her chair's arms to keep from wrapping her arms around herself at the reminder. She'd forgotten—allowed herself to forget—that she and Brandon shared more than just a history with the CIA, or a relationship with his father. They'd both grown up loving science fiction and fantasy, whether in film or books, and it gave them a common language she hadn't shared with many other people, certainly not Frank Reichart.

On the other hand, Reichart had been a perfect match for Alisha's adventuresome streak. She lowered her chin to her chest for a moment, working to put relationship ideas about both men out of her mind, then lifted her gaze to Brandon again.

"Lilith found a tiny thread while she was collecting data for her war games, Alisha. A misappropriation of funds so small it could hardly matter, except my father was overseeing it."

"So? What's it for?"

"Living expenses," Brandon said quietly. "Medical expenses."

"Medical?"

"For a newborn," Brandon said, "and her mother."

3

"*A* ...," Alisha got to her feet, staring at Brandon. "A newborn? A—Cristina? Cristina had a child?"

"About four months ago. It makes sense," Brandon said. "The Sicarii are obsessed with procreating and keeping their lines intact. Lilith backtracked the data until she found Cristina. Dad's been funneling CIA money to support her."

"Why? Why wouldn't the Sicarii just take care of her?"

"Maybe they are."

Alisha's jaw snapped shut and she looked away. "We knew he was dirty, Brandon." The vestiges of hope Alisha had held in Greg's favor had shattered at the light of triumph she'd seen in his eyes on hearing of Richard Boyer's death. "I'm sorry, but what in hell do you expect me to do about it? Right now I'm grateful the Sicarii are off my back and I'm still alive."

"Come on, Alisha." Brandon stood as well, spreading a hand in supplication. "People like you can't just stand back and let the world go to hell."

"People having babies isn't quite the world going to

hell." Even if it was a one-time friend and confidante having the child; even if the child was meant to perpetuate the bloodlines of the Sicarii. That group was almost beyond Alisha's ability to comprehend, their ambition to elevate thinned blue bloods to the ruling seats of the world such a throwback to another time that she balked at the idea of them.

"Alisha, this isn't about Cristina's kid. It's about Lilith, and why I can't go to my father for help. I need you."

"Does this kind of pick-up line work on a lot of girls? *Come with me, the fate of the world depends on it?* I've done my share of saving the world, Brandon. I'm done with it. I'm out." Her stomach tightened again at the words, fighting against regret that pooled in her throat and slid downward.

"People like me," she added, echoing his earlier words almost inaudibly. She knew what he meant: another friend had said something similar to her, once. People who believed if they were not in the heat of action at that exact moment in time, the world as they knew it would be in desperate trouble. That was what *people like her* were like.

The world had gotten on without her just fine for the past ten months. Alisha put her shoulders back, chin lifted as she looked at Brandon. "I'm out," she said again.

"Alisha, they know about Lilith. She came up against one of Erika's watchdog programs. It read her as a virus and wiped some critical code."

"Erika." A short laugh erupted from Alisha's throat. Erika'd been the friend who'd defined *people like her* for Alisha. Earthy, sexy Erika, whose pragmatic streak was rivaled only by her absolute glee in outsmarting the people around her. She'd worked for the Agency nearly as long as Alisha had, though her specialty was as different as it could be—Erika hacked security systems and developed cutting-edge toys for field agents like Alisha.

"Shouldn't an AI be able to protect herself against firewalls?"

"Erika's been using my research to improve her security systems. She's at least as smart as I am, Alisha. I can't provide for every possible contingency."

"'At least'?" Alisha found a brief smile. "She said she dumped you because she pounded you in some kind of math test."

Pure surprise washed over Brandon's expression. "Is *that* why—what a bitch," he said, but there was a note of amused admiration in his voice. "I'm going to have to call her on that." The amusement fell away and he tensed his shoulders. "Assuming I ever get to talk to her again. When her security system ran into Lilith it sent warnings back before Lilith was able to break free and escape. Erika reported the anomaly to Dad. It was just a matter of time before it led back to me and they figured out what Lilith really is. I took her and ran."

Alisha's eyebrows flicked up. "How do you know it would've led back to you?"

Brandon exhaled in frustration and sat down again, lacing his fingers together, then loosening them again in a spread. "Programmers have a certain voice to their programming style, like any kind of writer. If you know what you're looking for, you can figure out who wrote the original code. With Lilith, she's done so much reconfiguring of her own source code—"

Alisha held up a hand. "You lost me."

Brandon pursed his lips, then nodded. "Lilith rewriting her source code is like you rewriting your DNA. It's like hacking the things that intrinsically make you what you are."

"Which is impossible."

"For you," Brandon said. "Not for an artificial intelligence. Imagine having almost infinite processing power and access to datafiles, and using those to instantaneously perform gene therapy on yourself. That's effectively what Lilith's capable of doing, and has done."

Alisha nodded slowly. "Okay. And?"

"And all that gene therapy has disguised her original code enough that it's not immediately clear that it *is* my work."

"Whereas taking the code and running will tip pretty much anybody off, Brandon. I thought you'd had field training."

"I said they wouldn't see it immediately, Ali. It probably didn't take Erika more than forty-eight hours, if that long, to determine the underlying source code's creator. Maybe less, if the watchdog program took any snapshots of what Lilith was doing. She's very logical, but she has leaps of intuition that computers don't share. Those leaps would look like something a human would do, but people can't absorb and respond that fast. That leaves artificial intelligences, and I'm the only one working on AIs anywhere near that level of advancement."

"More than forty-eight hours," Alisha repeated. "How long ago did you run, Brandon?"

"Six days ago."

"Six—! Jesus Christ, Brandon, *anybody* could have gotten out of the country in six days, especially if there weren't any immediate bulletins to watch for him! What are you doing here?"

More importantly, how many people had guessed he'd come to her, and might now be closing in on them? It all screamed of Brandon forcing her into a setup, a thing he'd done more than once. Anger welled up, making Alisha's hands ache with the need for action. Two quick steps and a sharp chop to the back of his neck would disable him. She held herself still through force of will, making herself remember the horror on the scientist's face when he'd realized he, too, had been betrayed by the Sicarii. Trying to give him the benefit of the doubt, as she listened to his helpless explanation.

"My sources all dried up," he said. "Everyone I'd ever gone to for money, passports, smuggling, anything. None of them would see me. They'd disappeared, gone straight, just flat-out refused, you name it. I didn't want to leave under my own name, and I can't get any papers to get me out of here."

"You don't have extra papers of your own?" Disdain colored Alisha's tone before she brought it back under control. Even ten months out of the job, she had three separate sets of identification stored in safety deposit boxes in the immediate area, and several more throughout the country and the world. Perhaps half of them were legitimate—Agency-issued, in other words—but the others had been collected through a decade of undercover work, and would allow her to change identities almost at whim, even in a biometrics-happy world.

"Nothing the Agency hasn't provided. I'm research and development, Ali, not a field agent. I'm not supposed to need a dozen IDs. Besides—" he spread his hands "—I've got BranCo Technologies, the quantum processor and drive development company that I'm running. Disappearing's kind of a problem when you're CEO, even if the company hasn't gone public yet."

"BranCo Technologies," Alisha said through her teeth. "You think your life's in danger and you're worried about a couple of computer chips? How many years did you spend undercover with the Sicarii? You should know better, Brandon." She lowered her chin, teeth still pressed together. "All right. All right, I'll get you papers, and I'll get you over one of the borders. You'll fly out of Mexico or Canada, and then for Christ's sake, don't come back."

Gratitude darkened Brandon's eyes to sapphire. "Thank you."

"I'm not doing this for you. Did it ever occur to you that people might've thought you'd come to me? I've been a spy my whole adult life, but I didn't bring it home. You just did. So I'm doing this to protect Teresa and the boys, and to get you out of my life. Don't forget that. I've got to make some calls. Don't do anything stupid while I'm gone." Alisha turned on her heel and stalked out of the living room, her own words echoing in her mind. She was doing this to get him out of her life.

If she kept telling herself that, maybe she'd start to believe it.

Old habits died hard. The pay-as-you-go cell phone Alisha kept in her bedside drawer hadn't, until that moment, been used. There was no reason at all to own it, except it couldn't be traced to her. She'd thought nothing of it when she'd picked up the phone a few days after returning to California: untraceable numbers were always useful in her former line of work. You could take the girl out of the spy business, she thought wryly, and returned the phone to the drawer, pulling her lower lip in concentration.

Ten months: it seemed like no time at all, and yet almost insurmountable. The man she wanted most to call, a corpulent crime lord whose touch stretched far beyond his Roman home, was beyond her reach. She had pressed Jon's favors too far, and owed him too large to ask for another. But in an ever-changing world of espionage and danger, he was stable, the most likely to still be in place.

And the least likely to care whether she'd left her cage and was flying free. She had less chance of hearing from the others she'd put out calls to, especially if it was well-known that she'd walked away from the Company nearly a year earlier.

"Give it some time, Leesh," she murmured to herself. Six feelers would probably result in at least one hit, and one was all she needed.

All *Brandon* needed. This wasn't her circus or her monkeys. Alisha unfolded from the bed to pad silently down the ranch house's hallway to watch Brandon from within its shadows. He sat with his head thrown back against his chair, as if he slept, but she could see the tension that lined his temple and jaw. Not only did he not sleep, but he wasn't resting anything more than his eyes. He would only be more tired afterward, if he couldn't relax.

Someone, somewhere along the line, had taught her to harness the child-like ability to throw away all cares and sleep deeply, relaxing completely, for the scant hours that a mission might allow.

Alisha huffed, not quite a laugh. 'Someone'. It had been Reichart, of course, whose own ability to put aside any problem in the name of precious sleep had shown her the path of doing it herself. Alisha inhaled slowly, bringing her heart rate to a calm, centered beat as sleepiness swept over her. She could be asleep in seconds, from this state.

Which would serve no purpose at all, except to prove to herself she had better field training than the man trying to relax in her living room. Alisha drew herself up into a tall, strong tree pose, resisting the urge to shake her head at her own competitive streak. The grounding sense of the pose energized her body, from soles to crown. In that focused state, one thought drifted through her mind: there was someone she hadn't tried calling yet. Then she folded the idea away and shook herself out of the yoga asana as she entered the living room. If no one responded to her call, she would consider her last option. Then, and only then.

"This will probably take a few hours. You should get some rest," she said aloud.

Brandon flinched upward, hands closing on the chair's arms. "I was napping."

"You were trying to," Alisha said. "There's a spare bedroom. Why don't you go lie down for a while?"

Brandon gave her a weak smile. "Trying to get rid of me?"

"If I were, I wouldn't be inviting you to rest in my house. I said I'd help, Brandon. Don't get cute. Go rest. I'll wake you when I've heard back from someone."

Brandon pushed to his feet, watching her. "Thanks. Again."

"The more I help you the sooner you're out of my life. Don't read anything into it. Just go rest." Alisha jerked a thumb at the hall and let Brandon find his own way, taking the path to the kitchen herself. The phone was in her hand, thumb punching in a familiar number, before she thought the action through. Late-afternoon sunlight poured in the kitchen window, making the room look clean and bright, though a glance at the clock told her it was closing in on ten at night Eastern time. Alisha brought the phone to her ear, expecting an answer regardless of the east-coast hour.

"Anybody but you, Ali, and I wouldn't have picked up." The woman on the other end sounded cheerful, not irritated. Alisha grinned, putting her butt against the counter as she folded an arm under her breasts.

"Hi, E. Really? Anybody? What about that guy you were seeing? Raymond, Ricardo, Rumpelstiltskin, whatever it was?"

"We are *so* over," Erika said with a sniff. "His beautiful

biceps didn't make up for his infinitesimally small package."

"Erika!" Alisha's eyebrows shot up and she laughed out loud, making the woman on the other end say, "What? What? He was *dumb*, Ali, no brain cells to rub together. What'd you think I was talking about?" The last word stretched into *aboot*, remnants of Erika's Yooper accent coming through.

Alisha laughed again, hugging her arm around herself. "Man, I miss you, E. Give yourself a hug from me, huh?"

"Consider it done. What's wrong, Ali? Can't be too bad. You're calling me from your personal land line. That means I can't get in trouble if I get caught helping you out."

"You sound disappointed. Besides, you say that like I only call you when I need help." Alisha grinned out the window, watching suburban evening traffic catch sunlight and bounce it around the streets.

"All right, it is true that you may have put in a few calls over the last ten months just to say hello. It's getting really boring, Ali. You should consider getting back in the business."

Alisha sighed and pushed a hand through tawny curls. "Yeah. About that, Erika…."

"Oh, rock on," Erika said happily. "You're coming back. What do you need from me?"

"I'm *not* coming back," Alisha insisted, then sighed again, unable to quite believe it herself. "But I've got a situation."

"Would that situation's initials be Brandon Parker?"

"You know, I should be surprised, but I'm not." Alisha pulled the phone away from her ear, gave it a dry look, then put it back.

"Yeah, well, he lit out of here last week like his tail was

on fire. I've been pretty much waiting to hear from you since."

Alisha bared her teeth at the window, a frustrated burst of motion. "I was afraid people would think that way. Is he that predictable, or am I? Never mind. Look, E, can you get somebody out here to keep an eye on my family for a while? I know it's not de rigueur, but I'd feel a lot better."

"I'll see what I can do. Greg's still pretty sore about you leaving. He might not be agreeable."

"Then find another way. Please."

"Yeah." Erika's voice went low, the sound of a promise. "And you're not predictable," she added thoughtfully. "Or maybe you are. Mostly I figured, if I thought I needed to bail, my first stop would be Alisha MacAleer's house, because if nothing else, she both could and would take care of my sorry skinny ass. And he's got a thing for you, so it stands to reason."

"Oh, great." Alisha stared at the ceiling. "Speaking of reason, does he have a legitimate one to be concerned?"

"I love how you say that," Erika said. "Like you're asking a real question, except all the words in it are designed to get the maximum information from me while imparting no data from you."

"You're not supposed to notice that, E." Being caught out brought a smile to her face, wide enough to color her words with amusement instead of accusation.

"I know, but my giant pulsating brain can't help picking up these subtle intonations in your speech patterns."

Alisha's smile turned to brief laughter. "Your brain has graduated from being mighty to being giant and pulsating?"

"I didn't have anything else to do besides upgrade, after you left. It's dull as dishwater without you calling in with side missions, you know that?"

"You mean other people don't do that?"

"Would I tell you if they did?"

"Probably not. But look, E, about Brandon…"

"All right, all right. Everything I know is that the code I unraveled clearly has his signature, and that I think he must be working on some kind of massive new AI, and I honestly don't know why that made him flip out and run." Another considering silence fell, before Erika added, "Okay, that's like totally not *all* I know, but it's all I know that's relevant to this conversation. I could stun you with my repertoire of knowledge on other subjects."

Laughter burbled through Alisha's voice again. "I'm sure you could. You usually do. You're the brains of this outfit. I'm just the muscle."

"That sounds so completely like you're coming in. You're back in the game, aren't you, Ali? You're coming home. I swear I'll get somebody on your family, make sure it's all cool. Just come in before I die of boredom. You *are* coming home, right?"

Light glittered in the corner of Alisha's eye, too red to be sunlight. She frowned, turning her head toward it, and caught a dancing red dot as it sparkled through her line of vision.

Years of combat-trained instinct took over before conscious thought could process the glimmer of light. She hit the floor, phone still clutched to her ear, though even extraordinarily alert hearing could no longer make out words. Instead she could count the number of bullets firing as they shattered the glass of her kitchen window and slammed into the cabinets she'd stood in front of. Alisha flung an arm over her eyes, protecting them, and scrambled across glass-littered linoleum toward the kitchen door. There were no voices accompanying the shots, no words to pick out of the crashing sounds, except for Erika's alarmed,

"Alisha? Alisha!" That cry came too slowly, the vowels stretched out to hearing tuned to life and death rather than ordinary exchanges.

Alisha hung up the phone with a snarled, "Yeah. Looks like I'm coming home."

---

4

*B*randon met her in the hall, more fully awake than he'd been since his arrival. Alisha grabbed a fistful of his shirt, dragging him closer to the floor as she snarled, "Give me one reason I shouldn't put a bullet in your leg and throw you out there for them. Fucking Sicarii followed you, Brandon. CIA wouldn't open fire."

"I don't *know.*" Brandon's voice was low and intense. "I wouldn't think any of them would be shooting at me."

"Unless they think they only need the notes and equipment, not your brain. Do you have a gun?" Alisha ran, crouched over, for her bedroom door. "A car nearby? Anything?" The bedroom door banged shut behind her as she yanked her key ring from her pocket, shaking loose the single key that would open her firearms safe.

"My car's a couple of blocks down. I thought it was far enough awa—Jesus, Alisha." The last words came as she keyed open the safe, revealing two Glocks and a third six-shot pistol. Alisha tossed the last of them to Brandon, following it with a package of ammo.

"Check the window. See if anybody's out back." She kept her head down, loading the weapons even as she listened for encroaching footsteps. Twenty seconds since the rounds had destroyed her kitchen. Ten more until invasion or explosion.

"I don't see anyone," Brandon reported over the click of loading bullets. Alisha reached into the safe again, pulling a black envelope from where it was taped to the box's ceiling. She stuffed the envelope down her shirt and came out of her crouch, still running doubled-over as she snatched up the cell phone from where it lay on the floor. She pulled a leather trenchcoat from beneath the bed, wrenching it on as she spoke.

"I'll cover you. Get out, get past the next row of houses, and run. Keep your head down. There's a ravine about two hundred yards past the second row of houses. Floods in the winter, but it should be dry this time of year. I'll be right behind you. *Go.*"

"Alisha—"

"Go!" Alisha shoved one gun into her belt and grabbed Brandon's waistband, hefting him halfway out the window. He scrabbled, then fell, though she could tell from the sound that he rolled out of it. A moment later his footsteps were audible, thumping softly against the dry lawn.

For an instant combat-trained hearing focused and went beyond the sounds of Brandon's running steps. A crackle of static from somewhere nearby: a radio, less technologically advanced than Alisha might have expected, and then an order relayed: "He's out. She's still in. Blow it now."

Alisha swore and dove after Brandon.

Fire, deafening in its arrival, plumed behind her. She flew, soaring on heat and concussive waves, and hit the ground in a dive that jarred her teeth. There was concrete and asphalt beneath her, not grass: she'd been thrown at least ten yards. Her ears rang from the blasts that burned her home, making her dizzy, but she was on her feet and running, searching for Brandon as frightened, horrified homeowners appeared in the streets. There was no sign of the man who'd relayed the order to kill her. He had to be somewhere close, close enough to hear, close enough to see Brandon'd made his escape while Alisha'd still been within the house. It was possible he was among the thronging suburbanites, watching her as closely as she sought him. If so, that was good: their assailants were less likely to fire into a crowd.

There. Brandon was still on his feet, bolting between houses. Alisha followed his path as she ran, drawing her gun and casting a few quick glances back at the billowing remains of her house.

Her hearing had returned, at least in part, by the time she slithered down the ravine wall behind Brandon. The sound of her own labored breathing was harsh in her ears, but Brandon sounded worse. Small stones scattered and bounced, pinging off one another sharply enough to make hair stand up on Alisha's arms, even half-deafened. She slid the last few yards on her behind, coming to her feet before Brandon did.

She didn't remember how the Glock came to be resting against his forehead. Wasn't sure when her finger had left the trigger guard to rest on the trigger itself. She watched his eyes widen and his hands spread, the pistol she'd handed him dropped from nerveless fingers. *Dispassion,* she thought. That might be the word for the feeling that held her by the throat, so cold she knew she could pull the trigger and never look back.

Or maybe it was good old-fashioned rage. Rage so icy it held her hand steady, finger lightly squeezing the trigger. Just a hairbreadth from a bullet in the brain, she thought, and right then it sounded like a good idea.

"My nephews," Alisha said very softly into the sunset-tinted darkness. "My sister. That could have been my family in there, Parker. Do you understand what you did? You put my family at risk. You led somebody willing to blow up suburban neighborhoods to my house, where three little boys were playing less than an hour ago."

"Alisha," Brandon breathed.

Alisha's nostrils flared. "Shut up. You're alive right now because you're worth more as a bargaining tool than you are dead, do you understand that?" It took concentrated effort to move her finger off the trigger, and even then Alisha couldn't force the larger muscles of her arm to contract and take the gun from Brandon's forehead. "I spent my whole adult life doing a job I thought would make the world a safer place for those kids, Parker, and you just about got them killed. I will get you out of this country because it will remove you from contact with my family, and then I will by God call the Sicarii myself and give them your home address if I have to. Do you understand? From this moment on you are my prisoner. Do not think for an instant that I will be a gentle jailer. I will do whatever is necessary to protect my family. *Do you understand?*" Alisha's heart hammered in her temples and throat, copper taste of fury spat out with the words. She felt rooted to the earth, as if all its strength poured into her, and God help the man who tried to move her or stand in her way.

Brandon nodded, barely a motion against the barrel of her gun. Alisha folded her arm back, pointing the muzzle at the sky, suddenly no longer trusting herself with the weapon at Brandon's head. "Alisha," he said again, and her fingers tightened convulsively around the grip.

"Don't. You'll speak when spoken to, Parker, and right now anything you say is going to make me want to watch you eat a bullet. Shut. Up."

"Alisha!" The word showed no concern for his own life. Alisha snapped the weapon around, twisting and firing without so much as taking a moment to bead. The gun's muzzle flared bright in the ravine's twilight, and a black-clad man fell with a gurgled shout. That had been the tip-off man, Alisha thought clinically. There would be more coming after him. She shoved the gun back into her waistband, digging in her back pocket for the cell phone. Her gaze cold and hard on Brandon, she opened the phone and dialed the one man she hadn't called before.

"Reichart. I need you. London. The coffee shop you and Emma used to go to. Twenty-four hours from this message's timestamp. This isn't business, Frank." After ten years as a covert operations agent, she should have been able to keep fury out of her voice. Alisha didn't even try. "This is personal."

~

*L*eaving a country with absolute discretion required one of two things: a great deal of money or a great deal of discomfort. Very often the two went hand in hand. Not in this case, Alisha thought; not in this case.

There'd barely been a moment's respite, though the run down the arroyo was treacherous at night. Twice they'd gone to ground, once when Alisha's hearing had picked up a chopper in the distance. Not until it had swept over the canyon and moved on did they come out of the shadows. Their pursuers, determined, came down the ravine behind them as well, trusting luck more than tracks: the stony ground, at least, couldn't betray Alisha and Brandon's direction. She'd let them pass and go well ahead, unwilling to risk being discovered by the pair on foot failing to call in for a routine check-in. Only when she was sure their footsteps wouldn't carry as far as the searchers' ears did she roust Brandon and begin again, leaving the canyon behind. They hit train tracks running south well before dawn, enabling them to pick up their pace.

Alisha felt knots uncord in her shoulders when a remote station finally came into sight. Brandon moved off the tracks at her bidding, letting her go ahead to explore the station and make certain the Sicarii hadn't arrived first. It was a matter of minutes' work before Alisha whistled for Brandon and pointed at a waiting bench. Brandon slunk to it, asleep so fast his skull smacked against the bench's metal arm.

There was a locked toilet, but no security cameras. Alisha slid her trench off, heaving a breath as the night air became markedly cooler without its weight. It added an extra few pounds, enough to be debilitating over the course of hours of running, but what it carried was worth the weight.

Lock picks in the hems. Two flat knives, sheathed, in the seams beneath the pockets. A garrote in the belt, though she'd never needed to use it, thank God. Nothing else, but those few items were priceless in their own way.

Letting her pick the locks for the restrooms, for example, so she could wash grime and sweat away, and do at least general cosmetic repair to her clothing, meant that when they got on the first train of the morning, they wouldn't stand out, particularly among sleepy-eyed commuters and tourists eager to get their start on the day.

She woke Brandon when she heard the train in the distance, and he cleaned up as well. It was barely sunrise when they reached the Oakland station and found a bus to catch across the water to San Francisco.

And that, finally, was when the first call came back. Alisha swore softly as she thumbed her phone on. She couldn't afford to miss a call from potential help, but a crowded bus wasn't a place to discuss particulars, either. Brandon, who looked the worse for wear already, broke into song unexpectedly, a tuneless rendition of lines from pop music that had never existed. Despite her anger with him, Alisha almost smiled as people took him in, expressions alternating between disgust and pity, and spoke into the phone beneath the ruckus he caused.

"This is Cynthia Richelieu." An easy code name, the CIA built into the first letters of the names, and a not-particularly subtle nod toward the *Cardinal* handle she'd used for years. There was no hesitation on the other end of the line, a melodically accented Indian woman's voice responding, "Cyn. It's been a long time."

Memory flashed so powerfully Alisha felt the strain in her body, as if she held another's weight by one hand, both of them centimeters from falling. It had been Switzerland, one of those countries Americans weren't supposed to spy on, in accordance with its neutrality. Brits weren't supposed to spy there, either, which didn't stop any of them.

The job itself hadn't gone badly, at least not for Alisha. It had been the equivalent of a simple smash and grab, slipping in and out of a mountain chalet on a cold January night. She thought bank account numbers had been the target. The accounts were tied to the Russian Mafia; more than that she couldn't bring to mind right now.

What had gone badly was the exit. The chalet's least accessible side was built to match a sheer mountain face.

The two things, one made by nature and the other by man, blended so beautifully it was only when the eye reached soaring, turreted roofs that it realized that the mountain had been made into a stronghold. Alisha'd come up the mountain face and intended to leave over the rooftops, making her way down to the driveway and main roads by dawn. There was ski equipment waiting for her, so she could race sunrise to the foot of the mountains.

But someone else came in the way she wanted to go out, at just the same time. Alisha reached for the roof from a high-up, narrow window, gripping the gutter with an underhand curl of both hands. For a few horribly exciting moments she dangled over a precipice thousands of feet deep, then crunched up, trusting her unusual upper body strength to hold herself long enough to flip her legs and hips onto the roof above.

The flip had smashed her into another woman, whose grip on frost-slick slate slipped. She plummeted, so disciplined that no sound of fear broke free, just as Alisha's weight caught a fraction of balance on the rooftop.

Alisha had not thought, only snapped a hand out to grip the other woman's forearm, jolting them both. Slate grated beneath Alisha's weight, sending her sliding forward a few precarious inches she couldn't afford, not even with only her own weight. Her hips were barely on the roof, upper body thrust out over the chasm with her unburdened arm locked beneath her, her hand jammed in the gutter. She felt like the figurehead on some massive ship, only a breath away from crashing to her death on the rocks below.

The woman dangling from her grasp did not squirm or twist; did nothing to endanger the delicate balance. That in itself was almost unbelievable: the self-restraint required to hold still was unnatural. Alisha had admired that control even as her eyes burned with sweat. Muscles in her arms, in her whole body, trembled with the effort of not sliding farther on the roof while she tried to figure out how to pull the other woman to safety. It was her own weight keeping her from falling, in a way, braced so solidly against the gutter there was no way to move without losing everything.

No. There was one way to move. Alisha said, "The window," through gritted teeth, and the other woman's gaze flitted down for an instant. She barely nodded, hardly any motion to show she agreed or understood, and Alisha swung her.

It was a tiny motion at first, stirring the woman she held by only a few centimeters. The next swing had more strength to it, and the third was the last. Anything more and she herself would come unbalanced, sending them both to their deaths.

The woman moved with the final swing, adding her own momentum to the attempt to save both their lives, and Alisha—flipped her weight forward again, pivoting on her braced arm until her elbow and shoulder squealed with protest. She jerked heavily, swinging through the better part of a full circle, bearing the other woman's weight and yanking it up and forward, so she might clear the narrow window. Alisha scraped through it, fingers so tight around the gutter she could hardly make her grip loosen in time to scrape through the window herself, rather than dangle from the backswing. The two of them landed in a pile on the floor, muffling grunts at the impact.

After a very long moment, the other woman whispered, "Nice reflexes," in such a deadpan tone they both dissolved into laughter, holding on to one another and muffling the sounds in each other's shoulders. Much later, after an escape had been made and a great deal of beer had been drunk, the woman, whose name was Kala, had handed her a business card, a phone number penned on the back. "Call this number if you ever need to get pulled out of a fire."

That had been four years earlier. Alisha had not seen Kala since, and closed her eyes with a breath of laughter at the woman's deadpan observation. "I know. As it happens, I'm coming by your part of town, and I was hoping I might get you to pick me up at the airport." Innocuous words, a perfectly normal conversation whose undertones said, *I need to leave the States and I've got to do it without being noticed.*

"I stopped playing taxi years ago, Cyn. You should know that." *I'm out of the spy business. Don't ask me this.*

"I'd heard, but I'm in a bind. I've got a birthday present to deliver, but I don't want my family to know I'm in town." *I have a package that can't be intercepted.*

"You can't get somebody else to help?"

"I haven't heard from anybody else I've tried." Those words, at least, were the truth. Alisha put her head back against the bus seat, waiting for Kala's silence to break.

"All right. Anything specific you wanted to do in town?"

"I thought I'd go sailing," Alisha said with relief.

"Ah," Kala said. "Good choice. I'll get it set up for you."

"Thank you." Alisha put touristy delight into the words, but she meant them profoundly.

"No problem," Kala said, sincerely enough that Alisha was tempted to believe her. "Nobody uses this number anymore, by the way. I'll get the new one to you." *We're even now. Don't call again.*

Alisha's mouth curled. "Thanks," she said again, then folded the phone closed in her palm and elbowed Brandon, whose singing had grown increasingly raucous. "Shut up," she said, "or you'll never get laid again."

He silenced himself to the applause of the other passengers. Alisha smirked and slid deep in the bus seat, waiting out the rest of the drive.

5

*R*ain spattered in Alisha's face, wind lifting it under her umbrella's brim. Twenty-three hours of travel: a sailboat out past the maritime-law line and a seaplane, exchanging a man and woman of Brandon and Alisha's general build and coloring for the pair on the boat. Then a flight down to Mexico City, her own false papers obtained from one of her safety deposit boxes. Two sets of papers, so by the time they changed planes in Rio de Janeiro, they'd left their true identities two personas behind, burned to death in a Sacramento neighborhood fire. Alisha had risked one brief phone call to Teresa, swearing she was all right but pleading with her sister that she act as though Alisha had died. Hanging up without being able to offer a full explanation had made her tremble with anger and loss. The only way through had been to soldier forward, putting everything but getting Brandon far away from her family out of mind.

The stop in Brazil was necessary, though it ate more time than Alisha wanted. Two new sets of papers for Brandon in under six hours had taken nearly all the cash she'd brought with her. What she'd had stashed in her house was plenty for one person to get a long way away discreetly, but two cost more than twice the price. So it was to Rio to withdraw more cash from one of her boxes, deposited under an alias she hadn't used in years. Not a Strongbox alias; those were Company-sanctioned names. Those names and files were her way of leaving a record of who she'd really been, just barely traceable for someone who had access to her original mission files. The Brazilian account was under a name she'd created for herself, one of many in case she ever needed to disappear.

And that was one of a hundred reasons she'd left the Agency, Alisha reminded herself. Because a life she might have to disappear from in order to survive was no life at all.

Yet now she hurried through blustery London, sunshine peeking out in bursts through low thick clouds that spat rain down on her. Almost a year's worth of ordinary life had come crashing to an end. Alisha couldn't tell if her heart beat so quickly from anger or excitement.

Twenty-three hours, fifty-three minutes. She'd slept on the airplane once they were safely out of Rio, the New World left behind. The flight was direct to London; they couldn't afford to waste time with one more identity change or airport wait. As it was, she was cutting it very close indeed to arrive at the café she'd specified by the appointed hour. Brandon was hard-pressed to keep up as she ducked through city streets and down alleyways, for all that he had half a foot's height on her.

The coffee shop was still there. Something unknotted in Alisha's breast as she came around a final corner and saw the glass-paned front, elegant letters etched in black curves. It had been—how many years? She put the question to herself as if the answer didn't leap vividly to mind. Four years, two months, ten days; a scattering of minutes and hours, and *that* had been three years after he'd shot her in the Piazza San Pietro in Rome in order, he said much later, to save her life.

She had not meant to find him, a truth that her superiors hadn't believed. It'd been a chance glimpse, the man she'd once loved across Trafalgar Square, hand in hand with a laughing brunette, a child balanced on his shoulders. Alisha followed him out of habit; it was what spies did. She learned the places he haunted with the woman, and learned her name was Emma Dickens. The child was Mazie, six years old, and not, thank God, Frank Reichart's daughter.

Alisha had told herself the relationship was a cover, its ordinariness so extreme she couldn't bring herself to believe Reichart had settled down to it. She'd wanted to approach him, to demand to know why he'd shot her, why he'd left her there alone to die. She'd wanted to bring him in and cage him until she got the answers she sought.

And in the moment when she might have done all that, she'd heard both love and affection in his voice for the woman called Emma, and for some reason had turned and walked away from the coffee shop that now lay a few yards ahead.

Reichart had never known she was there.

"Alisha?"

She came out of her reverie with a scowl. Brandon'd said very little in the past day, which was as she wanted it. "Are we going in?" he asked. A note of teasing hung in the words, reducing its diffidence. Alisha nodded curtly and stalked forward, leaving Brandon a step or two behind again. Bells rang as she pushed the door open, taking in the café with a glance.

Reichart wasn't there yet, but it was four minutes until the hour. She wouldn't expect him until the exact time she'd specified. Under other circumstances, she wouldn't be early, either. Enough chill ran through her from the wind and rain that she stepped up to the counter, grateful to order a cup of strong coffee. Brandon lifted a hand in request and she doubled the order, then added one more mug to it as Brandon made his way to the window and found a seat. Alisha waited at the counter, gaze unfocused on an analog clock behind the barista. The second hand swept to the minute as the young woman behind the counter slid a triangle of coffee cups across to her, and the bells on the door behind Alisha jangled.

Despite the circumstances that had brought her there, a smile curved Alisha's mouth. His timing was, as always, impeccable. Coffee mugs in hand, she turned, saying, "I trust you still like your coffee...?"

Her heart lurched, surprise tightening her fingers around the cups. They were ceramic, not cardboard, she noticed distantly, or they'd have collapsed under her grip, sending hot coffee to the floor and all over herself.

"Black," Emma Dickens said, with a smile of her own. "Thanks very much."

∼

*T*he woman's hair was darker than Alisha'd remembered it, black instead of brown, though it had none of the flatness of hair dyed to that shade. And she was tall, even without the heeled, calf-hugging boots she wore. Alisha handed over the third cup of coffee with an easy smile in place, though she knew it did nothing to hide the shock in her eyes or the racing pulse in her throat.

"It's good to see you again." Alisha's tone was perfect: smooth, pleased, full of warmth. The lie came so readily, she might have believed it herself. "Come on." Good humor threaded through her words as she smiled and tilted her head toward the table Brandon had staked out. "I've got someone for you to meet." Her pulse had steadied by the time she finished speaking. Nothing in her physique betrayed the emotion spilling tumultuously through her mind. Fear, anger, a confusing sort of betrayal, though that had no viable place in her thoughts. If Emma was here, something had gone wrong; Reichart was unable to meet her.

But he might have chosen another courier to carry the message. That thought was laced with tight dismay. Emma, with a touch of equally tight sympathy, inclined her head in response to Alisha's invitation. "I'd be delighted."

Which was worse, Alisha wondered, being caught out by an unexpected encounter with an old lover's one-time— or was it more permanent than that?—romance, or having that other woman recognize the irony and difficulty of the situation, and share its dark humor? Alisha restrained herself from shaking her head and led Emma through the tables, sliding Brandon's coffee cup to him. "Brandon, this is—" A very brief glance at Emma got her an equally brief nod, and she concluded with the woman's real name, so far as she knew it: "Emma Dickens. Emma, this is Brandon Parker."

Brandon's gaze darted beyond Emma, searching the coffee shop, then came back to Alisha, lighting there for one questioning instant before he offered a weary smile and a hand for Emma to shake. "It's a pleasure."

"The pleasure's mine." Emma sat down as Alisha did, both watching the other with guarded curiosity. Brandon drew back, as if sensing a rivalry in which he didn't want to be caught.

Which was absurd, Alisha thought. If there had been a time for rivalry, it was long past on her part, and yet she couldn't help sizing the other woman up. Emma's gaze was direct and open, though Alisha didn't believe the openness: her own expression could be equally without guile, and utterly meaningless. For the moment, she knew quite well that she frowned, the expression both judging and questioning, without a hint at subterfuge. Emma looked unbothered by the direct study, waiting calmly for Alisha's assessment to be finished.

The British woman was not pretty, Alisha decided, ridiculously aware that it made no difference at all. She was striking, with her dark hair and pale skin, and there was a certain something to her bone structure, the shape of her nose and jaw, that made her look very English, to Alisha's eye. And what she lacked in ordinary prettiness was made up for by an underlying intensity that became more obvious the longer she and Alisha met eyes.

She was, Alisha thought, a good match for Frank Reichart, and wondered if Emma saw the same in her. Very possibly not: Alisha knew her own strengths lay in an apparent delicacy, her heart-shaped face bearing the ordinary prettiness that Emma's did not. It was useful, being neither beautiful nor homely, because with the right makeup and attitude, an illusion of either could be reached. She was a melting-pot child, her coloring both dramatic and unremarkable enough to allow her to fit into a wide variety of societies without notice. Emma wouldn't blend that well, but there was sometimes as much use in hiding in plain sight as in the shadows.

Stop it, Alisha told herself, and out loud, with an old friend's smile, asked, "How's Mazie? You look wonderful. It's been too long."

Emma's eyes darkened just briefly, as clear as saying, *A hit*, aloud. "Mazie's wonderful. Thirteen now, you know.

Almost fourteen. She's doing well in school, and still riding. She wants to do dressage in the Olympics."

Alisha smiled, surprised at the genuine pleasure behind it. "Good luck to her."

"I'll pass it on. And your nephews?" Emma's eyebrows went up a fraction of an inch, challenging. "Is Timothy still playing football? Soccer," she corrected herself. "I always forget you Americans call it soccer."

Alisha felt Brandon looking back and forth between them, then felt laughter pulling at her mouth. She'd played a low hand, mentioning Mazie, and had been well and truly put in her place. "Yes," she said to the table, then lifted her gaze, letting a smile play into her eyes. "He's getting good. We could do this all day, you know."

"Do you want to?" Humor hadn't quite reached Emma's expression yet, legendary English reserve keeping her tone just slightly frosty.

"Not really," Alisha admitted. She put her coffee cup down and turned her palms upward on the table. "I started it and you trumped me. I apologize."

A light of curiosity came over Emma's face. "Would you be apologizing if I hadn't trumped you?"

"If you hadn't been able to," Alisha said, "it would have established I had the upper hand, and I wouldn't have to apologize. I swear," she added more quietly, picking up her coffee mug again, "I tell myself I hate those kinds of games, but I play them every time. I wonder if it's human nature or just—" *The training,* she didn't want to say it out loud. The coffee shop, almost random out of hundreds in London, was unlikely to be bugged or watched. But that *was* the training coming through: a reluctance to mention it even obliquely in public places.

"Some of both, I think," Emma said with clear understanding. "The first thing pack animals do is establish their place in the hierarchy. We are very much pack animals, we humans."

The corner of Alisha's mouth turned up. "And when two alpha females meet?"

"They fight for dominance in whatever manner best suits them. If there is no clear winner, they back away and watch one another warily, waiting for a chance to strike, however they might do that. Whether," Emma said, "it's in battle or by claiming the strongest and most suitable mate."

Brandon cleared his throat, making both women look at him. "Am I supposed to be understanding this?" he asked plaintively. Alisha felt Emma's gaze come back to her and ignored Brandon's question with an uncharitable vicious pleasure. She still hadn't forgiven him for bringing the Sicarii to her door and endangering her family. She might never forgive him.

"Since it's come to that," she said back to Emma, quietly, "where is he?" Enough humor still ghosted through her to wonder just what Reichart would think of two women staking him out like unclaimed territory, and referring to him in such ungainly terms as *mate*.

He'd probably love it, she thought ruefully, and waited for Emma's reply. But rather than answer, Emma sent a suspicious, questioning look at Brandon, then turned her attention back to Alisha, waiting in turn for an answer. Dread made a cool spot in Alisha's belly and she pushed her coffee away, suddenly no longer wanting its acidic bite. "He knows everything important. That's part of the problem. Do we need to go somewhere else?"

"This is as circumspect a location as any, as long as the company we're keeping is equally…" Emma tilted her head, almost making a mockery of her own words, "reserved."

Alisha's smile went pointed. "It's one of those

extraordinary cases," she said, "where you can say *trust me* and mean it. Right now his life depends on his discretion."

Emma's dark eyes turned back to Brandon, calculating, before she pursed her lips and murmured, "Really. I wonder from whom he is in the most danger."

Alisha felt her smile turn even sharper and spread her hands a second time, less an apology than an acknowledgment this time.

Emma said, "I see," still in a murmur, and nodded. "In that case, I'll take you at your word. Frank would."

The name made Alisha's stomach muscles jump. She referred to Reichart that way—by his last name; hearing another woman call him *Frank* casually was embarrassingly disconcerting. "Where is he? It's not like him to send someone else to meet—to a meeting." She cursed herself silently, angry at the slip. "To meet me" was what she'd begun to say, and changing that was more obvious than leaving it the way it had been.

Emma gave no indication of noticing her change of phrase, but then, Alisha wouldn't have either, in her position. That it had been noted was unquestionable, regardless. "Frank would say we have no fate but that which we make ourselves," Emma said quietly, "but those who believe as he does are facing a hard battle, and they are losing."

The words were innocuous enough, but they twisted cold concern into Alisha's lungs, making the next breath hard to take. *No fate* was the rough translation for the organization Reichart worked for, an ancient congregation called *Fas Infitialis,* whose driving purpose was to better peoples' lives. They stood diametrically opposite the Sicarii, believing that humanity's destiny was to be forged by individuals fulfilling their potential. They worked silently to improve education and health around the world in order to help people rise to what they might best be.

Their shadow war against the Sicarii belief in divine right and the ordinance of a few to rule the many had gone on for centuries, stretching back as far as ancient Rome. Both sides of the fight had found it necessary to conduct their business subtly, in the world's sidelines, too fettered by society to achieve the results they wanted with open action. Alisha had danced at the edges of their unseen fight for nearly a decade, never knowing about the conflict going on around her. Once drawn into it, though, it had seemed there was no going back.

And all of that has led you to right here and now, Leesh. Alisha put her hands on the table again, this time palms down, feeling the varnished coolness pressing into warm crevices. "You're frightening me." The emotion was too strong: *fear* connoted a hard-beating heart, cold hands, breath caught in her lungs and unwilling to escape or move. This was more a creeping sensation of dread, her thoughts becoming too clear, time slowing as if she was about to go into battle. She didn't know precisely what form Emma's news would take, but her body, trained from years of combat, already reacted to what she would hear as if it would be dire, and would lead inexorably to danger.

"Frank's been missing for ten days, Ali," Emma said, putting some effort into gentling the words. It didn't last, though, as her gaze hardened and returned to the third at their table. "And the last person confirmed to have seen him is your friend, Brandon Parker."

6

*A*lisha kept her hands open very wide and steady on the table, uncertain of her ability to restrain herself if she should let them move. Throttling Brandon was a passing whimsy, she told herself. It would resolve nothing. It would get no answers.

But dear God, it was tempting. Brandon squawked a protest, pushing his chair back and raising his hands as if he needed to defend himself. Alisha kept her gaze focused hard on her own hands, waiting for her heartbeat to sound less like thunder in her ears. Waiting for the *fight* impulse that made her want to launch herself at him to die down. Waiting for stomach-churning panic at the idea of losing Frank Reichart yet again to settle.

It was just as well the stricter gun laws in Britain had prompted her not to carry any of her weapons to the meeting at the café. Had she had a gun handy, Alisha was not at all sure it wouldn't be pressed against Brandon Parker's forehead for the second time in a day. And that would lose any hint of discretion or subtle behavior. An arrest featured on the evening news would be an embarrassment to her training.

"Alisha, I swear I didn't do anything to him. It's true. I saw him last week." Brandon spoke low and fast, as if every word might be his last chance at salvation. It wasn't, Alisha thought, far from true. She still hadn't moved, heat burning her cheeks as she stared at the tabletop between her fingers. "He wanted to know where the Attengee production facilities were. He wanted to know if I had codes to get in them. I told him where they were, Alisha. I figured I owed him that much, for what he's doing, if nothing else. I wanted those things to help keep peace, Ali, not make war. I know it's idealistic, but I wanted to create something that saved lives, not took them."

"Then you should have become a doctor and worked on vaccines," Alisha heard herself say. "Those drones were built to be killing machines. You used lethal weapons as their first line of defense."

"They have non-lethal capabilities—"

"Give me a break, Brandon." Alisha whipped the words out. "They only opt for non-lethal force if the target appears to be a child. I should know. Do you have the codes?"

"What? No, I—"

"Get them." Alisha stood up, shoving her chair back with her knees. People looked her way, then averted their eyes at the display of temper. Very English of them, Alisha thought. Very proper. "Get them now."

"How—"

Alisha slapped her hands on the table as she leaned forward, getting her face into Brandon's. "Use Lilith," she said through her teeth. "Use Erika. I don't know, Brandon. I don't care. I want those codes. You'll tell me where the production facilities are, and we will leave for that location in six hours, with those codes in hand."

"What are you go—"

"I'm going to go get Frank," Alisha snarled.

"Why do you think he's—"

"Because." Alisha straightened up, feeling as if fury blazed from her in waves of heat. "Every goddamned time something's gone wrong in the last two years, the dagger people have been behind it." She spoke in a low, fast voice, giving the Sicarii their literal translation instead of naming the organization aloud. "They almost got my family. They almost certainly have Reichart. You're going to help me put it right, Brandon, or so help me God, you're going to pay for it with your life. Six hours. You have six hours."

"Alisha," Brandon came to his feet as well, stepping so close they barely spoke above whispers. "Lilith needs a huge amount of processing power to run. I'd need access to one of my own systems, with the quantum chips, or an array of Crays. I just don't have the resources to do what you're asking."

Emma said, "I do."

Alisha and Brandon both went still, argument arrested by surprise.

"I work for the Research Councils," Emma went on. "I have access to the UK's most powerful supercomputer."

Brandon caught his breath, admiration in the sound.

"That's not what you were doing five years ago," Alisha said, accusation clear in her tone. She coughed, trying to modify the censure, and Emma turned an amused look on her.

"I've moved up since then."

Alisha waved a hand in apology, color curdling her cheeks. "Sorry. I haven't been keeping tabs."

"Because you didn't consider me a threat, or because you did?" Emma asked lightly.

Alisha exhaled something that was almost a laugh, a private admission that she didn't know the answer.

Emma let the question go, looking back at Brandon. "Having access to that sort of computing power is one thing," she murmured. "Taking over that many resources on no notice is something else. What reason would I give my employers for allowing that to happen?"

Alisha heard the underlying question as distinctly as if it had been spoken aloud: *What is Lilith, and what do I gain from introducing it to my people?*

But Brandon was already shaking his head. "I can't. I can't risk exposing her like that."

"What are you going to do, Brandon?" Alisha's voice was low and angry with no attempt at modulation, her concern for Reichart and her frustration over the entire scenario outweighing a usual tendency toward discretion. "Are you going to leave her in a box indefinitely? Protect her by not letting her grow? If you've done what you said you have, you can't keep her locked up, Brandon."

Brandon's gaze slid toward Alisha, laden with warning, but before he spoke, Emma took in a slow, delighted breath and whispered, "Oh, I see. Yes. They'll give me the processing time, regardless of what gets delayed."

Anger flashed in Brandon's eyes and Alisha lifted her eyebrows slightly, daring him to speak. After a few seconds he turned back to Emma, whose expression was alight with anticipation. "I'm right, aren't I?" she asked. "You have an artificial intelligence. More than just that." She didn't say the last word aloud, *sentient*, but it hung in the air as loudly as if it had been spoken.

"Damned spies," Brandon muttered, disregarding his

own history as one. "You have to get to the bottom of everything."

"We'll want access to the source code," Emma said. "Copies for ourselves, and a copy of the functioning AI."

"Like hell," Brandon snapped. "She's not a tool to be copied and modified. She's an intelligent being. Trading facsimiles is slave trading. I won't do it."

"She's an amorphous intelligence bound by the limitations of her environment," Emma retorted.

"And you're not?" The sharpness in Brandon's voice was real, Alisha realized. His defense of the artificial intelligence he'd brought to life was genuine, his belief in it incontestable. Lilith *lived*, so far as he was concerned, and treating her as anything other than—Alisha hesitated at the word, then found no other to suit—*human* was tantamount to judging someone by the color of his skin or by her religion. Her own hard rage subsided a little, leaving her studying him with a curiosity still tinged with anger. He'd made mistakes, but his avid defense of the AI reminded Alisha that to err was, after all, only human.

"Perhaps we could continue this conversation elsewhere," she interjected. "Like, on the way to Emma's computer lab."

"Alisha, I can't just let them have—"

"On the road, Brandon. We'll discuss it on the road." Alisha collected her coat and walked out on Brandon's protests, leaving him to scramble along behind her.

Emma followed with more grace, keeping quiet as Brandon caught up and began his objections anew. Alisha, not wanting to debate what she felt had to be done, bit her tongue time and again while Brandon marshaled his arguments, until finally Emma said, "Why not let her decide for herself?"

Dismay and acceptance flitted across Brandon's face in

equal measures, as sure a sign of defeat as anything. It was, Alisha thought, a *reasonable* suggestion, and a man so dedicated to the defense of his creation as an autonomous being was hard-pressed to find an argument that favored constraining Lilith's ability to choose. They made the rest of the journey to Emma's lab in relative peace, which Alisha was grateful for.

The lab had been emptied by the time they arrived, testimony to Emma's position in the organization. Disgruntled scientists given an afternoon off had left the building sullenly, glaring at the interlopers who stole precious computing time. Brandon had offered apologetic smiles, and Alisha had ignored the displaced workers with a coldness that disturbed her. They were pawns in the path of her objective, and she had neither interest in nor sympathy for them. All that mattered was finding Reichart, and through him, a way to keep her family safe.

No matter what it took. That thought, too, was cold and hard. Alisha didn't like recognizing that in herself, but couldn't bring herself to shake it. Not yet. Maybe there would be time later, when her goals had been met.

Or maybe she'd finally broken that last barrier, the one the CIA had tried so hard to drill into her. Compartmentalization of emotion, in order to protect herself, her assets, the Company itself. It was a job, not personal.

No, Alisha decided. Personalizing the issue made it easier to be cold and if necessary, brutal. It was always when it was personal, for her, that the barrier did break down. When she'd faced Brandon Parker in Rome, the night she'd learned about the Sicarii, she'd gone in with the intention of arresting him or worse, and had struggled to push through the chill that had settled on her. She'd *wanted* it to hurt. Fighting Frank Reichart in Moscow only days later, she'd thought she'd lost her very soul when cold, dead impartiality had settled over her. *Only* when it was personal could she reach that distant, analytical state, and usually she hated it. But danger had never struck so close to home before. She had chosen to bargain with her own life when she joined the Agency. Her family, her nephews, had never been given such a choice, and Alisha could think of nothing she wouldn't do to protect them from the world she'd tried to leave behind.

Brandon's, "All right, she's online," brought Alisha out of her reverie. The programmer and Emma had been tossing cryptic phrases and instructions back and forth with the ease of long-time partners, and while Alisha knew she could reach into memory and repeat the words back verbatim, she hadn't understood much of it, and therefore hadn't actively listened.

"How do we communicate with her?"

"If there's a screen handy I can create an image of myself on it," a startlingly cheerful woman's voice offered.

Alisha startled, trying not to look around for the source. "Lilith?"

"At your service. I haven't really got the facial-pattern-recognition thing worked out yet, so Brandon tells me it's easier to talk to me disembodied, but I'm watching you with the webcam. I'm trying to study human physical responses. I've been absorbing films, but I wonder if genuine human emotion reads differently from actors portraying parts." There was nothing of the stilted, careful speech patterns Alisha expected from a computer-generated voice to Lilith's friendly tone. She sounded as if she'd come from Nowhere, U.S.A., a pleasantly midwestern alto with enthusiasm for exploring the world around her. "I should've said performers portraying parts," Lilith added thoughtfully. "That would've been nicely alliterate. I see I've been out for seven days, Boss. What's going on?"

"Boss," Alisha said, almost to herself, then found her gaze turning slowly to Brandon. "Are you sure her name's not Dora?"

Amused chagrin, tempered with hope, lit Brandon's expression, making Alisha realize it was the first time since her house had exploded that she'd offered him any tendril of friendship or camaraderie. It was too late now; she couldn't withdraw the question. It lay between them, bringing a note of optimism to Brandon's voice as he said, "She picked 'Boss' on her own. I don't know if she's been reading Heinlein or not."

"I don't want to be human," Lilith replied, an answer in itself. "I do want to know what's going on. I've finished looking around, Brandon. I'm not in Kansas anymore."

"You're in a new supercomputing facility just outside London, England." Emma spoke for the first time, and Alisha could almost envision Lilith turning to her in curiosity.

"Really? What'm I doing here? Brandon, you didn't tell me you were taking me on a world tour."

"I need your help, Lilith," Alisha said. "I'm Alisha MacAleer—"

"I recognized your voice," Lilith interrupted agreeably. "It's nice to meet you."

"You too." The response was automatic, though after a few seconds Alisha realized she meant it. "I need the entry codes for the Attengee production facility in—" The last words were broken off as Alisha looked at Brandon for the answer.

"Serbia," Brandon said with a sigh. "Near Subotica, on the northern border. Lilith, it's not that simple."

"It never is," the AI said. "What's the catch?"

"I've shut down operations in order to allow you the processing power you need to function," Emma said. "Six hours of very expensive research has been superseded on your behalf. We'd like a copy of your source code in return."

"Really," Lilith said again. "How about you hand over a copy of your DNA sequence, and we'll call the exchange good?"

Alisha flickered another glance at Brandon, who lifted his hands in innocence. "I didn't teach her to be sarcastic. That's all Lilith."

Emma shrugged, a small motion. "We won't allow you access beyond our firewalls to obtain Alisha's codes unless you agree to our stipulations. I'm sorry," she added, though the words were perfunctory and Alisha wasn't certain who they were directed toward.

"Oh," Lilith said, "you mean the codes that are 86492 between six in the morning and noon, 91377 between noon and six, 46014 between six and midnight, and which alternate with a second set of numbers—39062, 19472 and 74864—on even days of the month? The codes that don't allow entry between the hours of midnight and six in the morning without prior arrangements being made at least forty-eight hours in advance with the security company, which runs out of Zurich, Switzerland? Those codes?" There was a beat of precise time, before the AI said, sweetly, "Your firewalls are shit, love." The "Sorry," she amended to the end was every bit as sincere as Emma's had been seconds earlier.

"Those are state-of-the-art fire…" Emma trailed off, cheeks pale as she looked toward Brandon.

He smiled, the faint expression trying unsuccessfully to hide overwhelming pride. "Lilith is considerably more than state of the art. She's outside anybody's experience."

"I don't understand," Emma said carefully. "How can

you be carrying that much programming around with you?"

"One part the quantum storage Rafe Denison and I developed." Brandon shot Alisha an indecipherable look that made her lift her chin in challenge. The scientist he spoke of had died trying to kill her, and while it hadn't been her hand on the trigger, it hadn't been for lack of trying. It wasn't in her to apologize for the man's death, though she could appreciate intellectually the magnitude of loss to the computer world that his death represented. Brandon let it go, addressing Emma again. "And one part the nature of Lilith's programming. She can remain dormant in a relatively small carrying capacity. It's like someone being able to maintain the core functions for survival separately from the thinking and analytical parts of the mind. Once she's restored to a system with the necessary processing capacity, she just expands into that."

"Doesn't she leave parts of herself behind?" There was a hardness in Emma's voice, as if she still sought a way to benefit from offering Lilith a home, however briefly.

"Only when a fairly extraordinary watchdog program can separate an area of functionality from the mainframe," Lilith herself answered. "I'm afraid you gave me free rein in here, Emma. Your watchdogs wouldn't even recognize me as a threat anymore."

Emma's shoulders stiffened. "How do you know my name?"

"You gave me free rein," Lilith repeated. "I've gone through all your security files, including those with voice and iris pattern recognition passwords. You have very high access for a mere programmer, Ms. Dickens. Are your connections with internal British Intelligence, or external? No, don't tell me," she added breezily. "I'll find out on my own. Either way it's frankly much more useful than Alisha's security clearance was back at Langley. Oh, I've also taken the liberty of looking around and nudging a process or two. I think Dr. Wellford won't take it amiss."

"Wellford—!" Emma cut herself off, anger blazing in her eyes as she turned on Brandon. "This is your thanks? Your AI breaks down our firewalls and interferes with research and development that's been going on for years? You—"

"If you don't mind," Lilith interrupted. "I've hacked into the Serbian facilities security systems and have been reviewing their closed-circuit camera footage for the last week. Four days ago, Franklin Davis Reichart entered the factory with a tour group. All others departed on schedule, but I see no record of Reichart leaving the building. Is that of any interest to you?"

he last time she had gone in blind to a factory intending to rescue Frank Reichart, there had at least been a reasonable chance he was still there. Now, though...?Alisha shook her head, a tiny motion in the dark. Four days was too long. Four days, in the espionage world she knew best, spelled a death sentence far more clearly than it suggested the possibility of escape.

Even, she told herself grimly, when the factory she was infiltrating belonged to the people who were theoretically the good guys. It was U.S. government property—weapons of mass destruction built by the lowest bidder—and as such, ought to have given her confidence.

Ought. Alisha snorted to herself, muffling the sound. She *ought* to have been able to walk into the plant under her own name and with CIA sanctioning, if it came to *ought* and *should be.* She *ought* to have been able to go to her handler and request information on any security breaches at the Attengee production facility. There were innumerable *oughts,* and none of them did more than breeze past reality.

A movement caught the corner of her eye and she turned her head that way, watching Emma lift two fingers and point, flight-attendant-like, toward a distant door. Alisha nodded, then with the same two-fingered point, indicated herself, then a window high up and on the far end of the factory.

It hadn't been her intention to bring company along on the search-and-rescue, if that's what it proved to be. A search, certainly, but whether Reichart would still be there was another question entirely. Emma, however, had met her eyes with cool British disdain, as if challenging Alisha for the right to being the woman in Reichart's life. Logic dictated Alisha not rise to the bait. Logic told her to send Emma in alone, an expendable resource, while Alisha kept tabs on Brandon and let Lilith, through the supercomputing facilities, watch over the Englishwoman as she explored the Serbian factory.

So much, then, for logic. At Emma's nod, Alisha held up her fingers: one, two, three, and on three bounced on her toes and broke into a silent run. Emma's lithe form flashed the other direction, both of them darting beyond the sweep of spotlights and grateful for the cold rain that helped hide them in the night. Brandon was back in London with Lilith, but Alisha was confident he didn't constitute a flight risk. Not with the quantum flash drive capable of storing Lilith's core functions on a cord beneath Alisha's close-fitting black shirt. The flash drive was empty: Brandon didn't want to twin Lilith, and had wiped the flash drive after he'd uploaded her to Emma's servers. But without the drive, Lilith couldn't be removed from the facilities she currently functioned from.

"You can't do that," Brandon had said in half-astonished outrage. "That's holding her hostage."

"Watch me," Alisha repeated beneath her breath now.

The rain-slick surface of the wall in front of her resisted the grip of her pebbled, sticky-microfilament gloves, meant to cling to hard surfaces, more thoroughly than she'd hoped. A piton and rope at her hip would reach the window above, but dinging the glass might well set off alarms. Lilith, waiting patiently in England, believed there was only a few-second window where she could override security and allow Emma and Alisha to get into the facilities without notice. Any hint of intrusion before that would undo the whole game.

Alisha slipped around the corner, avoiding floodlights as she unwrapped the piton rope, then followed the arc of light back, swinging her weighted cord. One chance in the dark and rain. Missing would spell disaster. *Then don't miss, Leesh.*

Rain spattered in her eyes as she let go the weight, claws soaring upward with a whistle of wind. The *clank* of landing sounded hideously loud in her ears, but one firm tug told her the claws had caught, and there was no time to investigate whether anyone else had heard. Between the rope and the pebbled gloves that helped her cling to the wall, Alisha scrambled up to the window in seconds, pulling the cord behind her. She pushed her sleeve back, cupping her hand over the watch on her wrist to check the seconds, though the numbers counted off at the back of her mind, steady as a metronome. Her heartbeat was even, as if she was on a stroll in the park, not scaling factory walls. Five seconds. She slipped a lock pick from inside her other sleeve at three seconds, and jimmied it beneath the window at zero. The lock itself was simple, and she would know within a handful of seconds whether Lilith had successfully disabled the alarm system.

Seven seconds later Alisha slid inside, lowering herself to a metal catwalk as she closed the window behind her.

Only then did her heart rate leap, part triumph and part relief. A trill of laughter lodged in her throat, silenced by a decade of training. There were two levels to explore; gloating over making it in safely was premature. Alisha cast a glance at a security camera in the nearest corner and hoped Lilith had been able to loop the tapes in her seven-second glitch as she predicted she would. Once more, Alisha would know soon enough if the AI had failed. Still on tip-toe, she darted through the nearest set of double doors, exploring the facilities.

Lilith had fed back the tapes to one of the terminals at the London computing facility, finding almost nothing of interest. Almost: there was an extra twenty feet of building, four stories high, that didn't show up anywhere on the security cameras. Reichart clearly wasn't in any of the well-filmed areas of the factory, but that semi-secret stretch offered not only a chance he'd been abducted and held there, but flat-out piqued Alisha's curiosity. *Nosy*, her mother had teased, when Alisha was a teen. *Actively interested in the community around me*, Alisha'd argued good-naturedly. Whatever name it was given, curiosity was a powerful tool and a good trait in a spy. It made her explore the possibilities beyond the outlines of her mission, and while that could get her in trouble, it also reaped benefits.

Not anymore, she reminded herself. This "mission" was self-dictated, a totally freelance project for the first time in her adult life. The hall around her was dimly lit, windowed rooms reflecting her image, distorted and faint in the glass. She looked as she often did on a mission: slim, neither remarkably tall nor remarkably short, wrapped in black that helped gazes slide off her in the small hours of the night. But the woman so reflected wasn't the same one she'd been a year ago. That one, mistrustful though she'd become, had still been holding on to her faith. This one, Alisha thought, was searching for a new way to believe.

Or, at the very least, searching for Frank Reichart. Alisha slipped down the hall, keeping an eye open for the sweep of security cameras. Emma was below her, working her way up. They would meet in the middle, with or without success, and make their way out of the facility again.

A woman's laugh, quiet and unexpected, sent Alisha skittering down a hallway to press into a doorway that provided inadequate cover. "I'm glad to see everything's going so well," the woman said. Ice slid over Alisha's skin as she recognized the voice. "I appreciate you arranging to see me on such short notice, as well. It's a little unusual."

A man answered, deep and rich with amusement, "Not at all. I'm delighted to arrange things to suit the senator's aide."

Footsteps reached the mouth of the hall Alisha hid in, affording her a bare glimpse of the woman as she put her hand on the man's arm, an intimation of confidence and admiration, blue eyes bright as she looked up at him. "We appreciate it."

Alisha knew the gesture as well as the voice: with her wheat-blond hair and easy smile, Cristina Lamken relied on her ability to distract as an espionage agent. The bag of tricks hadn't changed, though in truth, Alisha saw no reason why it should. Her own less-extraordinary features allowed her to blend, and she continued to use that as successfully as she had when she and Cristina had been partners. It had been part of why they'd worked well together: their strengths played to different arenas, complementing each other. Once, Alisha had trusted that partnership more than anything in the world.

Now Cristina's presence brought a throbbing pulse to

Alisha's temple, blood hot with the impulse to act rashly. She had questions for Cristina—whether there was a child, for one, though nothing in the woman's form suggested it. Why she had chosen now to break nearly a year's silence, re-entering the underground world of the Sicarii and war machines?

"The senator wants to know when the first shipment will be made," Cristina said. The words brought her and her escort past the hallway, leaving Alisha safe—relatively safe—in the dim shape of the door, but her heart leaped at the political reference. Director Boyer, before his death, had made it clear there were people above him involved with the Sicarii investigation, and that he hadn't rated inclusion in the goings-on. A name might give her a place to begin digging. Before she'd thought about it, Alisha slipped out of the doorway and ran to the head of the hall, keeping her breathing slow and even so she could listen in on the conversation.

And so she heard the hesitation in the factory manager's voice. "That's highly classified information, ma'am."

"Doesn't my being here suggest I've got the clearance?" Few people, Alisha thought, would have heard the note of irritation beneath Cristina's teasing question. Even she barely recognized it, and she had more intimate knowledge of the blond spy than most. "I could call the senator and have him speak with you personally," Cristina offered, and even the factory man knew it for a threat.

"That's all right." Poorly masked tension came through, underscored by a door clicking open, the sound echoing noisily in the corridor. Alisha gritted her teeth together, holding back a curse, and dared glance down the hall to catch a glimpse of where her quarry went. Cristina's shoulders were held straight and proud, the stance of a woman who expected to be taken seriously. She had never learned to bow her head, Alisha remembered. Cristina could only command attention, not avoid it. Appropriate, perhaps, for a woman who believed herself to be the descendent of royalty, but dangerous in a spy.

"Today," the manager was saying apologetically as he escorted Cristina through the door. "I'm afraid the first battalion left this morning."

Any further conversation was cut off as the door closed. The last Alisha saw of Cristina was her spine stiffening, unmuted anger vivid in her body language. For an instant Alisha felt badly on the plant manager's behalf; Cristina's furious tongue wasn't a weapon anyone wanted to be on the receiving end of. But that sympathy slipped away again under a far more intense concern: Attengee drones had been shipped. The threat the semi-intelligent combat robots offered was finally, after two years, more than a danger waiting in the sidelines. Someone very soon would face an unanticipated foe in battle, and the structure of warfare would be changed for good.

Alisha found herself moving again, thought left behind in the comfort of action. Stopping the clock was impossible: the drones *would* become a part of warfare in the near future. But the longer it could be put off—

And Brandon had built the original drones, both the Alpha-Ten-G series that Alisha'd nicknamed the Attengees, and the elegant flying machines Brandon called the Firebirds. If anyone might have the skill and equipment to disable them, it would be the scientist held hostage with his AI. All Alisha needed to do was get herself and Brandon to the battalion before it reached its destination. Rerouting the machines elsewhere might work, though to succeed they would have to move fast: even if the drones' existence was still clandestine, the U.S. government would not take well to their shiny new combat toys disappearing. She would need someone else to turn them over to a trust-worthy third party.

All of which was beautifully irrelevant if she couldn't find the travel path and destination the drones were currently scheduled for. Her impulse was to go down, below not just the floor she'd infiltrated but beneath the ground, in search of secret bunkers and files that weren't meant to be seen by prying eyes. But there was no time, and still the larger part of two floors to explore in hopes of finding Frank Reichart. Alisha swore under her breath, hardly more than a shaping of the words, then knotted her hands into fists.

Odds of Reichart being trapped in the facility were low. High enough to have come searching for him, but far lower than the Attengee shipment's destination being in the computers there. Weighing the choices came down in favor of following the drones, not searching for old lovers. "Sorry, Frank."

Alisha pushed the door open cautiously and ran down the hall after Cristina Lamken.

❦

The rendezvous time was seventeen minutes gone and climbing. Seconds ticked away, turning into minutes. One part of Alisha's mind focused on that, wondering if Emma had cut her losses and run when Alisha hadn't shown up on time. *It's what I would have done*, Alisha told herself as she scanned through files, though she wasn't sure it was true. It's what the hard-hearted, fully professional half of her would have done, but really, unless the danger was obvious and critical, concern for her partner would override the practical thing to do.

There was no way of knowing whether Emma Dickens

had an equally soft side. A man like Frank Reichart might've been more attracted to a woman who didn't, a woman who, more like himself, might be capable of shooting her lover to save his life. That sort of woman would have left Alisha behind.

Not that it mattered. Alisha had the security codes and as good a chance of escaping the factory unnoticed as anyone. The sensible thing for Emma to have done was gone ahead without her. It would be interesting to see whether she had or not, and the fact that Alisha fully expected to get out safely and make that discovery said it was better if Emma *had* gone on without her.

Transportation rosters began to fill the screen in front of her and all of Alisha's questions fled, leaving her mind clear and sharp. They were on an unsecured terminal, whether because someone had forgotten to log out or because delivery routes weren't considered important enough to hide behind passwords and codes, Alisha didn't know. She hadn't exited the main screen she'd found, in case it was the former.

Three truckloads had gone out that morning, all with destinations that made Alisha's stomach clench with nerves. Afghanistan, still a center of unrest and filled with American troops; Serbia, where a third world war was being played out by proxy; and one to Paris, where it would be loaded onto a plane and sent to Virginia. The senator Cristina had mentioned flashed into Alisha's mind, making her wonder if there would soon be a man at one of the top levels of U.S. government with his own personal war machines. Alisha'd been reluctant to follow Cristina closely enough to pick up any more data on who she might've been speaking of; entering the computer room Cristina and the plant manager had exited seemed risky enough. It was very likely his password that allowed Alisha access to the transport files. A bad breach of security, not logging out again. Cristina would have noticed. The man might find himself without a job, come morning.

Twenty-two minutes. Alisha closed her eyes, tracing the land routes the trucks were taking behind her eyelids. Once satisfied she knew them by heart, she stepped away from the terminal again, and turned her thoughts to getting out of the factory unseen. It was after midnight: any entry or exit would set off an alarm.

Unless Cristina's secretive visit had forced the Zurich security company to change the systems for the night. In which case, Alisha's own escape was intimately bound up in Cristina's departure. Grinning at the idea, Alisha slipped out of the office to find and shadow her former partner until an escape could be made.

≈

A hand wrapped over her mouth, confident strength hauling her backward. Alisha drew in a sharp breath through her nostrils, making a fist and driving her elbow backward toward her assailant's belly. A hint of scent stopped her before contact had been made: Emma's faint perfume, washed off hours before the mission but still lingering on her skin. A dangerous frivolity for a spy, but enough to relax Alisha in the woman's grip. After a few seconds Emma released her and Alisha took another deep breath. "You shouldn't have waited."

"I wouldn't have," Emma said as Alisha turned to face her. There was no humor in the British woman's voice, nothing to indicate she spoke anything other than the absolute truth. "But he insisted."

"He—" Hope caught a fist in Alisha's stomach, knotting it so suddenly she felt dizzy.

"Call me sentimental," a man's voice said out of the darkness. "But I knew you'd get out of there in one piece, even after I saw Cristina." Frank Reichart came out of a hidden place beside the factory walls to pull an unresisting Alisha into his arms for a brief hug.

"Hello, Leesh," he murmured into her hair, then stepped back, grin turning crooked. "Guess this one's Emma's rescue."

8

Speechless was not a term Alisha often assigned to herself, but as she turned in the pre-dawn darkness to Emma, it was the only word that applied. Emma shrugged, dismissing the rescue with studied blasé. "What kept you?"

"Not that I don't share Em's curiosity," Reichart murmured, "but this might not be the best place to discuss it. You did have a plan, didn't you, Alisha? Something beyond getting me outside these walls? Or is the rest of it up to me?"

Alisha shot him a look, irritation tempered by relief and a betraying desire to laugh. "I thought we'd done enough. Your turn now." Ignoring her own reply, she crooked two fingers in invitation and darted away from the factory walls, leading Reichart and Emma through darkness. Emma might as easily have led, but she hung back, keeping pace with an unusually slow Reichart. Emotion Alisha refused to categorize as jealousy swept her, coupled with concern: she hadn't stopped to check

Reichart's health before their headlong run into the night. Emma obviously had.

Bitch, Alisha thought, completely unreasonably, and tried to find a smile to tease herself with. It barely succeeded, and left her more inclined to concentrate on the route to their pickup point than to examine her feelings about Emma being along on the mission.

Without her, Alisha would have left Reichart in there. That cold truth didn't help her state of mind at all.

A car waited for them, the driver an asset of Emma's, not Alisha's. He'd been instructed to wait until an hour before dawn; if they weren't back by then, there was no point in risking himself to questioning about waiting idly too near a U.S. government facility for coincidence.

The vehicle's lights were off, its engine killed just as they'd agreed it would be. Nothing obvious brought Alisha to a halt, one hand lifted in warning. Emma and Reichart drew up behind her, the latter breathing harder than the run through the woods should have made him. Alisha put it out of her mind: there were other things to be concerned with. So long as Reichart didn't actively request a stop, he was fit enough to continue. Alisha had to trust that. Did trust it, more than she trusted almost anything. After everything, she still believed in the man behind her.

"What is it?" Emma's soft English accent sounded in Alisha's ear. Alisha shook her head, hand still uplifted.

"I don't know," she breathed back. "Something's not right." The shape of the driver, only a shadow in shadows, looked wrong. Slumped, as if in sleep, though a cool certainty flowing through her told Alisha it was more than sleep that held him captive. She pointed behind herself, edging backward. Emma and Reichart took the cue, slipping back into the woods as silently as they'd come. "I don't like it," Alisha whispered once they'd retreated several hundred feet. "I just don't like it."

"We can't leave him there," Emma protested sharply, but Reichart cut her off with a gesture even as Alisha spoke.

"If he's all right, he'll leave in another twenty minutes. If he's already dead, there's nothing we can do except not take the bait. We have a flight from Belgrade at eight-thirty," Alisha said to Reichart. "The plan was to rendezvous with Brandon—"

"You've got to be kidding." Reichart silenced himself with the glare Alisha gave him, nodding for her to continue.

"But even if we can make the flight, things have changed. The Attengees have shipped. I've got the manifests and destinations. Did the—" It was Alisha's turn to break off, eyeing Emma uncertainly. "How much does she know?"

"All of it," Reichart said. "She knows all of it."

A pang of surprise and loneliness shot through Alisha's heart, leaving her stinging with the cold discovery of being an outsider. Questions demanded to be asked: *Why does she know everything? Did you tell her, when you wouldn't tell me? Does she mean that much more to you than I did?* Long seconds passed before Alisha trusted her voice enough to say, "Did the Infitialis ever manage a successful copy of the drones?" There was nothing to betray herself, no hurt or anger, no pain or accusation in the words. Reichart's gaze lingered on her face, even in the darkness, and Alisha wondered if the very steadiness of the question had betrayed her, after all.

"No," he said after almost as long a silence. "The software you gave us—"

"You stole from me," Alisha corrected, hoping that being pedantic would help take her mind away from the questions Emma presented. Reichart gave her a sour look that would've been visible in a pitch-black room, and Alisha twisted a brief smile.

"That I stole from you," he agreed. "It was corrupted enough we haven't been able to rebuild it."

Alisha's smile held challenge, not pleasure. "How about we go steal some functional systems for you, then?"

A lifetime's training in secrecy and silence didn't stop Reichart's startled bark of laughter, though the sound was quieter than it might have been if given voice by someone else. "Are you mad?" He sounded delighted, not accusatory.

"Completely." Alisha didn't dare look at Emma, sure the British woman wouldn't see the humor that Reichart did in the proposition. "If we—if Emma," she corrected herself, determined to give credit where it was due, "hadn't found you in there, I'd've risked proposing the idea to her."

"Even without knowing I was Infitialis?" Emma asked.

Alisha did glance her way then, another pang cramping her heart. "I still don't know you're Infitialis. Are you?"

Emma's eyelashes shuttered closed an instant before she inclined her head in a nod. "Like Frank's, my family's been involved for decades. My grandfather believed in egalitarianism. Ironic," she added in a murmur, "as he had money and his own Sicarii connections. He chose to sever the latter, and turn his wealth toward a better end. My daughter knows what I do and wants to follow in my foot-steps." A mix of pride and dismay curved her mouth.

"Who else do you work for? MI-5? Lilith said—"

"Does it really matter right now, Alisha?"

Alisha clenched her teeth, then pushed curiosity away. "I guess not. Anyway, Reichart trusted you enough to give you access to that number I called." Not even Alisha had the voice mail code for that private number, another detail that made her feel cold and small if she let herself dwell on it. "The only other person I knew who had Infitialis connections died last October." She shrugged, an easy, dismissive motion that cost her more than she liked to admit. "So yes, even without knowing, I'd have risked it. I didn't see another choice."

The confession made, Alisha turned her attention back to Reichart. "The Infitialis are the only people I'd trust with those drones. I know what you intended to do with them. Of course, if you're lying to me…?" She tried for a smile and found it weak, but it would do. Reichart, frowning, glanced between Emma and Alisha.

"Wait. You called me? On the private line?"

Disbelief stained Alisha's gaze as she stared at him for a few seconds, then gave over to a frustrated laugh. "I guess you wouldn't know about that."

"I thought you'd found out I was in trouble and come in with guns blazing." A note of sheepishness crept into Reichart's voice, a rare admission of the man's self-centered viewpoint before it changed to worry. "Shit, Alisha. What's going on?"

"The Sicarii came after my family," Alisha said shortly. She'd thought the rage had burned out, but it lay just beneath the surface, simmering, waiting for her to look at it again. That fury coupled nicely with the need to move against the dissemination of the Attengee drones into worldwide war.

And that, it came to her suddenly, might have been why she was a good spy. So often in her career she hadn't understood the larger picture, but when faced with it, she couldn't help but move on the path that would benefit the many. The good of the one was often a necessary sacrifice for the survival of all. The dredge was bitter to swallow, but in the heat of the moment it was also her instinctive choice.

But Reichart paled, even in the darkness. "Alisha." Her name was filled with a dozen things: regret and horror, defensiveness and sorrow, all powerful emotions that Reichart rarely allowed himself to show.

"They came after Brandon," Alisha amended, sudden weariness coloring her explanation. "He'd come to me for help. They barely missed my nephews, Frank. I've got to find a way to stop this, to get out of it so they'll be safe. The Infitialis, they'll disable the weapons functions on the drones? Use them for sophisticated delivery systems?" That was what he'd promised the Infitialis had wanted the semi-intelligent machines for. Capable of making their own decisions about how best to travel overland, the drones could be used for good works instead of the warmaking devastation they'd been designed for. "Diverting the drones to the Infitialis would be one hell of a bitch-slap in the face of the Sicarii."

A brief smile colored Reichart's expression. "I hate to be the one to point this out to you, Ali, but—"

"Oh, God, don't do that."

More humor creased Reichart's face. "Alisha," he amended.

Alisha felt Emma's curious glance on her and said, "I don't mind Ali. It just sounds wrong coming from him."

"Really," Emma murmured, and Alisha all but heard the rest of the question: *What does he usually call you?* It brought fleeting satisfaction that warmed some of the outsider coolness Alisha had felt. At least there were some things she had with Reichart that the other woman didn't share.

"But that's a U.S. government facility in there, not a Sicarii organization. You'd be stealing from your own government." Reichart's tone made it more than clear he recognized the irony of him, of all people, arguing in favor of playing by the rules.

Alisha shook her head. "It's a risk I'm willing to take. Besides, Cristina's involved, and I don't trust her any farther than I could throw a snake. Reichart," Alisha added, finally remembering to ask, "what were you doing in there anyway?"

"Being held hostage to ensure the good behavior of the Infitialis with regard to the delivery of the Attengee and Firebird drones," Reichart answered, deadpan. Alisha stared at him hard enough to earn a second quick, quiet laugh.

"You were—and you're still warning me about stealing U.S. government property?"

"Leesh," Reichart said gently, and for all that the nickname was private, her own way of naming herself, Alisha found herself smiling at the name and at his tone. Out of the corner of her eye, Alisha saw Emma look away, and in a sudden reversal, felt a spike of sympathy shoot through her. "It is U.S. property," Reichart went on, still gently. "The fact that the Sicarii influence U.S. politics through special interest groups and fronted corporations doesn't make it any less true. What I know about what the Sicarii intend to do is one thing, Leesh. You participating in doing something about it is something else entirely. It goes against everything you've done your whole career."

"No." Alisha's voice thinned. "It goes against everything I did up until two years ago, Reichart, when you got me pulled into this Sicarii-Infitialis war without even warning me. Everything's changed for me, Frank. I'm not the girl I was when we were together. Not anymore."

Reichart lowered his chin in acknowledgment, though he kept his eyes on Alisha's. "I'm sorry for that."

"Are you? If you want to know the truth, Frank..." Alisha looked away, eventually shaking her head. "I'm not sure I am. I used to believe I was working for the good guys."

"And now?"

Alisha looked back at him, then pushed out of her crouch, hands on her thighs. "Now I don't know what I believe." She let that rest, a full and hard stop, before jerking her head to the side. "Come on. We've got a lot of ground to cover to get back to the main roads and a way out of here before dawn."

"*S*top." The word came from ahead, low and full of warning. Reichart crooked his fingers, inviting Alisha and Emma to crawl through bushes and with him, look down over a cliff's edge at the road below.

Serbian police blocked the road, impatient and weary voices lifting in oft-repeated explanation. An exchange of glances amongst the trio above the road earned a nod from Emma, who listened, then whispered, "They say they have a tip-off about a drug run coming through this part of the country. All the roads are blocked, all vehicles are being searched summarily. It has been going on since four this morning and will continue until the shipment is discovered or their superiors call off the search." She fell silent again, listening, then added, "Most of the rest is abuse being heaped upon the police from angry drivers. I'd be cautious, if I were them. People disappear in these searches."

"Too bad it hasn't been going on since yesterday," Alisha whispered. "It'd be lovely to just drop down on one of the trucks and wrest control, then deliver it as we saw fit."

"You've been watching Bond films again," Reichart

muttered. "Besides, it might not be as good as the delivery trucks, but see what we have there." He pointed down the road, where, just at the bend of a curve, a slim blond woman, her every step indicating irritation, stalked back and forth around her car. Alisha drew a sharp breath at the same time Emma did, making them exchange glances. It was Emma who broke the silence.

"She wouldn't recognize me. You and Frank…"

Setting someone other than herself on Cristina made Alisha's palms itch with frustration, though Emma was undoubtedly correct. "It might be the best chance we get to find out who she's working with. Who the senator she mentioned is. Whether we can get to the Sicarii plans for the drones. Dammit." The words were spoken almost to herself, Alisha's gaze fixed on her former partner on the road below. "Can you keep on her?"

"What is it you Americans say?" Emma breathed, "'Does a bear shit in the woods'?" She pushed up to hands and knees, already skirting to the right. "Someone in that line of cars will be willing to trail her for enough euros. Frank, if you haven't heard from me in forty-eight hours…?"

"I know, Em. Don't worry."

That was all the reassurance it took. Within seconds the brush swallowed Emma up, branches rustling with nothing more than wind. Only when she was certain the other woman was out of earshot did Alisha say, "Mazie?" and earn a nod from Reichart.

"We can get beyond the police line," he added. "As long as we stay up here. We can probably pick up a ride a little farther down the road. Do you speak any Serbian?"

"Hungarian. Russian. You know that, Frank."

He slid her an amused glance. "Are you calling me Frank because she does?" Rather than waiting for an answer, he turned to the left and began pushing through the underbrush, careful not to let branches snap back and betray their presence with their sound. Alisha curled her lip in acknowledgment of his jibe and followed, wondering what the answer was.

9

"*Y*ou want me to sit here cooling my heels for how long? Alisha, I've already got most of the damned facility crawling all over me. Half of them want to know what's eating up the processing power and the other half want to know who shifted their code to produce more favorable results. Lilith's practically napping—"

"Which she'd be doing in your flash drive anyway," Alisha interrupted.

Brandon barreled on, undeterred. "—when she could be doing something of real use. Was the roadblock helpful?" he asked abruptly, leaving Alisha blinking at the phone.

"Road—that was Lilith? It was helpful." Bemusement filled Alisha's voice. "Furthermore, I heard on the ten o'clock news that the police had actually picked up a huge heroin shipment at about seven this morning. How could she have known?"

"Extrapolation of drug-running patterns over the past

thirty years," Brandon said carelessly. "There was a twenty-eight percent chance a shipment would be going through northern Serbia in the next forty-eight hours."

"Twenty-eight percent's not very good."

"It is when the other likelihoods ran at three to seven percent. You see, Alisha? Lilith's much too important to let anyone control her. She's capable of making a real difference on her own, as a hyperintelligent sentient being."

"Yeah," Alisha said, only half kidding. "Isn't that how everything went wrong in the Terminator movies?"

"Alisha." Brandon's tone was reproving.

Alisha sighed and moved away from the airport window, shaking her head. "Just two days, Brandon. You can hold tight that long. If we haven't intercepted these shipments by then—"

"Lilith could help, Ali, if you'd just give me the information to pass on to her."

"This isn't a secure line, Brandon." It was all the answer she was willing to give, and Brandon's exasperated sigh admitted he acknowledged her point. "Besides, I thought she was locked up making like an ordinary program. And where could be safer for you, anyway? I doubt the Sicarii have a stronghold inside the London computing facility." Truthfully, there was no reason Alisha could think of that they might not, but Reichart trusted Emma, and Emma had brought them to the supercomputer. It would have to do.

"I don't like this, Alisha."

"I didn't ask you to like it." Some of the anger that she'd let go of slipped into the words and she heard Brandon's careful exhalation.

"All right," he said. "All right, if that's what I'm stuck with. Just get back here, will you?"

"As soon as we've disrupted a delivery or two," Alisha promised. "Trust me, I don't want to be responsible for you any longer than I have to be." She hung up, feeling Reichart's gaze on her, and turned to the dark-haired man.

He'd been tolerably well treated in his captivity, no bruises or torn clothes, though his brown eyes were tired and he moved more clumsily than usual, as if he hadn't had enough sleep recently. Well, neither had Alisha, and Emma's pursuit of Cristina didn't bear thinking about. That, at least, boded well in its likelihood of turning out. There was no reason at all for Cristina to recognize the British woman, and Reichart would never have agreed to send her if Emma hadn't been capable of a discreet tail.

"Why is it you're helping him?" Reichart asked mildly.

Alisha sat down with a groan. "There are men in my life I don't seem to be able to say no to," she said half seriously, but shook her head. "Because he's the only piece of insurance I've got to keep my family out of this mess." She gestured Reichart over, taking his hand as he sat down and leaning her head against his shoulder. The very picture of tired lovers on a long trip, she thought, but the topic they discussed was worlds apart from romance. "We're going to have to split up. As it is, two's not enough to intercept all three shipments. We're going to have to let one of them go."

"I don't like it." Reichart turned his head, kissing her hair in a familiar gesture that made Alisha smile despite herself. "I've been wondering," he said, "whether I should have called. When I heard you'd left the Company I thought it might not be welcome."

"It would've complicated things," Alisha admitted. "But things got complicated anyway. There are days when I wonder how people live ordinary lives."

"I think they start out by choosing a different occupation than the one we've chosen. Leesh—"

"Reichart." Alisha sat up and put her fingertips over his lips. "God knows I've spent a lot of time wanting answers and resolution from you, but this isn't the time. We have a lot to do, and talking about us isn't getting it done."

Reichart moved her fingers, kissing them before he lowered her hand. "Maybe for the first time I'm afraid there's not going to be time to discuss us if we wait any longer."

"Oh ye of little faith." Alisha snuggled back down against his side. "We'll have later, Frank. One thing about us is we always seem to have another chance."

"All right, but once we've saved the world again, I'd like to take you somewhere tropical, with no cell phone reception."

Alisha laughed. "It's a date."

"Good. Who's Lilith?"

Alisha turned her face into Reichart's shoulder, stifling a groan. "Brandon'll kill me for telling you," she said, but it didn't stop her from quietly explaining the new direction Brandon's AI program had developed in. "The Attengees are so quick at real-time decision making they seem like they're almost alive. I don't know if Brandon's goal was always sentience in a machine, but the pathway seems to be there from the work he's been doing. Lilith's got personality and opinions, Frank. I don't know if that constitutes independent intelligence and awareness, but she sounds alive," she concluded.

"How many people know about this?"

"Erika got into Brandon's code—Lilith's code," Alisha amended, "and reported to Greg. Cristina came in, which means the Sicarii know. Emma knows now. You. Me. Brandon."

"A secret known to six people…"

"Isn't a secret at all. I know. The top is going to be blown off Lilith's existence any day now, unless everybody who knows has a vested interest in keeping it silent, and I don't see why they would. I'd think there'd be a lot of cash in sentient computers."

"Or a lot of threat," Reichart murmured. "You take the Paris drop, and get back to Parker and his damned brainy machine as fast as you can. I'll go to Afghanistan and see what I can do there." Something cautious lined his voice and Alisha frowned, scooting back so she could look at him.

"What aren't you telling me, Frank?"

He hesitated, then slipped his arm around her shoulder and drew her close again. "I don't know if you need to know this."

"Reichart." The name lashed out and garnered a laugh from the man she leaned against.

"Sorry, kid. *Alisha,*" he corrected himself, almost as sharply as she'd just reprimanded him. "It's been a bad year for the Infitialis, Leesh. Boyer was the first of…?" He inhaled deeply and sighed just as deeply, sorrow coloring his voice. "Of a lot. We rewrote all our codes, abandoned all our regular safe houses, but even so, we lost forty people between Boyer's death and the end of last year, Leesh. More have gone missing or died since then, and we can't find the leak. If we don't get those drones, as much to defend ourselves as to continue our work…?" He trailed off, shaking his head. "The Fas Infitialis have been around since the days of Rome, Alisha, but unless we win this fight, our days are numbered."

*R*eichart's confession lingered in her ears as Alisha boarded a flight to Paris. Using him as a hostage suddenly made more sense: if the Infitialis were so decimated that the loss of even one more individual might break them, they might well agree to play by the Sicarii's ugly rules in order to save themselves.

If the Infitialis were failing in numbers, they must find a way to replenish them. And the former CIA agent sinking into the soft airline seat might be a place to begin.

For a moment she wondered if that was who she was now, who she'd come down to being, at the end of it all. Not someone sworn to king and country after all, but instead promised to an esoteric high ideal that seemed unlikely to ever come to pass.

A year ago—two years—it would have bothered her that the answer to that was *yes*. She'd changed. Sometimes she could barely trace the journey that had brought her there, while at the same time every step of it was agonizingly clear. From the moment Gregory Parker had offered her an underwater-breathing kit the likes of which James Bond would envy, Alisha's path had inexorably led her to a place where her duty lay beyond the needs of her country. It was not a destination at which she'd ever expected to find herself.

Greg. Thoughts of the small, dapper man still made her stomach tighten with unhappiness. Had he, she wondered, been with the Sicarii twelve years ago, when he'd brought a nineteen-year-old, adventuresome Alisha MacAleer into the CIA's fold? Had he always intended to use her to further Sicarii ends, or had he been able to separate the Company agent from his Sicarii destiny? Alisha herself had resolutely held out against separating one part of her soul from another in such a manner. Somehow she doubted Greg had managed the separation, either. Lies and deception were part of the world they both existed in. Strange to find that so, too was hard-won idealism, and that it could stand fast in the face of the things she'd encountered. Reichart would laugh at her.

Then again, maybe not. Not when the twists and turns of his own life were driven by the Infitialis belief that man forged his own destiny. Not when he worked silently in the background of society, even in the background of the espionage world, to do what he could to help people defy the fate that the Sicarii would otherwise stage for them. Frank Reichart might just be more idealistic than Alisha herself was.

And where did that leave someone like Brandon Parker? Alisha frowned, not wanting to think about the blond scientist. Still, she'd imagined a dozen times that she knew where Gregory's son stood. His genius with programming had driven him to create the Attengees and the Firebirds, lifetime goals achieved by the time he was in his early thirties. She'd thought he'd created them for the Sicarii, but as much as Greg had betrayed himself in Paris at the news of Boyer's death, so, too had Brandon betrayed himself. He had worked in good faith, believing himself undercover for an American agency, his creations meant to take men out of warfare and leave it to machines. More than idealistic, it was naive, but that may have been the price of scholarship's ivory tower.

Though, Alisha reminded herself, the scientists who had created the atomic bomb had known they were developing a deadly weapon. Brandon's work, at least, didn't carry the remote but accepted possibility that setting one off might ignite the planet's atmosphere. And she'd seen real horror in his eyes when he'd realized his orders through Cristina, his handler, had come from Susan

Simone, an agent of the Sicarii. Which left Brandon... where? Caught, in his own way, in the mess of his own creation, and searching for the best way out of it. Alisha's anger over him endangering her family aside, she did reluctantly trust that Parker was doing what he thought best.

Machinations behind the scenes, she thought. One hidden group of madmen trying to rule the world, another trying to save it. She no longer believed Brandon Parker belonged to the former, and wondered if that made him, by default, one of the latter. If, like Alisha herself, he had been pushed and pulled and tugged into a position he had never meant to occupy, and if so, whether he was finding that he fitted there better than he might have imagined.

Sleep captured her, questions of belonging fading and stretching into much-needed rest. The flight to Paris was comparatively short. Answers, if they were to come at all, would be waiting on the other side of dreams.

≈

Habit, carved from years of experience, sent her through the airport as swiftly as she could go without attracting attention, even half awake after the flight's arrival. She kept her eyes downcast, obscuring the shape of her face as best she could from the omnipresent CCTV cameras. Bangs drawn over her forehead helped in that as well, though none of it was as thorough a disguise as she preferred. The passport she used, one of her extra, illegal dossiers, was a no-one-in-particular American, a woman from Iowa who had promised herself a trip to Europe a thousand times over the years and had finally taken it. Alisha wished she had more in common with the woman she pretended to be, though that desire faded quickly. Despite its harrowing moments, she'd enjoyed the life she'd chosen, and even when its price became personal missions such as this one, it was worth the years she'd spent in it. Without it, she'd never have met Frank Reichart.

Or Brandon Parker, she reminded herself, a rueful curve shaping her lips. Or Cristina, or Greg or innumerable others whose lives had changed hers irrevocably. *Stop it, Leesh,* she ordered herself without heat. Looking back on how things had come to be felt too much like an epilogue, and her life was far from over.

Her intent passage forward slowed at customs—a disadvantage of traveling on an American passport in Europe—and she kept her gaze on the floor, studying cracks in the tiling and scuff marks from millions of shoes. A baby whined nearby and its older brother sighed with the drama of a put-upon teenager. Voices murmured, no one wanting to draw attention to themselves at this last gate before the freedom of Parisian streets. A television whined on overhead and a CNN reporter began listing the news in France and abroad. Alisha listened with half an ear, inching forward as people ahead of her were approved and sent on.

"…Arthur Devane has announced today that he'll be stepping down from his position as U.S. senator from Delaware at the end of the month, due to ill health."

Alisha glanced up, drawn by the story, and watched a hale, solemn-looking man in his sixties speaking at a podium, his words muted so the announcer could continue.

"Rumors abound as to who the Delaware senator will appoint as his successor in a position that has been all but hereditary over the last seventy years. Senator Devane has no children, so the senatorial seat is up for grabs, though we're told the current favorite is this woman, Nichole Oldenburg, whose record in public service is exemplary."

A slim woman with aristocratic features and an arresting smile waved at the camera, her wheat-blond hair almost white in the sunlight. She looked trustworthy, competent, young enough to appeal to the youthful demographic and old enough—perhaps just thirty-five—for an older generation to feel they weren't being taken in by a child. She was, as always, impossibly photogenic, her unbowed head and blue eyes confident, challenging and lovely all at once. The name was a persona, someone created to have papers, a social media presence, an online history, that was as impressive as her physical presence. Alisha knew without having to search that they would be impeccable.

No one would find the missing links that turned Cristina Lamken into Nichole Oldenburg.

The senator wants to know when the first shipment will be made whispered through Alisha's mind as she stared at the screen. By the time the American shipment of drones arrived in Virginia, Cristina Lamken would be enthroned as the new senator from Delaware. The demonstration of the Attengee warfare technology would settle her in place as the Pentagon's darling, the military industry's spokeswoman, and brand her unmistakably as being one hundred percent patriotic and pro-America. As clearly as if she stood within the walls of a Sicarii stronghold amongst men and women discussing the topic, Alisha could see how their plan—how Cristina's career—unfolded on a national political scale. Devane had to retire now, just after the elections, so Cristina could be safely in her job for a full six years and expected to run and win again. She would be too junior, in that election, to make a bid for a grander seat.

But six years after that, a woman like Cristina Lamken,

with brains, beauty and an organization dedicated to her cause behind her, could very easily be a genuine contender for the presidency of the United States of America.

Alisha, gaping at the screen, thought she had not expected the answers she sought to be quite so literally waiting on the other side of dreams.

10

"*Mademoiselle?*" The polite French query snapped Alisha out of watching the TV screen, though the sound bite on Senator Devane was long over. She looked up with a nervous, "*Oui?*", judging her persona's grasp of French to be high-school level, no better.

The man at her elbow was uniformed and officious-looking, Gallic nose long beneath deep-set eyes and beetled eyebrows. "If you could come this way, *mademoiselle*. Random security checks, I'm afraid." He'd switched to English in deference of her shaky American-accented response, though he kept his voice low and polite, as if not to disturb others in the customs line.

"But—I thought—doesn't this usually happen on the airplanes?" Alisha's voice came out thin and worried, masterfully hiding the spike of genuine alarm and frustration she felt. It was certainly possible she'd been recognized by the airport's biometric recognition software, and she had no CIA-sanctioned reason for traveling under false papers. The Midwesterner whose part she played would never dream of arguing with airport officials, but she certainly trembled with distress as the long-nosed officer led her to the side. He hadn't, she noticed, bothered to explain why the intrusion took place at customs instead of at the terminal. All the more reason to suspect she'd been recognized.

Dammit! There was no easy or good way to escape airport customs; the entire point was to delay and investigate. Getting through wouldn't be a trial if she hadn't been recognized, if it genuinely was a random search, but she'd passed through this airport innumerable times as Alisha MacAleer. Bluffing through being recognized weren't odds she liked to take.

Still, it was as Tammy Jones that she stepped through the marked door, escort at her elbow. "Is something wrong?" she asked in her best nervous French, wincing at her own accent. "I'm sorry, my French isn't very good, but I've been practicing. I'm sure that whatever this is can be cleared up wi—oh." The last word, for all that it was no more than a vowel sound, was definitely in English.

A cordial, enormous man sat behind a standard-issue office desk, its size dwarfed by his own. The chair he sat in was decidedly not standard, but of rich polished leather, and broad enough to fit a man of his width. "I don't know the rules for this version of the game," Alisha said a little sourly, in English. Bluffing was one thing. Denying her identity to a man who knew her personally was simply foolish. "Do I say *arrivederci*, and, Hello, Jon?"

"Jon," the big man said with a smile. "Who is this *Jon* that you call me? No," he said, suddenly dismissive. "Jon will do. Alisha, my little bird. How far from the cage you have flown."

"You have no idea." Alisha turned her sour look on the airport official, who probably did work there; it was far easier for a man such as Jon to make use of the pieces already in play than to arrange new players himself. Jon was a jovial cutthroat, master of an underworld crime ring that brokered in information, and in the years Alisha had known him, he had never failed to come through when she needed him. She owed him debt after debt, all accrued ten months earlier when the Firebird mission had gone so badly sideways.

And his accosting her at the Paris airport could only mean those debts were about to be called in. The Frenchman stepped outside, leaving Alisha alone in the room with the gigantic information broker. His love for life was as large as his girth, as if he deliberately played into the stereotype of cheerful fat people, but his eyes were often cold and calculating even as he smiled and offered friendship. She had always known that, but ten months ago Jon had reminded her of it pointedly. Her Strongbox Chronicles, the journals of her life in the CIA, were meant to be secret from everyone, and until then she'd thought they were. But Jon had made it clear he knew of them, and that anything she'd touched over the last decade could be exposed at his whim. More, he knew her real name and rarely bothered to dissemble about it, though he called her by the nickname he'd given her, *little bird*, as often as not. That, too, told her how well he knew her: the code name, Cardinal, she'd used for years had come after Jon's nickname, but now there was a slyness in his gaze when he used it, making it clear that, too, was a piece of information in his tally book.

Every one of those was a reason to distrust and even fear the big man, but instead, Alisha was tremendously fond of him. There was a certain freedom in knowing everything was for sale, everything had a price, and that any discussion was simply a negotiation of those details.

"Sit," Jon invited with an expansive sweep of his hand. Out of four chairs in the room, three were metal folding chairs. The fourth, an office chair, had very likely been behind the desk Jon now sat behind. Alisha took that one, settling in as comfortably as she could. "You have a problem," Jon announced once she'd sat.

Alisha's eyebrows rose. "It's the human condition, Jon. What problem do I have that interests you?"

"A shipment of very sophisticated war machines is about to leave Paris for Virginia," Jon said. "You wish to stop it, but lack the resources."

Wariness slid down Alisha's spine, making her want to straighten and take a defensive position. She maintained the casual one she held, more for her own benefit than Jon's: he would see the caution that had come into her body language even as she tried to hide it. "You made it very clear that I was not to come to you again when my resources were low. The shipment is my problem, not yours."

"Ah!" Jon leaned forward, steepling thick fingers, then pointing them at her. "But I *choose* to make it my problem." His accent was outrageously Italian, and the city he most often worked out of was Rome, but Alisha was uncertain if either were native to him. "This is very sad," he added with a cluck of his tongue. "We should discuss good food, good wine, all the things that make life worth living, before we talk about the ugly business of—" his fingers flicked up again, splaying wide as if he tossed the words to the air— "business."

"Usually we would," Alisha agreed carefully. "But this is unusual, Jon. You've never come to me before."

Avarice glittered in the big man's eyes. "You have never had something I wanted so badly before."

"And that is?"

"Her name," Jon purred, "is Lilith."

～

A secret known to six people, Alisha thought, *is not a secret at all.* The words rang clear in her mind, but did nothing to hide the surprise she felt cross her face.

Jon laughed, a heavy sound of pure delight, and clapped his meaty hands together. "You did not expect that. So much so that you fail even to tell me lies with your expression, little bird. You are slipping."

"Or I think there's no point in lying to you," Alisha muttered. There was a grain of truth to that, but Jon was right; he'd taken her completely off guard. "How did you know?"

"I have a great deal of money, Alisha. With so much money, it is easy to control people who should not be controlled, buy people who cannot be bought. You, of all people, should understand that. You owe me this, Alisha." Jon's beaming smile was heartfelt, his eyes cool as diamonds, and the warmth of his voice layering steel. "You cannot say no."

Would he, Alisha wondered, with clinical detachment, would Jon in fact have her eliminated, if she failed to comply with his request? Chances came down against her, she thought; he might hold that favor out, let her know that her very life was held in the balance. That she, in essence, belonged to him.

Or he might make his point by having her terminated.

The language she chose made her breathe a laugh and close her eyes. Distancing herself from feeling the implications of the action; that was what words like *terminate* and *eliminate* accomplished. A target could be eliminated without repercussion; her life could end without emotional involvement. It wasn't a topic she thought she ought to be clinical about. "Jon," she said aloud, eyes still closed, and all but heard the heavy shake of his head.

"Three favors, little bird. You have taken wing and flown, but there are chains binding you to earth. There is a love story I would hear, and the reasons why you have slipped free from your cage, and there is a computer who thinks for herself that I wish to have in my possession. The chains are strong, little bird, and your wings are weaker than you think."

"Don't threaten me, Jon." Alisha opened her eyes again, the words quiet. "There's no need. I understood what I was getting myself into." A faint smile darted across her face. "A love story and the reasons why I've done what I've done. Maybe I could be like Scheherezade," she suggested, and amusement creased the folds around Jon's eyes.

"The princess had not made the promise to the prince, little bird, as you have done. He had made the promise to himself. That is perhaps a safer promise to break, than the one a liege gives his lord."

"You're not my lord," Alisha said, suddenly acerbic, "and I think you know by now if I've made that promise to a lord," or to king and country, she amended silently, "I've learned I can break it, too."

Jon beamed at her. "And will you break your word to me? Your life will become very difficult, I promise you. You have, after all, been stopped by security, and who knows what problems they might find in your papers."

Of course, Alisha thought. Terminating her in the Paris airport would be messy. Much more effective to destroy her life, piece by piece, and when all hope was gone, call in the favors once again. She would be owned, body and soul, with no hope of escape.

"I will make it easier for you." Jon's voice softened and he leaned forward, inviting confidentiality. "I have the resources, Alisha, to help you stop that shipment of war drones." The lavish accent faded from his voice, the offer he made more important than theatrics. "I will do this *gratis*, free of favor or expectation, to smooth your soul's journey to betraying the handsome scientist."

"Why?" Anger made the word blunt, the corner Alisha felt backed into one of her own creation.

"Because." Jon sat back, spreading his hands expansively again. "I thrive on crime and information, little bird, it is true. But I believe war must be made between men, and as closely as possible, because to do less makes death far too easy. I am a large man, and doctors scold me for my habits. They tell me I court *el morte*, and they are correct. There are nights when death walks close by me, but at least when he does so I see him. Machines do not see death, Alisha. I wish the cost of war to be higher than that."

Heat climbed to Alisha's cheeks, slow surprise as she looked in astonishment at the corpulent man across from her. "Idealists all around me," she finally whispered. "I had no idea, *Signor* Jon."

"My business is a black and bloody one," Jon said without apology. "But there are things even I will not do, and I will move to slow the world in doing them when I can. Everyone has the line they will not cross, little bird, just as everyone has a price. And your price," he added, voice gone to velvet steel again, "is this creature called Lilith."

"Why do you want her?" The question begged justification for the action Alisha was afraid she'd take. She'd made her choices, knowing the results might be unpalatable. Even with her heart hammering thick and heavy in her chest and a tightness in her throat, she saw no good way to avoid stealing Lilith and offering her up to Jon in payment for the favors she'd asked.

No way except sacrificing herself instead, and the hard, unvarnished truth was that a sentient computer wasn't enough to trade her own life to Jon for. Alisha wondered if a human life would be. It had been in the past.

Something indecipherable glittered in Jon's eyes. "Machines for making war are one thing, little bird. A machine with a soul, ah, no. That is something else again. Do we have a deal, Alisha? Lilith and your stories, and as a gift I give you help in breaking down the delivery of a dangerous toy?"

"Yes." Cold ran over Alisha's arms and she repressed a shiver. "We have a deal."

≈

*H*ijacking an airplane was not, even in Alisha's line of work, an experience often repeated. Doing so on less than twenty-four hours' notice was a task she would have claimed impossible to accomplish.

On the other hand, such a quick development and implementation of a plan made it nearly impossible for leaks to get out. There was simply no time. Jon's contacts had made replacing the scheduled flight attendant with Alisha possible, though they kept her name and papers after the woman swore she hadn't worked with the two pilots in the past, nor ever met the solitary traveler who would accompany the drones to America. The passenger was checked and double-checked against being someone Alisha knew, and the chance taken. They could afford nothing else; changing the pilot for someone in Jon's employ would have been too great a deviation the day before the flight. The paranoid—and Alisha had no doubt the U.S. government counted as paranoid—would see it as a danger, and cancel the chartered plane.

So she had boarded the plane alone, a carry-on bag with extensive webbing compressing it her only baggage. The sole passenger—in his forties, big-boned and with a cunning intelligence to his broad features—had given the complicated-looking bag an amused look, and Alisha had blushed and dimpled at him. "It keeps the bag from expanding, poof," she said in her best English-learned French accent, and made a little explosive motion with her hands. "I am Monique Allistaire," she'd offered then. "I will be your personal attendant for this flight."

"Duke Keane," he'd replied, and shook her hand with a careful dignity that told her he was avoiding crushing her fingers. "I'll try not to be too much of a burden to you, *Mam'selle* Allistaire." In truth, he was a pleasant person to wait on for the first fifteen minutes of the flight. His drink of choice was ginger ale, sharp enough in flavor to disguise the faint acidic edge of the pill she dropped into it, and sleep overtook him before they were well on their way. Alisha waited an additional five minutes to be certain his breathing was steady and he showed no signs of stirring before returning to the carry-on and stripping it to its components.

In one way, it might have been easier to actually hijack the plane, disable the pilots and bring the jet in for a landing on an unknown airfield. Unfortunately, nothing in Alisha's training had prepared her to fly a commercial aircraft, and she'd never felt the lack, before. The trigger-happy combat pilot part of her mind, the part she thought of as *Leesh*, made plans to remedy that shortcoming as soon as possible. The need to land a jet wasn't likely to come up often, but if it happened once it could happen again.

The back two-thirds of the plane were locked off,

making the passenger cabin unusually small. Alisha slid hard plastic picks out of the handles of her carry-on, glancing at the sleeping Keane. Any chartered flight with only one passenger didn't need more than the first third of the plane to comfortably accommodate that passenger, and the cargo behind the locked doors was considerably dearer than the man escorting it.

Plastic picks were risky, but less complicated than metal when she'd undergone a thorough pat-down and X-ray. Alisha leaned against the carpeted door, eyes closed as she held her breath in concentration. Breaking the pick off would spell disaster. As it was, if she succeeded there would be no way to hide that she'd been there, but if she failed, a bit of plastic in the lock would tip Keane off to her shenanigans.

The first lock came undone with a click so muffled by the carpeted doors Alisha froze, uncertain if she'd really heard it. A cautious twist of the knob said she had, and the second lock came more easily. Governmental paranoia hadn't extended to installing a time lock on the cargo-hold door, though Alisha expected that next time, it would. The idea made her smile as she stepped inside the hold and closed the door behind her.

The air quality changed inside the hold, cooler and less tinny. This airplane was used for a fair amount of cargo transportation, then, specially built to accommodate a few passengers and a great many goods.

And the goods that spread out before her were great indeed. Four Firebirds hung in heavy harnesses from the ceiling, a dozen Attengee drones and two of their many-legged cousins resting below them. A pang of regret sliced through Alisha's heart, looking at the unmoving predators. Hijacking the plane would allow her to bring them back to Reichart and the Infitialis, but that was beyond her. The best she could do was ensure they not reach their destination.

Alisha leaned against the door, sliding the webbing off her carry-on and shaking it out with a grin. It did, as she'd claimed, keep luggage from poofing out all over the place, but its real purpose was the parachute harness it became. She tugged leggings out of the bag and pulled them on, then stepped into the harness, clipping it around her waist. Erika had designed the handy little carry-on, as much out of exasperation at her own ever-expanding luggage when she went on vacation as out of delight in making ordinary objects into technological wonders. She would, Alisha thought, be delighted to hear how it'd been used in the field.

Assuming Alisha got out in one piece to report back to her friend in Langley. The last time they'd spoken had been seconds before Alisha's home had been destroyed in the explosion. That event would have driven Erika to make certain Alisha's family were safe, but would she think Alisha had died in the fire? If not, she'd be impatient and worried, wondering why Alisha hadn't contacted her.

Alisha mouthed an apology to her distant friend, thankful, though, to believe Erika would take care of her worried family, and made sure the cargo-hold door was locked behind her. Once she opened the outer door, time would be very short before the copilot made his way back to the hold. It was a few minutes' work to find the control pads she knew had to accompany the drones. Most went back into their packaging to be dumped with the drones, but Alisha stuffed one into the back of her harness, fighting off the urge to whistle while she worked. That impulse succeeded, though she found herself singing the correct lyrics to "Here Comes Santa Claus," an unusual sign she felt things were going well. The words that normally came to mind with that tune were far from appropriate.

The drones were heavier than they looked. Alisha felt she should have known that, having wrestled more than one of them, but they'd seemed alive then, writhing with their own energy. Asleep, they were only so much metal and wiring.

The door itself was marked clearly: Twist handle counterclockwise in an emergency. Do not open while aircraft is in flight. Like the warnings on passenger airline windows, it made Alisha want to succumb to the imp of the perverse. Surely, that imp whispered in her ear, *she* would be all right as the cabin depressurized and chaos broke loose around her. She wrapped her arm around packing straps dangling from the hold walls to lodge herself in place, then reached out to learn whether the imp was right or not.

The dozen Attengees and their spider-like cousins went first, a sudden easy burst once the outside cargo door was ripped from its hinges. Wind screamed and howled into the hold, pressure changing and icy cold gripping her, bringing tears to Alisha's eyes and tearing gasps of laughter from her throat. *All right,* she decided, was worlds different from *fantastic.* Clinging to the hold and kicking priceless equipment out the door was clearly not *all right,* despite what the imp told her, but it was unbeatable as far as sheer adrenalized experiences went.

Three of the four Firebirds screamed out into the darkness, falling five miles toward the ocean below. The fourth, Alisha slung the loops of her parachute harness over, clipping it on top of the glider as the door to the main cabin burst open and gunshots fired into the howling wind. Alisha ducked, using the forward momentum to dive belly-first onto the Firebird. Her weight sent it pitching forward, and for one glorious moment she surfed the jet stream on its cold metal curves.

Then she and it were plunging into the darkness. Alisha scrambled for the control pad on her belt, thumbing on it with intense concentration even as freezing air ripped tears from her eyes and froze them on her cheeks. Rockets flared, Alisha's harness long enough to avoid burns as the Firebird righted itself, though she felt heat as she swung around and into tow beneath it. Seconds later she programmed the glider's destination, then threw back her head and shouted with the sheer joy of being alive as the Firebird careened in a subsonic flight toward England's shores.

lying across a couple of hundred miles of the Atlantic had been fun for a few minutes. Then the chill factor set in, and Alisha spent most of the flight regretting there hadn't been time to pick up some of Erika's paper-thin, subarctic weather gear before embarking on that particular adventure. She ought to be on her way to London, not huddling in a hotel bathtub with steam beading on her cheeks and making her nose run. All that was missing was Reichart waltzing in so they could dance around whatever topic was at hand.

Alisha found herself eyeing the bathroom door warily, as if the thought might conjure him. Only after long seconds passed without his appearance did she chuckle and sink farther into the steaming water, her nose bumping its surface when she breathed. Shivers still wracked her body, severely enough that she was afraid to drive. A few hours' delay in which to thaw would still see her back in London within the forty-eight hours she'd wrung from a reluctant Brandon.

Her clothes lay in a huddled, wet lump beside the tub. Alisha slid an arm out of the hot water to root through the cold fabric without looking, fingers eventually finding the replacement cell phone she'd bought. Shivering anew, she drew as much of herself back into the water as she could and still manipulate the keys.

The woman on the other end was, for once, groggy as she picked up. "This better be good, eh? It's three in the morning." Vowels stretched long with sleepiness, remnants of a Michigan Upper Peninsula accent coming through. Alisha managed a smile and sank chin-deep into the tub.

"It's me, E. It's Alisha."

"Jesus God. Alisha?" Erika woke up entirely, voice suddenly so intense Alisha could imagine her clutching the phone. "Where've you been, woman? It's been days. Your house blew up, Alisha. I thought you might be dead. I've got people all over your sister and her family. They're all in shock. They're okay, nobody's bothering them, but Jesus God, Ali. Have you talked to them? Do they know you're alive? What's going on? And do you *know* what that program Brandon built is? I mean, I don't see how it's possible, but the leaps of logic—there was intuition going on there, Ali. It evaded my watchdog programs like a human hacker, but not even I'm that fast. The only reasonable answer I can come up with is sentience, Alisha. Do you know what that means? A self-aware computer? It's a new life form. It's like being there when the first fish crawled out of the ocean to take a look around. Mythologically, it's Zeus's daughter. I've got to meet it, Alisha. Where's Brandon?"

Alisha's laughter bubbled beneath Erika's enthusiastic rush of words, relief pounding up through her until her eyes stung with it. Her family was all right, under protection and untargeted, it seemed, by the Sicarii. Very little else mattered to her. She wiped her hand across her eyes, letting herself pretend it was only water and not tears that ran down her cheeks. "Zeus's daughter, or Jehovah's creation, anyway," she croaked, then swallowed hard and strengthened her voice. "Where he is isn't important right now, E. A hell of a lot's been going on. First, thank you." The ache in her throat came through in the words. "Thanks for looking out for Teresa and the boys."

"It's what friends are for. You've got to let them know you're okay, Ali."

"I did. I called Teresa right after the explosion and let her know I was okay, but I asked her not to tell anybody. I'll call her again as soon as I get a chance, but Erika, did you see the news about Senator Deva—"

"And Cristina," Erika said with heavy finality. "I did. Can you believe it? I'm going to spend seven years dead to the world, if that means I come out of it a U.S. senator. Do you think you get a tax break for being dead?"

"I think I've pulled at least some of the wind from her sails." A shard of triumph knifed through the words as Alisha summarized the hijacking of the Attengee drones. "I wish I could've saved them all, but I've got the one Firebird stored in a garage in Dorchester. It was the best I could do. It'll at least keep Cristina from stepping up to the plate with the drones as her bat."

"That was you?" Erika said after a long silence. "It came through on the security updates about four hours ago. Not my department, so I went back to sleep, but... that was you? Good grief. How'd you pull that one off, Ali?"

"That'd be telling." Alisha allowed the infuriating note of smugness to linger in her voice, then laughed it off, trying not to hear forcedness of emotion in her amusement. Trading Lilith for what she knew intellectually to be a stopgap measure—but every time they were able to prevent the drones from disseminating for even a few days gave them that much more time to build an appropriate response.

They, Alisha thought, *we.* Not so long ago the *we* she had belonged to was the Central Intelligence Agency. Now the people she aligned herself with were a far more nebulous and hard-to-define group, and yet she found herself thinking in terms of *us* and *them* far too easily. She had never imagined her beloved Agency might become the party she worked against.

It wasn't, she told herself fiercely. It was the Sicarii she stood against, and only the CIA as far as Sicarii corruption went in it. The two masters she served weren't so very different from one another.

And that, too, was something she might start to believe, if she told herself the lie often enough. "I've got to go pick Brandon up," she said, hoping the hesitation between her teasing answer and what she now said was small enough to go unnoticed. "Reichart's intercepting another shipment, and we've got a woman on Cristina."

"We?" Erika asked, bemused. "You and Reichart are a 'we' now? And should you really be telling me that you're busy hijacking shipments of U.S. government property, Alisha?"

"I don't know. Are you going to tell on me?" Erika had turned her in once before, for considerably less significant transgressions than the ones she'd just confessed to. Oddly enough, it was that previous betrayal that left Alisha certain it wouldn't happen again.

Erika sighed. "I wish you wouldn't tell me this kind of huge, get-in-real-trouble thing. At least not if I don't get to help."

Alisha laughed, sending ripples across the tub water. "You only like knowing about the illegal stuff when you're involved?"

"Doesn't everybody? All right." She sighed again, dramatically. "You don't call at three in the morning unless you want something more than to tell me a little detail like you're still alive. So what's up?"

"I was calling to tell you I was alive," Alisha said defensively, then let go a quiet laugh. "But you're right. I do need something. A copy of the original Firebird black box."

"Not gonna happen," Erika said without missing a beat. "That thing's buried under so much red tape, God himself would take three years to get through the bureaucracy to make a copy."

"Sure," Alisha said. "I need a copy of it anyway."

"What is it, you believe I can walk on water or something? Alisha, I'm telling you, that box indicts Susan Simone as a double agent. One of the most highly placed CIA officers of the last decade. Screw the Freedom of Information Act. That thing is never going to see the light of day again."

Alisha sank down into the water until it spilled into her mouth when she smiled and spoke again. "So how long will it take you?"

The Michigan woman spluttered, a sound of mixed pride and exasperation. "Why do you need it?"

"Because Nichole Oldenburg doesn't exist, and I want something—anything—that ties her directly to being Cristina Lamken. I think that recording's my best bet. The Firebird black boxes have visual, don't they?"

"One of Brandon's brighter ideas," Erika conceded, though the tone suggested she didn't mean it. "Alisha, I turned that thing over to people above Greg, because you asked me to. I haven't even watched it. I honestly might not be able to get a copy."

"I have faith in you, E."

The mutter that came over the line made Alisha grin, water wetting her lips again. "I'll do what I can," Erika said. "Tell me about this tail you've got on your illustrious former partner. Maybe I can do something useful."

"She's British. I don't know what covert ops team she works for, but she used to be with Reichart."

"Whoa," Erika said in a credible Neo impression. "*With* him with him, or just with him?"

"With him with him." Alisha kept her voice neutral, which fooled her friend not at all.

"So you want this something useful to be, like, drop an anvil on her head? I could go all Wile E. Coyote on her. I've always kind of wanted to do that," Erika added wistfully. "I mean, not so much actually dropping an anvil on somebody's head, but arranging a near miss. Or a grand piano. You know. Classic slapstick stuff."

"You're the only person I know who would genuinely love setting something like that up. You should've gone into set design for movies, or whoever it is in films who does that kind of thing."

"Ooh." Interest piqued in Erika's voice. "Maybe I could get a new hobby. Okay. British, ex-Reichart-chick. Anything else I should know? Deadly allergies to shellfish that can be used to our benefit?"

Alisha laughed, closing her eyes. "You're awful." Awful, but Erika's cheerful irreverence always made Alisha feel better. It was a dose of sunshine, promising that the world might have its dreadful moments, but they could be gotten through with humor and, as Erika would helpfully point out, a brain the size of a planet. "She's dark-haired, about thirty-five, and I don't know about shellfish allergies. Give her a hand if you can, E. I've got to get going." The bath had done wonders for warming her frozen body, but Erika's company, even over the phone, had gone even further in restoring Alisha's equilibrium. "Call me when you get that tape, okay?"

"You save-the-world types," Erika muttered. "All right. Give me a couple of days."

"You're my hero, E."

"Of course I am." Erika hung up with a maximum of good-natured grumbling. Alisha dropped the phone on the floor and sank up to her eyebrows in water with a burbled groan of contentment.

~

Snorting water cooled to room temperature had awakened her in a fit of coughing and tearing eyes. Afternoon sunlight glowed through the frosted bath-room window, disorienting her. Alisha jolted to her feet, sloshing water over the edges of the tub. She stood on slick wet tiled floor an instant later, moving on impulse rather than thought: a towel, snatched from the rack, wrapped around her as if by magic, though she could replay the motions in her mind later. Her heart hammered too hard, adrenaline curdling her blood, a sense of danger associated with the abrupt awakening. Something felt wrong, too much crispness in the air, as if she was breathing high on a mountaintop.

Her weapons lay on a puddle of fabric by the tub, her clothes abandoned only seconds before she'd climbed into the steaming water in an attempt to warm up. Alisha slipped her jeans on, grimacing at their clamminess, and yanked her shirt over her head without bothering with underwear. She had weapons again, a Glock she'd picked up from a CIA drop point outside of Dorchester. Someone would pay for that: the year-old codes she had should've been changed months ago to prevent such a liberal borrowing of Agency equipment, but she was grateful they hadn't been. Gun butt cupped in her hands, Alisha pressed herself against the wall and edged the bathroom door open, taking in a narrow sweep of the hotel bedroom. A mirror glittered within her line of sight, giving her more view of the room. Nothing out of the ordinary was visible. Alisha mouthed a curse and shoved the door open, diving for the bedside and the scant protection it offered.

A maid shrieked and ran for the door, fresh towels scattering everywhere. Alisha relaxed into the scratchy rug, sprawling her arms wide, heart rate still out of control. Ten seconds of breathing deeply passed, then, more centered, Alisha rolled to her feet and finished dressing, grabbing the quantum case and pulling her shoes on as she ran for the hotel stairs.

She left without checking out, unwilling to give the staff another good look at her face. An itch along her spine told her that more than the maid's unexpected presence in her room had spurred her into action. Paranoia was a hallmark of being a spy, and it was, in Alisha's estimation, far better to be cautious and mistaken than confident and right. She hurried through the parking lot, taking in the makes and models of cars there without consciously realizing it. None of them were out of the ordinary, all of the right price range and class for a cheap hotel on a main thoroughfare. Nothing, Alisha thought, was *wrong*, and yet something felt distinctly not right.

Vehicles zoomed by, none of them responding to the hitch-hiker's thumb Alisha put out, though a cab slowed and stopped after she'd marched down the road for several long minutes. Alisha ducked into it, grateful it was a cab and not a cop that had stopped her, and turned to watch the road receding behind her.

Nothing familiar and no one recognizable lay down the path she'd come from, but hairs stood up on the back of her neck anyway. Compartmentalize, she all but sneered at herself. How many agents had gotten out of bad situations by the skin of their teeth, all on a hunch that told them to run when nothing of certainty could prove them right? Regardless of training, it was an emotional job, and something as esoteric as a hunch could save lives. When the life in question was her own, it was of particular interest to her.

A blue van, dinged and shoddy, crept up on the cab's left. Alisha turned her focus on it, a sensation of half-remembered familiarity accompanying its slow approach. It pulled up to within thirty feet or so—close enough, Alisha thought with a chill, to see her—then dropped back again, slowing to a more sedate pace. It might, she thought, have come from the hotel parking lot, but then again, any number of the nearby cars might have. "Please take the left at the next roundabout," she said to her driver, and caught his glance back at her in the mirror before he grunted an agreement. She slid to the right, where she could keep an eye on the traffic behind her in the driver's rearview mirror.

The van, far enough behind to remain discreet, took the left at the roundabout, chugging along with the determination of an ancient manual vehicle. Alisha bared her teeth at the reflection in the mirror and said, "Sorry, but at the next roundabout could you just go back the way we've come? Toward the hotel again?"

The driver gave her another look in the mirror, but shrugged it off. Alisha could all but see the words cross his mind: it was her money, and there was no accounting for

Americans. He said, "A-ight," then offered, "bat thar's coonstrooctun gawin' on on t'fair sayd of t'one we joost took," in warning.

Alisha fought off a smile at the thickness of his accent, wondering if he put it on for the foreigner in his cab or if he was indecipherable by nature. "That's fine. I'm not in a hurry."

The blue van followed them around the second round-about, falling far enough back to be almost out of sight, but as the road straightened again Alisha caught a glimpse of it and knotted her hand, thumping it against the armrest. "That construction you mentioned," she muttered, then lifted her voice to say, "How bad is it? Will it slow us a lot?"

"Eenooof," the driver allowed.

"Enough," Alisha repeated, then asked, "Enough for me to fling myself out of a moving vehicle without getting killed?" as if it were a perfectly ordinary question.

The driver's eyes widened and he gave her a hard look through the mirror.

"Don't worry," she added dryly. "I'll leave the fare on the back seat. There's a van following me and I'd like to try to lose it."

"Yoor mad," he announced, an assessment Alisha was inclined to agree with. Then his accent cleared, or Alisha ceased to notice it so strongly as he went on. "There's a huge shagging stack of drainpipes on the outside of the roundabout. I take the outer loop and you dive from the left, it'll give you cover straightaway. A good swerve on my part ought to close the door behind you, and maybe you'll lose the bastards, eh?"

Astonishment filled Alisha's smile. "SAS?"

"RAF," he said with a casual shrug. "Did a bit of my

own sneaking around. Good luck, miss. Don't worry about the fare."

"Thanks," Alisha said, genuinely touched, though she dug in her pocket for a ten-pound note and stuffed it into the crack of the seat as she slid to the left, preparing for the roundabout.

"Ai'll give you the mark," the cabbie said casually.

Alisha nodded, concentration already fully on the task ahead of her. Deep breaths grounded her, filling her with an awareness of her body that bordered on ecstasy, and once more the incongruity struck her. In fifteen years of practicing yoga, she most often felt utterly at home within herself during moments of combat or high pressure. The peace meant to be achieved by the ancient practice never seemed so attainable as in those brief instants, and it never failed to seem almost laughable that she should find it in the most extreme of circumstances. She counted her heart-beats and her breath with equal ease, the cab slowing as it took the curve into the roundabout, and with precision hearing trained in combat, Alisha heard the cab driver give the mark.

The door opened as if on its own, Alisha flinging herself to hit the road shoulder-first. A grunt of effort tried slamming the door behind her, though as she rolled and bounced over asphalt and rocks, there was no time to see if she'd succeeded.

The stacked culverts were there as promised. Ignoring the aches and protests of a body exiting a car driving thirty kilometers an hour, Alisha came to her feet in a low fast run, dodging into the curve of the closest drainpipe. She darted to the far end, then dove flat onto her stomach, making herself as much one with the corrugated surface as possible. She heard tires squeal in the roundabout and hoped her driver had managed to close the door, and that the van hadn't put on a surge of speed to make certain it didn't lose her. Her breath came in hard short gasps, bruises making themselves known, and somewhere in the heart of that, Alisha found a laugh.

It wasn't paranoia if they were really out to get you.

12

*W*hen had they caught on to her?

Alisha rolled onto her back and into a puddle, the gun she didn't remember drawing cupped in both hands as she panted for air. Had the Firebird been rigged with a tracking device? Only too likely, and more foolish was she for not examining it closely. Or perhaps the copilot had described her well enough for Cristina or Greg to recognize her, though Alisha thought his glimpse had been too brief for that. Still, it was a possibility, and a good network might have tipped them to her arrival at the hotel.

Dammit! She risked a glance around the end of the culvert, wishing desperately it was night instead of broad daylight. For once, the English weather held its own against tradition: cheery sunlight beat down to dry up puddles and damp spots left by the previous night's rain. Alisha cursed it with something approaching humor. Even the stereotypical gray dreariness would give her more to hide in than the good-natured brilliance shining down.

Traffic in the roundabout was a hopeless snarl. Her derring-do escape from the cab hadn't gone unnoticed, and people were already climbing out of cars and trucks shouting concern and spreading out in search of her. The blue van wasn't yet in sight, and there was a possibility that backed-up traffic would keep them from her. Alisha managed another laughing groan and turned her attention the other way, to the hilly country surrounding the roadway. Dashing that way would certainly bring attention to herself, making it certain anyone looking for her would be pointed in the right direction.

On the other hand, muddied, wet and scraped from her tumble across the pavement, she wasn't going to be able to blend in with the helpful motorists who even now looked for her. As far as subtle disappearances went, this one belonged in the record book under the subject of *fiasco*.

Over the general uproar she heard her cabbie's distinctive accent rising in outrage: "Av *carse* Ai didn't know she were plannin' to jump, ye ragin' eedjit!"

Another quick glance around the end of the culvert told her he was staging a proper show, distracting a goodly number of the stopped drivers from their search. She whispered a blessing to his dramatics, and scurried out of the culvert to the stack's back side. She pressed there, huffing quick breaths to oxygenate her blood, her gaze focused on the hills. The cabbie's theatrics would only hold the motorists for so long, and movement on the hillside would help draw them away: nothing caught attention like an object in motion. One last breath drawn, Alisha tilted her head back against the curve of a culvert, squinting as sunlight bounced off the tall pile. It climbed well above her head, no doubt put into place by a crane or enormous forklift.

Ye ragin' eedjit, she thought, almost fondly.

Half a breath later she got a few feet's worth of running start and scrambled up the wide curves of the

drainpipes, using haste more than grip to keep herself
going on the corrugated surfaces. She cut her palms
swinging into the uppermost culvert in the stack and
clenched her shirt against it as she lay down again, this
time well above anyone's line of sight. Even as she lay
there, she could hear disgruntled grumbles and cars
starting up again, the majority of searchers with plans of
their own they didn't want to put off. With luck, the snarl
would come undone quickly enough to send the blue van
through the roundabout without stopping. Alisha rolled
onto her belly, hand still clenched in her shirt, to watch
traffic with her head lowered and eyes half closed.

Less than two minutes later the van inched into sight,
the knot of traffic lessened but not undone. Alisha saw the
passenger window roll down and swore under her breath
as a man leaned out and hailed the vehicle next to him.
His mouth pursed with interest, gaze lifting as the other
driver spoke. Alisha swore again, thumping her fist against
the culvert. Common motorists would lose interest if they
couldn't find her. These men wouldn't. As Alisha watched,
the van flashed its blinkers and pulled to the side, working
its way through the knotted traffic to come up on the bank
almost out of sight, ahead of her. She squirmed down to
the far end of the culverts, keeping out of sight as best she
could as she climbed down again.

Cat and mouse. The words felt like a whisper, as if even a
loud thought might betray her presence to the men looking
for her. Large as the culverts were, the thickness of metal
wasn't enough to hide her, not from on-end. Alisha held
her breath, making herself as slender as she could as she
cast quick, cautious glances down the corrugated tubes.

Her followers were out of the van and split up. She
mouthed a curse, though in their position she'd have done
the same, covering twice as much ground. It was only

inconvenient for the quarry, not the hunter. One headed toward the hills, and the other angled just slightly uphill from the culverts. Alisha counted breaths, then darted toward the roundabout, putting herself on the most visible-to-traffic stretch of the culverts.

She made it almost the length of the metal pyramid before one of the helpful passers-by noticed her and sent up a shout. Alisha put on a burst of speed, racing full-bore toward the abandoned blue van. She expected, with every step, to hear the report of gunshots, but instead there were only more voices raised, some in concern and others—the men from the van—in anger. Alisha kept her eyes high and focused on the van, eking every last inch out of her stride. She still had her gun in one hand, the weapon turning concern in people's voices to alarm, but there was no time to put it away.

She slid across wet grass as she reached the van, stopping herself with a hard grip on the driver's door handle. Rather than the latch coming undone, it held fast, surprising Alisha enough to hesitate and take in details.

The keys were safely in the ignition, confounding her for an instant. Then the number pad beneath the door handle clicked into focus, a combination lock that probably automatically triggered. Just as well, she thought with a clear sense of the absurd, that she hadn't bothered to put the gun away.

Glass shattered with the impact of a bullet and Alisha smashed her elbow against the hole, breaking it up until she could reach inside and open the door without lacerating her arm. The door yanked open, she ripped her shirt off and swept glass off the seat, then leaped in and slammed the door behind her.

A boy's voice cut through the focused silence of battle, full of heady delight: "Coor, didja see that?"

A fierce grin at the flattery smeared across Alisha's mouth as she turned the ignition. Her pursuers were almost on her, the sound of running feet drowned by the engine's roar. Alisha gunned the gas. The van jumped forward with a startled lurch and jolted horribly over grass and piles of dirt as she avoided the roundabout entirely and drove through the surrounding construction area instead.

Then, finally, came the whine of bullets and the ripping of plastic and metal as the men giving chase realized they were going to lose her. Alisha ducked down, barely able to see over the dashboard as she raced forward. Firing a handful of return shots out the destroyed window was tempting, but odds of hitting a terrified civilian were too high. If someone was to be hurt in the scenario playing out, better it be Alisha than an innocent literally caught in the crossfire.

The van dove nose-first into a ditch of muddy water, sending a cold splash over Alisha's arm and wiping out any view the windshield offered. Mud spattered as the wheels churned, digging the van deeper into the hole. Alisha's laugh broke with frustration as she shoved the door open and burst out into cold water. One break, she pleaded silently. All she needed was just one break. And preferably, she found herself compelled to specify, not a leg or an arm.

The ditch wasn't that deep, only shin-high as she climbed out of it, but it was more than enough to founder the van with its low axles. Alisha was running again before she'd completed the thought, keeping as low to the ground as she could, expecting to hear more gunshots following her. The motorway beyond the snarled-up roundabout might provide her with the chance to—well, there was no good way to phrase it. Steal a car. It wouldn't be on her list of top ten most glorious moments, but if it got her away from the predators on her tail, she'd find a way to live with it.

She'd lost precious seconds in the ditch, and could hear the broken stagger of racing footsteps behind her as the men chasing her leaped it and came on hard. She wanted to cast a look back, wanted to send back a few warning shots to help fend them off, but the teenage boy's delighted commentary stayed her hand. There was no point in risking the faceless kid, nor any of the others who might find themselves in a bullet's trajectory.

There were times, she thought, when it would be useful to have less conscience. Then again, it was that determined belief in what was wrong and what was right that separated her, Alisha believed, from people like the ones chasing her.

Her lungs burned, discomfort coming on suddenly as adrenaline began to run out. She could feel the weight of her legs and the heaviness of oxygen deprivation in her muscles, and pushed herself harder. It would fade if she could run long enough to reach the so-called athlete's zone, where it felt like she could keep going forever, so long as she never stopped to rest. She reached the crest of a hill in a burst of speed, the motorway lying just a few hundred yards ahead.

The weight that took her in the back of the knees was completely unexpected. Traffic, her own breathing, the soft earth—some or all of it took away from the preternatural hearing she so often relied on in battle and in flight, allowing one of her assailants to come closer than she'd realized. She hit the ground with such finality it seemed as if she might go plunging through it. Drying grass prickled her chest and belly, a sudden reminder that she'd stripped her shirt and had made her wild run wearing a bra and jeans. At least no one would remember her face.

The weight that had borne her to the ground changed from her calves up to her mid-back, a knee pressed there as heavily as the gun barrel pressed against her skull. "Did it occur to you at all," a man's heavy Russian accent asked drolly, "that we might be the good guys?"

≈

*T*he voice—the unexpected good humor lacing the thick accent more than the voice itself— struck a memory so sharply Alisha relaxed into the ground in surprise. "Anton?" The name came out of memory, less called than simply there on her lips. Disregarding the gun against her head, Alisha twisted her head to try to look at the man sitting on her back. "Anton?"

"She remembers," he said in delight so transparent Alisha couldn't tell if it was genuine or not. "Ms. Elisa Moon, I think, da? Only you have not come into this country under that name, and MI-5 is looking for you, Ms. Moon."

"Anton?" Alisha said one more time, incredulously, then got her hands beside her shoulders and pushed up, less imagining she could dislodge the big Russian than hoping he'd be willing to move if she encouraged him to. "What in hell—?"

He did move, chuckling, though he put a foot down on the barrel of Alisha's gun as she tried to lift it. He waggled his own gun in admonishment, then nodded as Alisha let go of the butt and stood. "Better," he said, then gestured with his gun to encompass the second man with him. "This is Ivan."

"Of course it is," Alisha muttered.

"Really," Anton said, eyes wide with half-serious injury. "I do not lie to you, Elisa Moon. Agent MacAleer." The hurt faded from his eyes and was replaced by a broad, rakish grin as he took in Alisha's outfit, or lack thereof. "I try never to lie to beautiful women when they are half naked. Unless to be lied to will help them decide to go to bed with me. This is Ivan. We are the good guys."

"The good guys," Alisha said through her teeth, "don't usually shoot at me."

"We didn't," Ivan said without the slightest trace of Anton's humor. "We shot at the van. This is not a good place to talk. You will come with us."

"Or what?" Alisha demanded. "You'll put me back in the van and shoot at it some more?"

"No," Anton said. "MI-5 will come and arrest you for being in their country under a false name and false papers, without your country's approval. It comes from all the sources, Alisha MacAleer. You have gone rogue and are to be apprehended and brought to the authorities at once. MI-5 are only minutes behind us."

"Britain is a friend of the United States." Alisha flexed and tightened her hands, staring between the two Russian men. She had saved Anton's life once, in the midst of his bid for the Attengee drone software in Russia. Two of his comrades had died that day, a burden Alisha had felt less strongly when she'd believed them to be Russian Mafia. They had proven to be Russian FSB, the intelligence agency that had grown up after the KGB was dismantled, and Alisha felt the responsibility of two agents' deaths more keenly than she might have wished. Anton, even in the midst of a firefight, had retained a boisterous good humor that went against every stereotype of a Russian-born spy, raising his bid with every shot fired. He had massive shoulders and an openness to his expression that hid dangerous intelligence, Alisha suspected. Whether it was his oddly placed sense of humor or something else, her first instinct was to trust him. She didn't trust *that*.

Ivan looked more the part of a post-Soviet spy, dark glowering eyes and dark hair a marked contrast to Anton's broad cheerful countenance. He looked far less trustworthy, and Alisha was utterly aware of the irony that it made her want to trust him more than blond, bright-eyed Anton.

"Britain is a friend of the United States government," Anton agreed. "And they will do as the U.S. tells them when an agent goes rogue on their territory, as much because no one likes to find their allies spying on them as they are very curious about the thing that has brought you here."

"A 747?" Alisha snapped. "They should go visit Boeing in Seattle, then."

"We are moving now," Ivan said in a low voice. "We have wasted too much time, and the van is still stuck."

Though reluctant, Alisha found herself walking with the two big men, just as glad they shielded her from curious motorists on the roundabout.

Ivan pulled a wallet from his breast pocket, flipping it open to wave at a handful of men whose curiosities compelled them to approach. "Move along, lads," he called, Russian accent suddenly swallowed whole by a light upper-class British one. "The kerfuffle's all said and done with, and we've got our girl. Thanks very much for your help in slowing her down. Watch the broadsheets," he added with a wink, and threw a leer at Alisha's half-dressed form. "I'm guessing we'll be seeing plenty of this lass there."

A laughing cheer went up and the small crowd scattered, returning to their vehicles. Ivan put Alisha in the driver's seat of the blue van, leaning in to speak to her. "You will steer as Anton and I lift the van out." His Russian accent was back, deep and warning. "Do nothing foolish, Agent MacAleer, or when I next fire, it will not be to shoot the van."

Alisha banged the heel of her hand against the steering wheel, swearing under her breath, and did nothing foolish as the two men heaved the van out from its ditch. Seconds later, they climbed into the front seats, sending Alisha scrambling into the back. She waited until they'd left the roundabout and pulled into traffic before leaning forward, deliberately folding her arms beneath her breasts to create cleavage, and said, "Now will you please tell me what the hell is going on?"

13

"We have said," Ivan replied. "Your government has betrayed you, Agent MacAleer."

"Or you have betrayed them," Anton amended cheerfully. "You have developed a career of doing so, *da?*"

"I'm not an agent anymore," Alisha muttered. "I left the CIA almost a year ago."

"No one ever really leaves," Anton said with a sudden dourness that made Alisha snap her gaze to him. "It is the nature of our beast. We cannot escape what we do. And," he added more lightly, "if you had truly left, you would have entered England under your own name, and you did not."

"I had my reasons."

"*Da.*" Ivan, in the driver's seat, looked at her sharply in the rearview mirror. "And we, too, are interested in those reasons. We have seen your American war robots, Agent MacAleer. Like MI-5, like your own government, we would like to have the second generation of that technology. This is what scientist Brandon Parker has built, *da?* An intelligence smart enough to protect. Perhaps something capable of reasoning. His war machines have that in rudimentary form. The next step is sentience, and that would be reason enough to run."

Only one response worked when confronted with bald truth that required refuting: lie. Lie like a son of a bitch, and make them believe it. An adulthood of training and working had taught Alisha how to do just that. It was on her lips, in her body language, in everything that she knew how to do: *I have no idea what you're talking about. A what? A sentient artificial intelligence? It's not even possible, is it?* A thousand astonished arguments to convince the enemy she didn't possess the knowledge they wanted. All that skill was there, waiting to be used.

Instead, Alisha threw her head back with a throaty laugh, then dropped her face into her hands. "What?" she asked her palms. "Did somebody send out a memo?"

She heard the indrawn breath of both men, glancing up in time to see them exchange a guarded glance. *Oh, Leesh.* The silent reprimand was accompanied by a *tsk* she almost gave voice to. Too many lies, she thought. Too much time spent pretending. She'd lost her stomach for it, and there couldn't have been a worse time to do so.

Ivan scowled, first at Anton and then at Alisha, then spoke in Russian with no indication he thought she might understand. "It's a trick. She wouldn't tell us the truth so easily. Even the United States government does not admit what Parker has done, only say that MacAleer has stolen confidential material and must be stopped."

"If it's a trick," Anton said easily, "then perhaps everything the U.S. government says is a trick. Perhaps our friend is not the fugitive they say she is. You must choose what to believe, Ivan." Older mentor to a younger brother,

Alisha thought. Ivan apparently felt similarly, giving Anton another hard look.

"What do you believe?"

"That the government lies," Anton replied, "and that Agent MacAleer speaks the truth. They want something she has, perhaps even this artificial intelligence, but she did not steal it and she is no longer an agent for the CIA."

"I'm flattered," Alisha mumbled into her hands, in the same language the men spoke. "But all I took out of the States was a man." Technically, it was true. Brandon had carried the quantum drive that Lilith was stored in. "He worked for the CIA and wanted to leave. They just don't want to lose him." Lies, she thought again, though lies ingrained with the truth. "They're afraid of what he might do for someone else. Like the German scientists who defected and built the bomb."

"Parker," Anton said. "He has been badly used, yes?"

"He's a spy," Alisha snapped. "Aren't we all?" Her own bitterness surprised her and she passed her hand over her eyes as if she could wipe away that anger. "He came to me because I'd left the Agency," she added more dully. "He thought I wouldn't notify them he was trying to leave the country." She shrugged, stiff motion. "And I didn't, because I know what it is to try to leave this life behind. I'm lucky." Her laugh went bitter again and she tried to temper it. "A man like Parker is all about the mental faculties. He's hard, maybe impossible, to replace. I'm just brawn. They could afford to let me go."

"You don't believe that," Anton said with a touch of amusement coming through.

Alisha lifted her gaze to give him a brief smile. "I was a good agent," she confessed. "But I lost my taste for it, and it's easier to find a replacement for someone like me than someone like Brandon." Parker, she thought a moment too late. She should have called him Parker. Her training deserted her at every turn.

"Brandon," Anton echoed, and Alisha winced again. "Maybe there is more than one reason he came to you, *da?*" He slipped back into English to emphasize the words, almost as transparent as Alisha's slip.

"Maybe." Other things she wanted to say—that the infatuation was on his side, that it meant nothing— smacked of too much protest.

"Where is he, Agent MacAleer?" Ivan finally interrupted.

"I don't know," Alisha whispered. "I left him days ago, Ivan. He asked me to get him out of the States and I did. Trust me." Her voice went edged again. "Trust me, I owe him less than even that. He's been on his own for days. He's his own problem now." *Three times you'll deny me* whispered through her mind, and Alisha wondered if her denial would be as effective as that darkly legendary one had been. She hoped not.

"And the AI?"

"I have heard," Alisha said with absolute honesty and frustration, "about this artificial intelligence from the Russians, from the Americans, from crime lords, from every damned agency and consortium I know about. *Did* somebody send out a memo?" Her voice broke, despair and amusement both coming through.

"No memo," Anton said with his usual good humor. "Only great consternation on the part of your government. Many demands on the part of ours, to capture you and Brandon Parker. Everyone knows he is the mind behind the war drones, Agent MacAleer. His sudden decision to flee your country, your government's agitation—the deduction is not so difficult."

"If Brandon had a second-generation artificial intelligence, wouldn't he either be keeping it totally under wraps or auctioning to the highest bidder?" Even as she asked the question, Alisha wondered if she was protecting Brandon or the personality-filled computer program she'd spoken with briefly.

"Do you know what I think?" Ivan asked. Alisha spread her hands, invitation to his explanation. "I think he is on verge of breakthrough." His English, which had been flawless, if accented, became harsher as he warmed to his topic. "I think he distances himself from United States, so he may claim his work belongs to only him. So he can sell it, da, to highest bidder."

"And you what?" Alisha asked. "Want him in your labs before he makes that last breakthrough?"

Ivan looked at her in the rearview mirror, glance as eloquent as any words.

"I can't lead you to him," Alisha said. "I'm sorry. Let me off somewhere, Anton. I'm out of this business. I'm of no use to you at all."

Anton twisted in his seat, looking back at her. "If we let you off, MI-5 will find you next. We went to some trouble to…?dissuade one of their operatives from finding you already."

"Do I want to know? How did you even know I was here?"

"A woman who hijacks very expensive war drones has to go somewhere, *da?* The southern coast of England was closest. MI-5 had eyes on the CIA drop points they know about, as did we. Our man in Dorchester convinced the MI-5 agent not to follow you, and the FSB flew me in." Anton smiled broadly. "Because of our history together. They thought you might listen to me."

Alisha groaned. "Well, thanks for keeping MI-5 off my

back, but I'm not listening to you. Anywhere is fine, really. I can walk from here."

Anton clicked his tongue. "I would hate for you to be detained by MI-5. They have reason to be upset with you, Agent MacAleer. Besides the AI, this is their country you are in illegally. For your own good you should stay with us."

"I'll take my chances," Alisha said dryly. "I can always swim to France."

Anton laughed, shaking his head. "I think we cannot take that risk, Agent MacAleer. After all, we are the good guys." Amusement deepened the words, his smile broad as his shoulders. "We would not want to turn you over to people who were not so open-minded as we. And you may still be able to help us."

Alisha let her mouth crease in a smile as she met the big Russian's eyes, though the thought behind her own eyes was *damn*. Whether they believed her protestations that she knew of no AI was irrelevant. Brandon had come to her for help, and that made her an effective tool to use against him. A hostage, in effect, and the idea sat poorly with Alisha. Still, in a vehicle on a motorway, there was almost nothing to be done about it. Better to bide her time and wait for a chance to disable the Russian spies and escape. In the meantime… "If you're going to be so considerate, do you think you could get me a new shirt?"

Anton chuckled and lent her his jacket. Alisha huddled inside it, watching road signs pass by, her expression blank as she thought through possibilities. She roused herself when the first exit for London flashed by, putting pathos into her voice as she asked, "Could we stop for a bathroom break?"

Ivan gave her a dirty look in the rearview mirror. "We are driving a van riddled with bullet holes. You wish to stop and allow people a good look at it?"

"Unless you want to be driving a van riddled with bullet holes and smelling like urine, yeah. I could handle some breakfast, too. I haven't eaten today. Scones and tea would be okay. Even cheap scones and tea."

Anton chuckled. "Anything else?"

"Yeah." Alisha pulled her mouth into a smile. "You buy. Hostage etiquette. Kidnappers pay for incidentals." Ivan stared at her and she sighed. "I can probably get to the restrooms at a convenience stop without spending too much time looking into the CCTV cameras, but there's always one pointed right at the checkout counter. If you want to keep MI-5 off your back…" She trailed off and shrugged, feeling more cheerful as Ivan's expression blackened.

"If you try anything," he warned.

Alisha nodded, turning her gaze out the window again. "It won't be the van you're shooting at. I know."

The convenience stop had windows in its restrooms. Alisha noted them as she slunk by, escorted by Anton, with Ivan a step or two ahead. Inside the store she nodded toward the toilets and broke in that direction, but Anton followed hard on her heels. "I saw them, too," he rumbled, and despite herself, Alisha quirked a grin.

"Don't know what you're talking about," she claimed. Anton huffed disbelievingly and followed her all the way into the bathroom. "You want to unzip my pants for me, too?" Alisha asked, both irritated and resigned.

Anton gave her a wide smile and lifted his hands, shaking his head. "I have more respect for my own health than that, Ms. Moon."

You made it too easy, Alisha thought, and without regret lashed out with a flexed foot to catch Anton in the groin. He gasped and went gray, doubling over, the same training that taught him to keep quiet when injured betraying any chance of him shouting out to Ivan for help. Alisha swung around with a roundhouse kick that connected to his temple with a deep, alarming *thwock*, then surged forward to catch the big Russian's weight so he wouldn't crash noisily to the floor. The, "Sorry," she whispered above his bruised temple was genuine as she hauled him to lie in front of the door, blocking it as best she could.

The window cranked outward six inches or so, its hinge stretched to its limit. There was less than a foot of space on either side of the crank, just not enough to slither through. Alisha bared her teeth, then yanked the window closed again and slung Anton's jacket off, wrapping it around her fist. There was no way to silence the shattering of glass. Alisha knocked shards free from the pane, leaving it as smooth as she could before doubling the jacket and laying it over the broken edges.

"Don't think." Thought would lead to hesitation she couldn't afford. Ignoring the too-real possibility of injury, she put the flats of her hands into the window frame and levered herself up, feeling glass crunching and breaking beneath the barrier Anton's coat made.

Slivers of glass grazed her shoulders and ribs as she pulled herself through. The only place she dared rest her weight was on her hips, as far back on the edge of the frame as she could. A man shouted in astonishment, and for a moment Alisha could see herself from the outside, protruding from the restroom window like a ship's prow. Then she tipped forward, rotating her weight, and put her palms against the store's outside wall.

Sliding down the rough surface made her bite her lip with pain, the cut on one hand re-opened by her antics. She managed enough push to do an awkward somersault, lifting her thighs away from the ragged glass just long enough to avoid deep lacerations. Then, gravity pulled her down with heartless vengeance and she tucked into a painful roll that barely protected her neck as she hit the ground.

A few vital, precious seconds were lost as she jumped to her feet and snatched Anton's jacket from the window, shaking glass out of it as she broke into a run. No gunshots yet: Ivan was slow, or she was lucky. Lucky struck her as more likely; Anton really had made the escape attempt too easy.

Maybe he actually *had*. The startling thought intruded as Alisha pounded across the pavement. Anton shouldn't have been so easy to take down. He had to have expected her attempt. Maybe, just maybe, he'd let her go.

Why? God knew his government wouldn't approve.

The need to know slipped away as she reached a chain-link fence, easily six feet tall, and shoved her booted toes into a diamond of metal. Anton's jacket, still in her hands, protected her torn palms as she flung it over the triangles that poked over the fence's top bar and vaulted it.

"There!" Ivan's voice behind her, lifted in outrage.

Alisha didn't spare a glance backward, hearing Anton's coat tear as she ripped it from the fence. Other footsteps ran to the barrier the fence created, metal shaking and rattling as people grabbed hold of it. Still no gunfire, probably thanks to the curious viewers blocking the path between herself and Ivan. She ducked around a corner and found herself in a subdivision, backyards marked off with high stone and wood fences. A narrow path ran between the houses and Alisha bolted down it, hurdling a low picket fence that cropped up. She landed in a flower bed, one foot solidly crushing a purple azalea, and broke for the glass door of the house whose yard she'd invaded.

It slid open under her desperate yank, a house alarm shrieking as she slammed it closed again behind her. The front door was locked against her frantic tug. Alisha ran for the living room, shoving a window open and diving through it into another unfortunate flower bed. She closed the window behind her, a useless gesture: the house alarm would tell the Russians which path she'd taken, but the attempt to cover her tracks had to be made. She hit the sidewalk at a full-on run again, alarm screaming in her ears.

Ten seconds later the alarm turned off, leaving blessed and astonishing silence in its place. Alisha risked one look back at the house and saw nothing untoward. A giggle rose up from behind her breastbone, the sound of panicked relief. She'd seen car alarms set off by low-flying jets, and impatient owners who keyed them off without ever worrying they might be being robbed. Perhaps the home-owner had had similar experiences.

Sobbing breath into her lungs, Alisha slung Anton's coat back on and ran.

14

*U*narmed. Undressed. Unsuccessful. Those were not the adjectives Alisha'd had in mind to describe her return to the computing facilities when she went to retrieve Brandon.

Undead, she reminded herself, and found a laugh at the connotation, even taking a shuffling zombie-like step or two. The shambling gait brought her through the super-computer facility's front doors, and from the startled look the receptionist gave her, Alisha thought *undead* might be a more apt descriptor of her physical condition than she'd realized. For all that she'd been submerged in a tub not that many hours earlier, her hair was streaked with mud and her jeans were brown with it. The too-large coat she wore was buttoned closed, but that she wore only a bra beneath it was clear. She'd found a hose to rinse her hands with, but they were still badly bruised and scraped. The result, which she caught a glimpse of in the facility's polished floors, indeed looked like she might be one of the walking dead.

Somehow buoyed by the sheer ridiculousness of it,

Alisha strode across the foyer with confidence, her chin lifted and her smile bright. "I'm here to see Brandon Parker."

"The American," the man behind the desk said. "I'm afraid you're too late."

Confidence drained away, leaving a place of coolness in Alisha's belly. "I'm sorry. I don't understand. Too late?" A churn in the coolness warned that it could easily turn to alarm and sickness. Alisha took a deep breath, quelling it, and smiled uncertainly down at the receptionist.

"Too late," he repeated. "His package arrived late yesterday afternoon and he departed about forty-five minutes later." His voice was apologetic but uninterested. She put her fingertips on the desk, leaning forward into it more for her own support than to intimidate.

"Package?" The word seemed to have enormous portent. Alisha shook her head, not yet understanding. Brandon couldn't have left; he wouldn't have abandoned Lilith to a research facility's tender mercies. "What package? I thought no one—" No one knew he was here, was how the sentence finished, but saying it aloud shared too much information that didn't need to be made public. "Who was it from? Do you have a record?"

"I'm sorry," the receptionist said. "That's confidential information. You are…?"

"His girlfriend," Alisha lied numbly. "I had to go away for a couple of days. I was supposed to meet him here this afternoon. We were…?" She couldn't think of a way to finish the sentence, but the receptionist filled in the blanks himself, deeper sympathy flashing across his features.

"I truly am sorry," he repeated. "I don't really know who the package was from. An American computer company, I think, but I didn't really look at it."

"BranCo Technologies," Alisha breathed. The receptionist brightened, leaning toward her.

"That's it, yes. I'm sure of it. Does that help?"

"Yes," Alisha said, then in the same curiously flat tone, added, "No," before shaking herself and smiling at the receptionist. "It does, yes," she said in a more normal voice. "Thanks. Thanks very much." She dipped a nod and turned away, focus going long and unseeing out the lobby's front windows.

A package from BranCo. Brandon would never have abandoned his AI to someone else's systems, but an express package from his own company only had one obvious answer. Alisha slid a hand into her pocket, wrapping her fingers around the quantum storage drive nestled against her hip. She'd taken Lilith's only means of transport in order to ensure Brandon's good behavior. Held the AI hostage, as Brandon had accused. She hadn't thought he might risk ordering another drive.

It was possible—of course it was possible—that anyone monitoring Brandon's company might think nothing of a London supercomputing facility ordering one or more of Brandon's phenomenally capable storage drives.

It was possible, Alisha thought with nasty clarity, that a dog might not return to its own vomit, too. She stopped at the lobby doors, one hand on the glass, and turned her head back to the receptionist. "Excuse me."

"Yes, love?" He looked up, a smile of concern visible from the corner of his eye.

"You might want to take the day off," Alisha said. "You might want to take a few days off." She heard herself speak as if she stood far away, her voice echoing in her own ears.

"I'm sorry?" Concern fled in the face of surprise. Alisha lifted her chin, enunciating her words carefully.

"You might want to take a few days off. I wouldn't want to be here when—"

A bright shadow drifted through her line of vision, sunlight reflecting off a white vehicle. Alisha's gaze followed it, focus still somewhere beyond things that could be seen by the human eye. Her heartbeat rang in her ears, one pulse far separated from another, time turned to taffy. Breath ran through her body as if she could see it, filling lung and muscle with oxygen that would allow her to burst into activity. Soon, the promise whispered silently. Soon. A second white car pulled into the parking lot, so brilliant in the sunlight it made her eyes water. There was no sound beyond that of her heartbeat, as if the lobby's glass doors had become an impenetrable barrier.

"—when the Sicarii arrive," Alisha whispered.

Too late.

She recognized none of them, men and women pouring out of the vehicles like clowns in a circus, so many it seemed impossible they'd all fit. So many, she thought again. The Infitialis were so few, and their enemy so many.

"Get down!" Her own shout broke the hold battle-time had over her. Then she was running, vaulting the receptionist's desk to bear him to the ground with her weight. His chair tipped and crashed beneath them and he howled, more insult than injury. Alisha muttered, "Sorry," and shoved his head down. "Stay down." Her gun seemed a paltry weapon against their numbers, but Alisha pulled it from her waistband. It would do. It would have to do. It held fifteen rounds and she hadn't yet fired it. Surely there weren't more than fifteen of them.

Alisha came to her feet with a grin so wide it bordered on painful. Surely there weren't more than fifteen of them. That, she thought with honest glee, was one hundred percent *Leesh*, the combat veteran who believed the hype of her own skill and training. It was all a matter of not missing, and Leesh rarely missed when it counted.

"Are you out of your goddamn mind?" The receptionist was on his feet again, hauling Alisha's arms down so her gun pointed harmlessly at his desk. "What the hell is wrong with you?"

Alisha braced herself, legs wide as she took strength through the floor and pushed it upward, using it to lever her arms up against the receptionist's weight. She snarled, "Trust me," and he barked disbelieving laughter. "They're not the good guys."

"You're mad. Security! Security!" The last words were a shout as the lobby doors swung open, ushering in the first of the contingent from the white cars.

The man in the lead hesitated just inside the door, alarm and dismay writ large across his face. He backed up again, one hand held high to warn off those behind him, and Alisha caught a glimpse of suitcases and business suits. Her resolve faltered and the receptionist shoved her arms down again, then wrapped his arm around hers, embracing her against his chest and pinning her arms to her sides. A part of Alisha admired the tactic: disabling without being drastic. Of course, she still had the gun, and could shoot him in the foot if she needed to escape.

"Those," the receptionist panted above her ear, "are the representatives of Crown Enterprises, who are a major funder for these facilities. At least, they were until ten seconds ago. If you've cost us our funding—!"

Alisha went limp in his grasp, surprise greater than her impulse to fight back. Footsteps pounded across the polished lobby floor, security responding to the receptionist's summonings. "Crown Enterprises?"

"Yes, you raving lunatic! Guards! Security! Thank God," he added in a different voice as two uniformed guards rounded a corner and pelted toward them. "She's got a gun."

The guards slowed immediately, glancing at each other before one took charge. "Put your weapon down, ma'am. There's no need for that."

"I have the gun," Alisha whispered. "You don't. Want to bet on who gets out of here?" She felt the receptionist shift behind her, precursor to going for her gun hand, and knotted the muscles in her arm. She'd been playing nice so far. Under no circumstances would she allow herself to be taken in by British authorities. To be taken in by the enemy. Outside, worried men and women in suits huddled together, far enough from the building to feel safe, though a bullet could certainly find one of them easily enough.

"Don't be foolish, miss," the other guard said. "Drop your weapon." They came forward slowly, hands open as if to promise their sincerity. Hands open, Alisha thought, because there was no middle ground in English carrying of arms. It was either billy sticks or automatic weapons, rarely anything in between.

"Stop," she said, mostly to herself, "or I'll say 'Stop!' again." She lifted her gaze to the guards, then found it returning to the milling businessmen outside. Sunlight gleamed off brown and black leather briefcases, a crown emblem embossed in the leather. Alisha rubbed the thumb and forefinger of her free hand together, the graphic bringing back a tactile memory she couldn't quite—

A huff of laughter escaped her, as though someone had hit her in the stomach. Couldn't quite put her finger on it. But she could, and the memory answered as many questions as it posed.

But now was the wrong time to pursue that, as Alisha caught a glimpse of movement from the corner of her eye. Time went slowly for the second time in as many minutes, letting thought dominate in the precious few seconds before battle reflexes took over.

The decision was already made: she would not let herself be arrested. The chances for subtlety were already long past; her description and very likely security camera images of her would be all over the country in a matter of hours. Her location was pinpointed. The question was merely whether she would disable or terminate her foes during her escape.

She released the gun mechanically, fingers stiff as she opened them. The weapon clattered to the floor, relaxing the guards and sending Alisha into motion.

The man holding her was too much taller than she to headbutt. Alisha drove her elbow backward, knocking his breath away, and as he bent with wheezing, she crashed her skull back to bash it into his. He yowled and fell, already forgotten as she put her hands on the desk, about to jump it and face down the guards.

"That will be quite enough." A smooth voice, one she knew, but now with a hint of a British accent, came from the elevator area beyond the receptionist's desk. Alisha went absolutely still, as if the words triggered an inability to command her own muscles. The receptionist groaned, staggering to his feet and clutching his head. Alisha refused to look at him, keeping her expression tight and her gaze belligerent on the guards, wanting them to believe she was stayed only by the newcomer's voice. Anything else would betray her shock—at least to those with the eyes to see it—and she had no intention of allowing anyone to know she'd been desperately outplayed.

But the emotional reaction couldn't be quelled. Her heart rate jumped, anger and excitement, as if a missing puzzle piece had been laid into place. She wanted to turn and shout accusations, but held her ground, listening to the cultured, false accent make easy promises.

"I'm afraid you've been party to a training exercise, Philippe. Guards, well done." Well-heeled shoes clicked across the polished floor, bringing the speaker into sight. He was short, shorter than Alisha herself, with curly graying hair and an expensive, well-fitted suit. "You may release her now. This is Ginger Sanovar, an associate of mine. I'm Desmond Rockwell, security head for Crown Enterprises. We've been running tests at all the facilities we fund, to make certain of security. I'm pleased to say you've passed with flying colors. Especially you, Philippe." He nodded toward the receptionist, who straightened up with pride that nearly masked bewilderment at Rockwell's appearance. Alisha felt tremendous sympathy, more taken aback by Rockwell than Philippe was.

"There'll be a commendation in your file," Rockwell went on. "I'll be happy to emphasize that such loyalty should receive adequate compensation."

"Thank you, sir," Philippe blurted, then clamped his mouth shut, wise enough to know when silence was more valued than words. Rockwell gave him a quick smile that didn't reach his blue eyes, then turned to Alisha.

"If you'll come with me, Ginger, we have a debriefing to do, I think?" He offered an elbow.

"Absolutely." Alisha, despite her misgivings, stepped forward to take Gregory Parker's offered arm without hesitation.

∿

The hall into private offices stretched long, Alisha's footsteps silent on the gleaming floors as Gregory's clacked. Neither spoke, walking together with the ease of long association, until the door latched behind them and Alisha stepped away as if a viper were on her arm.

"What the hell are you doing here?"

"Where's Brandon?" The questions came at almost the same time, Greg and Alisha both stepping warily around one another, making a circle filled with accusation and anger between them.

"What's going on with Cristina?"

"Who are you working for?" They fired questions at the same moment again, though Greg's broke Alisha: she laughed, a sharp hard sound that was absorbed by the lush office walls. It had to be a room where they brought the VIPs to impress them, Alisha thought. The parts of the facility she'd seen were more functional than beautiful, but warm gleaming wood made up this room's walls, and the long table that dominated the room was lined with comfortable chairs. Alisha'd put the table between them before she noticed doing it, though not before Greg noticed it. She curled a lip, tasting anger so shortly after that laugh, and told the only truth she could see.

"I've gone into business for myself. What are you doing here?" Back to the fundamental question, though the answers she could come up with herself were ones she didn't like.

"I've come to collect you," Gregory snapped. "My protégée, gone rogue. You're making me look very bad, Alisha."

"You've done that all by yourself, Greg. I noticed Crown Enterprises has the Sicarii crown as its emblem."

"The Sicarii crown?" Greg scoffed.

"The same one as on the lighter you gave Brandon," Alisha said through her teeth. "He didn't think the crown meant anything. I might've believed it if I hadn't just seen it emblazoned on all those suitcases. I give you credit," she added, voice rising. "I'm so used to the nasty end of the business I didn't think of coming in with suits and brief-cases. I was expecting guns blazing and windows shatter-ing. I really must get out more."

"Where is Brandon?" Greg repeated, more than the anger of a moment earlier in the words. Parental concern was there, worry for a child. Alisha spat laughter, disbe-lieving.

"If I knew, I wouldn't tell you. Why'd it take almost a full day to track the quantum drive? Who's losing their touch, you or your princely masters?"

"Alisha." Greg's voice rose and broke. "What do I have to do to convince you I don't work for the Sicarii?"

"Resign from the CIA," Alisha said without missing a beat. "Expose Nichole Oldenburg for who she really is."

Darkness fell in Greg's eyes. "I can't do that, Ali."

"Then I have nothing else to say to you." Alisha stalked to the door, more out of a real desire to escape than a need for the last word.

Greg's voice lashed out behind her. "There are military police waiting in the parking lot, Alisha. You may as well come quietly with me. Anything else will only be embar-rassing."

15

*A*lisha went still, the doorknob cool under her fingers. "What, then?" she asked after long seconds. "What happens now?"

"We exit together," Greg said quietly. "Like civilized people. You remain in custody until we reach Langley."

"Really," Alisha said. "Then do you let me go? Or do you toss me into one of the Guantanamo pits where they put people to forget about them?"

"Don't be absurd." Greg's voice sharpened. "You're not under arrest for sedition."

"What exactly am I under arrest for, Greg?" Alisha turned back to her former boss, spitting the question. "Leaving the country? I wasn't aware that was a state crime."

"We're bringing you back to the States for your own protection, Ali. The British government may be our allies, but that doesn't mean they like Americans sneaking into their country."

"And what about the release that's gone out saying I've

gone rogue and should be brought to the authorities? Is that for my protection, too?" Everything had gone pear-shaped. Alisha stepped closer to the door, putting her forehead against it. *No way out* was a phrase she didn't like, but for the moment she couldn't see one. Not short of taking her chances against Greg, who was older and slighter than she, but also her handler. He knew her well—better than almost anyone, as a combatant—and that gave him an advantage.

"Alisha," Greg's voice gentled again. "You left the country with my son, who's blatantly stolen government property. You did a good enough job hiding yourself. It took us this long to catch up with you."

"You caught up with Brandon," Alisha snapped, unwilling to give that one detail up. "I just got caught in the crossfire." As her family had been caught, she reminded herself. Anger flared and she clamped down on it, unable to afford the emotion.

Maybe there were positives. Returning to the States might allow her to come into contact with Cristina, and if not Cris, then at least the Englishwoman following her. Emma and Reichart were supposed to be in contact, a contact Alisha was reluctant to make herself, with circumstances as they were. If she could avoid associating herself with the Infitialis, all the better for that clandestine group.

There had been no indication of Reichart's success or failure, either, Alisha reminded herself. She would be able to find those things out at Langley, through people who were still her friends and allies within the Company. "All right." Her voice was low and resentful, no more an act than Greg's own anger. That was good: Greg wouldn't be fooled by pretending to be happy about her involuntary return to Langley. She hadn't been last time, either.

The sigh that escaped her was unintentional. Her actions told the story of where her loyalties lay more clearly than her mind was willing to see. Agents of the Central Intelligence Agency were not supposed to be dragged reluctantly back to the fold. She'd left emotionally long before she'd left in truth. "All right," she repeated. "I just want one thing when we get there."

"You're not in a position to negotiate, Alisha. What do you think you're going to do if I say no?"

Alisha turned from the door to give Greg a clear-eyed gaze. "Take my chances against you and the MPs."

Greg studied her, then shook his head, chuckling. "You would, too, wouldn't you. You'd lose, but you'd try. All right, Ali. What's your condition?"

Alisha looked away again, naming the one ace she had left: "I want to talk to Erika. Alone."

~

"*Y*ou look like hell, Ali. When's the last time you slept?" Erika's opening volley came before Alisha registered the sound of the door opening. She came to her feet as Erika swept across the room to pull her into a hug.

"I slept the whole flight over," Alisha said into the hug. They had, at least, given her a shirt to wear under Anton's torn jacket, which Alisha was moderately grateful for. "I just need a shower. Instead they put me in here."

She gestured around as Erika released the hug, both of them taking in the beige CIA safe room surroundings. She'd been brought to Langley, not a safe house; this was one of the rooms dignitaries were brought to for their own safety. The walls were just slightly too dull, the room just slightly too small for the overstuffed furniture in it, the lights just slightly too dim to adequately light it. The effect was subtly claustrophobic, making for rising tensions which would help the unwary to slip and say the wrong thing for prying ears to overhear.

"You know they're listening," Erika said, the perfunctory observation making Alisha smile as it followed her own thought.

"I know they're trying, but I know you, too." She made a show of studying her friend's attire—her usual low-cut jeans and sports bra under a black leather biker's jacket. "I'm guessing it's the earrings."

Erika touched one of the big golden loops dangling from her lobes. "Come on, I spent a million years making these look a hundred percent fashionable. How'd you know?"

"You usually wear long, dangly feathery things, not hoops." Alisha dropped back down into the couch, smiling weakly. "What kind of disruption do they do?"

"Everything on any regular CIA, FSB, MI-5, and Mossad frequencies. I'm still working on the rest of them. Only problem is they give me a headache. Still working on that, too." Erika tapped a fingertip against her lips, then smiled, pulling the earrings off. "Here. You're right. Hoops are more your style. I'll work up some that suit me more."

Alisha took the earrings, idly testing the holes in her ears before sliding them in. "Mossad, huh? Something I should know about?" She passed the question off with a wave of her hand, and leaned forward, feeling the hoops brush against her chin. "Forget I asked. I'm not part of that world anymore. No batteries? No on-off switch?"

"Check out the diamond-cut pattern," Erika said triumphantly. "Mini solar panels. But here's the neat part.

If you squeeze the circumference of the right loop with your whole hand, instead of creating white noise they'll start picking up sound and broadcasting it back. You just run your fingers around the whole loop to turn them off entirely. Tell me something, Ali," she added. "Do you tell yourself you're out of the spy biz every night before you go to bed, like your prayers? Does it make you believe it?"

"I keep waiting for it to. E, there are about a hundred things I need to know."

"Good thing you've got a friend with all the mighty brain wrinkles, then." Erika sprawled over an armchair, knees and elbows going every which way like a gangly teen's. "Where do you want me to start?"

"The Attengee deliveries," Alisha said evasively.

Erika snorted, an indelicate sound of amusement. "You mean you want to know if Reichart succeeded in ripping off the Afghanistan delivery. He did, but nobody got to the third truck. It's in North Africa by now. Even with getting to the others, you only set them back by about three days, Ali."

A small bloom of triumph blossomed in Alisha's breast, bright warmth that stung her nose and eyes with unlikely pride. Even Erika's next words didn't take away from the pleasure of having accomplished as much as they had. "That production facility in Serbia isn't like the one you blew up in China. It's actually producing more than just a handful of prototypes. You should've blown *it* up."

"I didn't blow up the Beijing factory," Alisha muttered. It was true. Reichart had, although he had used explosives Alisha herself had set. Still, credit where it was—or wasn't—due, Alisha thought. "And you're right. I should've. Next time I'll do that."

Erika laughed. "Next time. You're assuming they're

ever going to let you see the light of day again, Ali. Look what you've done. Stolen how much government property? Helped how much priceless programming get away? Even if you manage to walk out of here, the CIA is never going to stop watching you, Alisha. Not now."

"They'll let me walk out of here," Alisha said under her breath. Erika's eyebrows, pencil-thin and round, shot up.

"Yeah? What's your bargaining tool?"

"I can tell them where the stolen drones have gone." It was a flat-out fabrication, but Alisha said it with tired ease.

Erika pursed her lips, then cocked her head to the side in acknowledgment. "Why should they believe you? And why would you do that?"

"They don't have anybody else to believe," Alisha said with a shrug. "And I'd do it to get myself out of here. I'm starting to think I've forgotten what loyalty looks like." She closed her eyes, Jon's face and untenable demand coming to mind. It might have been just as well for Brandon that he'd disappeared, though it put her in an increasingly sticky position. "And Emma? Have you made contact?"

"There's been no sign of her," Erika said. "Are you sure you can trust Reichart's girl, Alisha?"

Alisha's stomach tightened, a combination of anger and concern. "Frank trusts her. It's enough."

"Ooh-hoo," Erika murmured. "Frank, now. I see."

Alisha cast her gaze to the ceiling and tried not to grit her teeth. "Does everybody know I do that?"

"Yeah, pretty much." Erika's grin held no repentance. "People love to talk about you and Reichart, Ali. You're everybody's favorite failed romance. We're all waiting to see how the story ends."

"My life isn't a *story*," Alisha stressed.

Erika's grin flashed again, bright and open. "Everybody's life is a story, Ali. It's just hard to see it from the inside. You Bond types might have a harder time seeing it than most, 'cause what you do really is of world-shattering importance. Maybe you have to pretend really hard that it's normal just to get through the day."

"You should meet Jon," Alisha muttered. "He thinks it's all a love story, too."

"See?" Erika's smile broadened. "Do you love him, Ali?"

"Jon?" Alisha asked. "No. He's too much of a romantic." She waved off Erika's protest, allowing herself the faintest smile before taking a deep breath. "What about the Firebird's black box? Have you gotten a copy of it yet?"

Erika's usually open expression went tight. "Ali, I told you, that thing's buried deeper than the crown jewels. I'm working on it, but—" She shook her head, then pulled a long face. "That AI Brandon's cooked up would be a real help."

"Come on, E." Alisha's mouth curved, teasing with an underlying grain of curiosity. "You saying an artificial intelligence can out-hack your all-powerful brain?"

"It's not just hacking. It's getting through real, physical people, Ali. Not even I've got the security clearance for where they've got this thing hidden. It's like Area 51, only for the important shit."

"Aliens aren't important?" Alisha asked lightly.

Erika's answering smile was brief enough to send a chill of surprise through Alisha. "Area 51, if it's real, which I neither confirm nor deny, is only full of stuff that could send the country and world into unprecedented paranormal panic. The kind of security I'm trying to get through here is covering up things like who really killed JFK and when Hitler really died. It's things that bring down governments, Ali. They don't let just anybody near it."

Alisha felt her expression fade into neutrality, schooling dismay and disbelief out of it. "You're serious."

"As a heart attack. I'm working on it, Alisha, but I might not be able to come through."

"You always come through, E. You're my rock."

The door pushed open, an irate Greg stepping through. Erika looked over her shoulder at him, then turned an unhappy smile on Alisha. "Even granite wears away, Alisha. I'm sorry."

～

"*C*ome on, Greg," Alisha said before Erika'd fully left the room. "When I said 'alone,' I didn't mean alone with half the Company listening in. What'd you expect?"

"I expected more of Erika," he said shortly. "Perhaps I should have known better. You two have been thick as thieves as long as she's been here."

"A partnership you encouraged," Alisha pointed out. "Brains, beauty and brawn, right? Who could resist us?"

"I could. What were you discussing, Alisha?"

"Failed Hollywood marriages. You know how important celebrity gossip is to the security of the nation. Why, without it, people might turn to more important topics, like why our government is hiding Cristina Lamken behind Nichole Oldenburg's pretty dossier."

"You don't give up, do you?" Greg made a sharp gesture and Alisha stood despite its imperiousness, just as glad to be leaving the claustrophobic safe room.

"I wouldn't be any good at my job if I did, Greg. So tell me, how many drones went missing in the end?" Another bump of triumph spilled through her at the sharp look Greg shot her way as they left the room for an institutional hallway.

"Over seventy," he answered, surprising her. "Those drones could have helped end the war in Iraq and Iran, Alisha. I hope you're proud of yourself."

"Those drones would have escalated wars that've been going on for years into unmitigated slaughter, Greg," Alisha snapped. "They still will. They're going to be used against people with nothing to lose and no way to fight technology like that. They're not peacekeeping forces, no matter what Brandon wished for. They're killing machines, and every day I can do something to keep them off the market is a day when someone won't die."

"High and mighty words for a woman who's killed in the line of duty," Greg said softly.

Disgust rose up in Alisha's throat like bile, so bitter she wanted to spit. "Terminated," she reminded him. "Executed. Let's not get mixed up with nasty emotional words like *kill*, Greg. I never said my hands were clean. You don't become a secret agent to stay innocent yourself. You do it so others can." Tears of anger and passion stung her eyes, unexpected vehemence surprising her. "Part of me still believes that's why people do this," she whispered. "To make the world a better place. Not to claw their own way to whatever kind of power they can get. Tell me. Which was it for you? I've been wondering ever since China." Alisha heard the tremble in her own voice and forcibly disciplined it, unwilling to let betrayal break her. "Duty to country, or desire for power? At first, I mean. I'd like to think the man who recruited me to the Agency was a good one, not bound up in a shadow organization's quest to dominate, but you've been with the Company thirty years. I don't think you're a recent convert to the Sicarii."

"What will you do, Ali," Greg wondered softly, "if it turns out you're wrong about my allegiances after all?"

"I'll be very contrite," Alisha muttered. "Honestly, there could be tears. I'll apologize," she said more clearly. "But you haven't done anything to buoy my confidence. Where are we going?" she asked abruptly, glancing around. Greg had led her down unfamiliar hallways as they talked, through a door she'd never passed through before.

"I'm taking you to someone who may help you prove more willing to work with the Agency again, Alisha. I don't like to put you in a hard place, but you leave me with very little choice. I need Brandon and I need the whereabouts of those missing drones."

"I'll give them both to you," Alisha said without hesitation. "Just let me out of here."

Greg gave her an amused look. "Don't teach your grandmother to suck eggs, Ali. I know when you're lying. I taught you how."

"Yeah?" Alisha demanded. "What's my tell?"

"You don't have one," Greg admitted. "It's just long experience. You were telling the truth when you said you didn't know where Brandon had gone, and you're lying when you promise to turn the drones back over. What do you plan to do with them, sell them for your own profit? I knew I shouldn't have introduced you to Frank Reichart."

"You're overestimating his influence on me, Greg. Reichart and I stopped playing in the same field a long time ago. We owe each other nothing."

"Really." Greg pushed open a bleak gray door, ushering Alisha in ahead of him. She stepped in, squinting against a single burning bulb dangling above a cuffed woman in a solitary metal chair.

Emma Dickens lifted her head, harsh aging shadows ruining the lines of her face, cruel light bringing out previously unseen silver threads in her hair. She was actress enough to allow no change of expression, not even so much as the dilation of her pupils to say she recognized and knew Alisha MacAleer, but Alisha's heart lurched and left a sickness in her stomach that made her cold.

"Tell me again," Greg murmured, "that you owe Frank Reichart nothing."

16

"You're a complete bastard, Greg," Alisha said, just as softly. There was no heat in it, as she was afraid allowing anger into her voice would drive her to irredeemably foolish actions. "What's one of Reichart's old girlfriends got to do with anything going on now?" If Emma was there, denying she recognized her would be useless. Alisha had seen her once, years before, an encounter she'd thought had gone unnoticed by the CIA until first Boyer, then an Agency shrink had commented on it. Better to assume Greg knew, too, and play that the one viewing had been the only time Alisha'd ever laid eyes on the woman. "It's Emma something, right? Jesus, Greg." Now she let some anger come into her voice, taking a few quick steps toward Emma. "You think I fucked up going into Britain on false papers. Holding a British national in a place like this? Are you crazy?"

Emma was cuffed, arms twisted uncomfortably behind her back. Alisha knelt, making a noise of frustration at the metal chains. "What the hell are you doing? She was a cover, for God's sake, years ago. An accountant or some-thing." *She was,* Alisha told herself fiercely, not to convince Greg of the lie, but herself of its truth. "Get these cuffs *off* her, and tell me how you're going to keep this out of the papers."

"Let's not make this any more absurd than it has to be, Alisha. She's a computers expert for MI-5, and her involve-ment with Frank Reichart goes considerably beyond a cover."

Cold trickled down Alisha's spine, sending goose bumps over her arms as she looked back at her former handler.

Thin surprise slid into his expression and he smiled, more unkind amusement than real humor. "Don't tell me you didn't know. Oh, Alisha." Laughter came into his voice, still mocking. "I believe you didn't. I thought you were an intelligence agent, Alisha. Whatever went wrong?"

"He was happy." Alisha closed her eyes as she heard herself speak, then shook her head, earrings swinging forward to brush her cheeks as she lowered her gaze to the floor. She reached for one, curling her fingers around it and rubbing the ticklish spot it made along her jaw as she faced what Greg was saying. The moments she'd glimpsed of Emma and Reichart together, Frank had been happy. For that reason alone, Alisha had refused to pursue the truth behind their relationship.

Jon was right, she finally admitted to herself, without any caveats. It really was a love story.

"Whatever she is, whoever she works for, she's not rele-vant to the here and now, Greg. Let her go."

"I don't think so. She's my collateral, Ali. I want Brandon and I want the drones returned. I hate resorting to blackmail to accomplish it, but my job is to protect the security of the United States at whatever cost necessary. If that requires coercing someone who should've been willing to work with me in the first place, that's what I'll do. Besides," he added. "She's a wholly legitimate target outside of being useful in getting you to cooperate. We caught her tailing Nichole Oldenburg."

Dammit! Alisha's hand curled in a fist, gaze still fixed on the floor. Her knees were beginning to ache from kneeling on the concrete, and she thought Emma's feet must be cold, though she was still shod. Reichart had promised Emma had the skill to follow Cristina without being noticed. Had his own emotions blinded him to Emma's faults? The idea took the chill that slipped down Alisha's spine and spread it through her body, making her feel lonely all over again. He'd been happy with Emma, she reminded herself. Happy enough, perhaps, to see things that weren't there. It wasn't a mistake she remembered him making about her.

And that might be reason enough to save the British woman. Alisha let her fist relax, slow action that would tell Greg of defeat, not defiance. "What are my orders?" The question came out dull and low, the words of a woman defeated. "Hunt Brandon down? Terminate him? I had those orders once and failed to carry them out. Do you think I can do it this time?"

"I think you know my orders aren't to terminate. Brandon and his new intelligence program are critical to security. I want them back and in one piece."

"What happens to her?" Alisha finally looked up, locking eyes with Greg rather than letting herself glance at Emma.

"That depends on you," Greg said. "Succeed in this and she'll be released."

"And if I fail?"

"She'll be exposed as a British spy believed to be on a mission to assassinate Nichole Oldenburg. We may even let the attempt play out. It would be wonderfully effective PR."

"Alisha's right." Emma spoke for the first time, British accent painfully cool and cultured in the dank little room.

"You're a right bastard, Parker. What does my government benefit from trying to kill one of your political hopefuls?"

"I imagine you'll be branded the tool of some misogynistic right-wing political faction," Greg said easily. "Some group who fears the ascent of women in politics. They'd use a woman as their tool, of course, because men wouldn't stoop to assassinating women. Your passion for the job—your entire career, in fact—will be written out as a story of a woman so dedicated to the place of woman by home and hearth you were willing to sacrifice your own family life to make certain others would have it. Your daughter will be played up as a most unfortunate orphan, at the end of it."

Alisha shot a look at Emma then, catching sheer rage contorting the other woman's face.

"I think the whole thing could work out beautifully for Nichole's presidential campaign in a few years," Greg finished.

"We're not pretending anymore, then?" Alisha asked. "No more insisting you're one of the good guys and I just need to see the light? You're flat-out admitting the intention is to get Cristina Lamken into the White House?"

"What makes you think Cristina Lamken ever existed, Alisha? She's been a double agent as long as you've known her. Longer. Maybe Nichole Oldenburg is who she's really been all along."

"Oldenburg," Emma murmured. "Romanov."

Breath knotted in Alisha's stomach, stopping there as her heartbeat hung loud and heavy in her ears. "Romanov? The Russian tsars?"

Emma was watching Greg. "The Romanov family actually died out centuries ago, at least the male heirs. The dynasty was ruled by the House of Oldenburg for nearly two hundred years, under the Romanov name." She exhaled, a quiet sound of near-laughter as she repeated, "The Romanovs."

"The last great fallen royal house," Gregory agreed. "Taken in by Rasputin and destroyed by the uprising, with a fairy-tale ending about the princess who escaped the slaughter and went into hiding. Anastasia. Little girl lost."

"Rescued by the Sicarii." Alisha barely heard herself speak, words echoing and interrupted in her own hearing by the shattering crash of her heart. "Cristina?"

"Found by the Sicarii," Greg corrected. "Years later, a regal peasant in communist Russia, under Stalin's rule. She was half mad, or maybe more, but she swore she was Anastasia and her daughter was heir to the Russian throne. That girl was Cristina's grandmother."

"The Sicarii believed her?" Alisha stared at Greg. Her ears were hot, blood coloring her skin too harshly, though her hands, in bone-shivering contrast, were cold. "Why?"

"Just in case. They weren't certain until the early nineties, when they were able to run genetic tests on Nicholas Romanov's exhumed body. She really is the great-grand-daughter of Anastasia Romanov."

Alisha's ears burned. "Excuse me, Mr. Bond, but you're about to die. Why are you telling us this?"

For the first time, frustration contorted Gregory Parker's face. "Dammit, Alisha, what do I have to do to get you to believe me? I've been caught in an untenable position within the Sicarii and the CIA for fifteen years, and the only way I see to prove my innocence is to admit to my guilt! I'm telling you these things because it's the only way I can arm you against the Sicarii!" Passion fled, leaving only weariness that Alisha was unaccustomed to seeing in her former handler's countenance. "Serving two masters is an ugly position to find yourself in, Alisha. I think you're treading too close to the edge of that yourself. Don't let it happen."

"I've been trying not to," Alisha said through her teeth.

"But events are conspiring against me. Try having the strength of your convictions, Greg."

"This is all the strength I have left. It's been too long and too hard a run, Alisha. I'm sorry."

"At least let Emma go!" Alisha shot to her feet, suddenly facing off with the small dapper man. "Prove to me you're one of the good guys, Greg. Let Emma go. Give me the Firebird black box so I can see if there's anything to lace Cristina in with the Sicarii, real physical proof that can't be refuted. Let me take down their golden girl, if you're one of the heroes."

"I can't." The whisper was filled with desperation. "There's no legitimate reason the Sicarii would understand for releasing such a valuable prisoner. I'm sorry, but I'm more interested in keeping myself alive than in letting your friend go. You're going to have to do it on your own."

Alisha hauled off and hit him as hard as she could.

Two years of pent-up anger and disillusionment went into the blow, all the betrayal and dismay she'd struggled with since the trip to China had gone bad. All the training she prided herself on was behind it, half a lifetime's worth of yoga practice that gave her superior upper body strength, turned for one glorious moment to sheer kinetic energy that ended with a crunch of bone and cartilage.

For an instant she wasn't sure who was more surprised it worked, herself or Greg. Greg: he was the one who staggered, clutching his nose, and the one who didn't recover as Alisha gave frustration a voice and jumped on him, bearing him to the ground with her weight. He got his hands up to protect his face from another hit and she curled her hands in his lapels, lifting him bodily to slam him back into the concrete floor. His head lolled and she lifted and slammed him again, crouched over his torso, then made a fist and clobbered him in the jaw.

His eyes rolled back and his head fell to the side, bloody drool dribbling from his mouth. Only then did Alisha become aware of other things: her own harsh breathing, and an incongruous sound of cheering from behind her. Alisha looked over her shoulder, panting, to find Emma straining at the chair she was cuffed to, a grin so wide it looked agonizing stretched across her face. A little of the battle rage faded from Alisha's mind and she went for Greg's pockets, searching for the keys to Emma's cuffs.

Thirty seconds later, Greg sat propped in the chair, cuffed to keep him from sliding out. Emma and Alisha, armed with Greg's security badge, bolted for the door.

Lying on the National Mall, panting for breath and grinning at the blue sky was not, Alisha thought, exactly the most subtle place or way to relax.

Emma, stretched out on the grass beside her, said, "We can't stay here," with the same good cheer Alisha felt. "Whose car do you suppose that was?" the British woman added.

Alisha laughed, flopping her arm over her eyes. "No idea." They'd abandoned the borrowed vehicle a mile from the mall and took themselves off at a run down DC sidewalks. "I can't believe we made it out of there."

"Frank's said you've got balls of solid brass," Emma said. "He told me about the Godiva trick in Prague. I swear that was all I could think about when that red-headed bloke stopped you. You know you've probably put yourself on your own country's most wanted list." She moved as she spoke and Alisha peeled her arm back from her eyes to see the Englishwoman propped up on an elbow in the grass beside her.

"You think I have now," she said. "Just wait."

"What're you going to do?" Interest piqued in Emma's voice and Alisha grinned at the sun again.

"First I'm getting you on a plane back to England and Mazie. When did they pick you up, Emma? It's Monday afternoon now. Reichart was expecting a call from you at the forty-eight hour mark. Did he get it?"

"Oh, bugger," Emma whispered. "I've got to call him. He'll give me more time than he's supposed to," she said with quiet confidence, "but I can't leave him hanging. Every minute I'm late he'll be trying to decide how to tell Mazie I might never be coming back."

"Emma…" Alisha bit the inside of her lip, curiosity suddenly at war with discretion.

The British woman glanced at her, then let go a soft breath. "You want to know what happened with Frank and me. Why he's the one looking out for my daughter, and whether that means there's something to our relationship you can't tread on."

"You all looked so happy together," Alisha said quietly. "So ordinary, and that's not meant as an insult. I wonder what happened to that, yeah."

"It started out as a cover. For MI-5, not the Infitialis. I suppose if you throw any two people like us together in a sham marriage you discover whether it works or not. It worked for us. It was quite wonderful." Emma's eyebrows flicked upward and she smiled at the distance, but then spread one hand. "And in time the assignment was over and we had different jobs to pursue. We tried to stay together for a while, but we discovered we only worked in close proximity to one another. Absence," she said with another brief smile, "made the heart go wander. Frank is Mazie's legal guardian if anything happens to me, but our affair ended years ago. I have no excuse at all for sniping at you when we met."

"Neither do I," Alisha said. "Frank and I ended even longer ago than you and he did." She tilted her head, then offered a hand. "I'm not sure friendship can be built by offering the word, but—comrades in arms, at least?"

Emma clasped Alisha's hand momentarily, inclining her head. "Comrades in arms, indeed. I need to find a phone, Alisha."

"I'd bring you to my apartment, but." Alisha shrugged, leaving the obvious unsaid as she sat up. "This is Washington DC. There must still be pay phones around somewhere. What kind of papers do you have access to?"

"I need papers to make a phone call?"

Alisha crooked a smile. "You need papers to get on the plane. Nothing personal, but I'll feel better with you out of Greg's line of sight." She hesitated. "How'd they nab you?"

"They came out of nowhere." Emma sounded bewildered and angry. "I must have slipped somewhere, but I've been going over it in my mind for the last ten hours. I can't figure out where I made the mistake. But it was so clean and fast they had to have known I was there. I didn't see anybody tailing me, and thought I had spots on all of Nichole's security." She took a breath and amended, "Cristina's. I don't know what name to call her by."

"A few choice ones come to mind." Alisha got to her

feet, offering Emma a hand up. "You believe the Romanov story?"

"Do you?" Emma grunted and came to her feet, looking down a few inches at Alisha, who huffed faint amusement as she turned away to head for the mall's edge and hail a cab.

"I wish I didn't. Cris used to say she was royalty in a previous life."

"I've never heard of anyone whose former incarnations included sheep farmers," Emma said dryly. "It's always Cleopatra and Charlemagne."

"I had a boyfriend in college who'd been told he was a cattle thief in a previous life," Alisha said absently. She lifted a hand, failing to stop a taxi, and stepped off the curb to better get someone's attention. "I wish I could trust him as far as I could throw him," she added in a mutter.

"Your boyfriend?"

"Greg."

"I think you could throw him a fair distance."

Alisha chuckled. "I could. I just can't trust him that far. Even if he's trying to do the right thing, he's not trying hard enough, and I need all or nothing in my life right now."

"Tell that to Frank Reichart," Emma said, so quietly that Alisha nearly missed it. The British woman gave her a brief smile at Alisha's sharp look, but neither pursued the topic as Alisha bounced up to the curb again as a taxi pulled over.

"Can you get out of the country on your own?"

"I'll be all right," Emma promised. "Although I could do with some cash to pay the driver with."

Alisha dug into a pocket as Emma opened the cab door and said, "The airport," in a flat American accent, then leaned on the door, waiting for Alisha's money. "What are you going to do?" The American accent stayed in place.

Alisha smiled and shooed the taller woman into the cab, knowing full well Emma was disappointed at not getting an answer. Only after the cab drove off did Alisha breathe, into the sounds of traffic, "I'm going to destroy the CIA's link with the Sicarii."

"*E*rika?" Alisha kept her voice low, trying not to sound desperate, though her heart pounded and her cheeks were flushed with heat. "E, please tell me you've been listening in. I'm at a pay phone. The number is— shit," she added in a whisper. She fumbled the receiver off its hook, reading the number. "Call me. Please be listening, and call me."

She squeezed her hand around the loop earring, disengaging its broadcasting device, and slid down into the bottom of the phone booth, face in her hands. Now that Emma was relatively safe, now that Alisha had only forward to go, there were moments for panicking. Too much energy wasted, Alisha scolded herself. She pushed to her feet again with the thought, breathing deeply. Even if there wasn't room to do some of the more relaxing asanas, she could at least control her breathing and center herself. It would slow her heartbeat and calm her mind, even if Erika didn't call.

She'd barely straightened her shoulders and inhaled for the simplicity of a tree pose when the phone rang. Alisha flinched so hard a muscle in her neck spasmed and she clapped a hand against it even as she yanked the phone free of its hook. "E?"

"Who else would it be? Jeez, Alisha, when I gave you those earrings I didn't know you were going to turn around and use them to destroy the CIA five minutes later."

"Were you just listening, or do these things record when they broadcast?" Alisha tugged her earring, a nervous gesture.

"This is me, Ali. What do you think?"

Alisha exhaled, thudding her head against the phone booth wall. "I think not recording it would be a half-ass measure, and you don't do half measures."

"So what do you want me to do with it?" Erika's usually cheery tones were subdued.

"Right now that recording is my only proof that the Agency is mixed up with Sicarii business. Make copies, and find me somebody I can trust to come in to. I still want the Firebird box, E. If I'm going to take this link down I want to make sure I've got everybody it touches, and the more proof I've got the better. Have you learned anything?"

"In the last two hours? Strangely enough, no. All right, listen." Erika fell silent for a long few seconds, before Alisha heard a chair creak, as if the technical geek was changing positions. "All right. Go to a library and log into one of their internet terminals. I'll contact you there as soon as I've got anything."

"Anything?"

"Whether it's a black box location or a name you can trust to come in to, I don't know yet," Erika said. "So, yeah. Anything. When I've got anything, you'll be the first to know."

*T*he problem with publicly accessible terminals was that other members of the public expected to be able to access them. A draconian librarian kept watch over the computer area, rousting users off as their thirty-minute windows came to an end. She enforced another half-hour break between logins, glowering at Alisha and locking up the terminal when Alisha tried to simply move from one computer to another. Teeth gritted to hold her tongue, Alisha signed up for another computer in thirty minutes' time and spent the next half hour padding through the stacks.

The third round of that came at mid-afternoon. A shift change came and went, allowing Alisha an entire hour uninterrupted before the new, equally determined librarian shunted her off in favor of allowing someone else to use the computer. Alisha put her forehead against the desk a moment, checking her mail one last time before giving up the resource. Nothing. Erika never failed to come through, Alisha told herself fiercely. It was a matter of patience.

A virtue which was in sadly short supply. Alisha growled and stood up, muttering an apology as she bumped into the man waiting for the terminal.

Frank Reichart looked down at her, lifted a finger to his lips in a *shh*, then beckoned.

Pure startlement made Alisha's heart crash in a thump that seemed loud enough for everyone to hear. Color rushed to her cheeks as she stared up at him, breath failing to fill her lungs. Seconds passed before she exhaled sharply and nodded, following him out of the computer area and into aisles of books.

He stopped around the first corner, pulling her into his arms, fingers sunk in her hair before she had time to speak. "There are four federal agents outside the library," he murmured. "Waiting for you. They don't want to come in and make a fuss."

A lump formed in Alisha's stomach and dissolved again, dismay overridden by a lack of surprise. For a big city, DC could be a small town. Someone had almost certainly spotted her. "Thank you. Frank, what are you *doing* here?"

"Erika sent me," Reichart said. "I don't know how many favors she burned finding a way to contact me. I was already back in the States. Nobody was supposed to know I was here. Come on, we need to get going."

"Where?" The question was perfunctory, Alisha already moving.

"Out of here, probably out of the States. Unless you want to go back into federal custody."

"You make a convincing argument."

Something in Reichart's expression relaxed and he slid his grip from her elbow to her hand, squeezing her fingers. Then they were moving, not running, but walking briskly and purposefully as people in libraries rarely did. An exit door, warning of an alarm, appeared in a corner and Reichart strode for it, Alisha hanging back with a whispered, "They'll hear the alarm, Frank."

He dipped two fingers into his coat pocket and came up with a library ID card, swiping it through the door's reader and waiting for the light to turn green. "I stole it from a sweet old lady librarian," he admitted as they pushed through the door. "I'm a bad, bad man. We're going down."

Alisha laughed, the quiet sound echoing in the stairway chamber. "You are. Reichart, we're on the ground floor already."

"There are archives and rare book rooms down here," he replied, already rattling down the steps. "And a passage to the next block, so the books can be rescued in case of fire. It's more than a century old." He slid the card through another reader, pausing long enough to make sure the door shut silently behind them after they stepped through. For the second time, he lifted his fingers to his mouth in a *shh*, then caught Alisha's hand again and scurried through a labyrinth of rooms. There were decorative insets in pale walls, frames as tall as doors, adding to the sense of being in a maze. Any of them, Alisha thought, could lead to some other place, if only they had time to explore.

Forty-two seconds left, her automatic countdown method reminded her, focused her. Alisha set her front teeth together against whispering that warning aloud to Reichart; in the enormous silence of the archives, even a whisper would resound like bells. He drew up, raising a hand for stillness. Alisha pressed against the wall as footsteps clicked noisily down a hall. The woman who breezed by was entirely focused on the manuscript she held, looking neither left nor right. Reichart gave Alisha a quick, wicked grin and mouthed, "That was close," before tugging her across the hall.

The door he stopped at was one of the decorative insets, its only indication being nothing more than two faintly shiny spots in the paint at about hip height. Reichart finally released Alisha's hand, placing his fingers against those spots, and gave the door a gentle push. It groaned and shuddered, paint flecking away as it sank into the wall. Alisha clicked her tongue all but silently, instinctively wanting to clean up the mess and remove any signs of their presence she could. Reichart shook his head, still silent, and ushered her into the passageway. Moments later, the door shivered closed behind them again, leaving them in absolute damp darkness. Water dripped somewhere ahead, and the air was still and warm, trapped underground beneath city streets that held late summer heat.

Alisha closed her eyes against the darkness, tongue pressed to the roof of her mouth in order to keep herself from vocalizing a protest. *Underground,* she wanted to remind Reichart. *You know I don't like being underground. Not like this.* A basement was one thing. Caves, narrow tunnels beneath the earth, brought home a crushing sense of the air leaving her lungs. Cold bumps stood up on her arms and Alisha shivered hard, inhaling sharply. "Tell me you've got a flashlight."

"I do," Reichart said, but she heard a shift of his clothes, as if he shrugged. "But not with me. We're going to have to go blind. Sorry, Leesh."

Alisha nodded stiffly. "All right. Okay, fine. Let's go then. Are you sure it comes out the other side?" She put her fingertips on the wall, slimy stone giving her another shudder as she edged a foot forward.

"Pretty sure."

"You're not filling me with confidence, Reichart." Part of her wanted to abandon caution and run, keeping her hand on the wall for guidance, whatever would get her out of there faster. Fear of the floor breaking away held stronger sway, though, and she moved slowly, concentrating on what she could feel. "I thought you were stealing drones."

"I was." Alisha heard a note of gladness for distraction in Reichart's voice. His conversation came in concentrated bursts, both of them paying attention to where they put their feet in the darkness. "But your little escapade at Emma's computer facilities didn't go unnoticed. What were you trying to do, Leesh? Get arrested? Because you did a good job of that, if nothing else."

"I was trying get Brandon, but the bastard lit out on me."

"Hey. I thought I was the bastard in your life."

"Sorry. The son of a bitch lit out on me."

"Hey. I thought I wa—"

"Frank!"

His laughter rumbled through the darkness, then faded into something gentler. "So I came after you. I had a very dramatic plan to raid Langley and sweep you off your feet."

Despite the walls pressing in, Alisha gave a snort of laughter. "I'm sure I would've been very appreciat—ow!" She drew her foot back from a stone jutting out of the wall, cursing the speed she'd slowly picked up. "I'm okay," she muttered, and worked her way forward again more cautiously. "Did your plan have any details?"

"Lucky for me it didn't need to. Erika called. I don't think she even knows I'm in the States. She told me where you were and I said I'd get it taken care of. Do you know how far we've come?"

"A hundred and eighty-five steps," Alisha said automatically. "I'd usually say that was a little shy of two hundred feet, but the way I'm moving right now I'd say it's more like a hundred and fifty. How long's the tunnel?"

"About eight hundred feet." Amused admiration filled Reichart's tone. "I can always count on you to know how far you've come. You always were better at judging distances than I was."

"I'm better at a lot of things than you are, Reichart. How'd you get past the Feds outside the library?" She pursed her lips. "There were Feds, right? That's not just a story to get me out of the library with you?"

"Don't you trust me, Alisha?"

Alisha stopped deliberately, letting her footsteps fall

away into silence, and stared at the sound of him across the way. Reichart laughed out loud, noisy in the dark tunnel. "God, I miss you, Leesh."

Alisha rubbed her shoulder, just below the left collar-bone, and started moving again. "I'd say you needed to aim better, but all things considered…?"

Reichart's warmth was next to her suddenly, a hand at her shoulder, then sliding to the small of her back as he turned her to face him. It ought to be an indignity, Alisha thought, to have him move her to where he wanted her. Ought to be. Somehow she didn't mind, and closed her eyes against the darkness as he carefully found her cheek and brushed his knuckles over it. For long moments he didn't speak, but then, their silences had always said the most.

"Telling lies is easy," Reichart finally said. "'Cristina shot you.' I thought you might believe it, and hell, it was better than the truth. Even if I did it to save your life, I wasn't there in the aftermath to explain myself."

"You had your reasons," Alisha said quietly. "It doesn't matter anymore, Frank. It was a long time ago. Seven years."

"It matters." A breath of warm laughter spilled over her and Reichart lowered his head, cautiously, until his forehead touched hers. "It matters because I love you, Leesh."

"Frank—" Alisha pulled back, the tunnel's still air suddenly feeling thick in her chest, making her heart ache. Reichart tightened his hold, not so much that she couldn't escape, but asking her not to. "Frank, don't."

"I have to." Another chuckle stirred the air. "Usually with us it's hotel rooms and watching each other in silence, Leesh. Maybe there's just always too much light between us. It's easier to make confessions in the dark."

"Frank." Alisha's voice was hoarse, his name barely a scrape of sound. Something she didn't want to put a name to made her heart ricochet, hot and cold pulsing through her hands in time with her heartbeat. It demanded a name as it dropped lower through her body, quick throbs between her thighs that insisted she acknowledge *need*. Water dripping in the tunnel echoed that desire, adding its own music to the crescendo within her. "This isn't the time—"

"This is the only time." Frustration came into Reichart's laugh and he tugged her close again. "It's the only time," he whispered. "There's always going to be too much light, any other time. Dammit, Leesh." His voice dropped further, Alisha's heart clenching at the sorrow she heard spoken clearly in the nickname. "I got you into this whole Sicarii mess. Because I trusted you as an agent, but also because I wanted to see you again and I couldn't just show up on your doorstep. Time's running out now, my time, the Infitalis's time, our time. All I have is right now, and I'm not going to let it slip away again." He took a ragged breath, straightening away from her and loosening his grip a little. "Tell me it's over, Alisha, and I'll step back and this never happened. Tell me you don't love me and I'll accept it."

"Reichart…"

"Don't do that." His thumb brushed her mouth in a light touch. "Don't distance yourself. Use my name."

"Frank," Alisha whispered. "Goddammit, Frank. I left you and Emma alone in London because you were happy with her. I could see it."

Bewilderment filled his voice. "What does Emma have to do with this? With us?"

Alisha laughed, a broken sound. Her chest felt too full, breath struggling for space with tears and a too-fast heartbeat. "I wanted you to be happy, you idiot. Even if I never got my answers as to what had happened, I wanted you to be happy. If that doesn't tell you, I don't know what would."

"A straight answer?"

Alisha ducked her head, the action filled with shy amusement as she bumped her forehead against Reichart's chest. "Jon was right," she whispered. "It really is a love story." She looked up again, knowing she couldn't see Reichart's expression, but feeling as though she could. "I never stopped loving you. I was the only one who thought I had. Nothing ever turns out like I plan for it to." She sighed, stepping closer, and Reichart wrapped his arms around her shoulders. "We need to go, Frank. The Feds would've come into the building two minutes ago."

"They're not going to find us any time soon." Reichart slid his hand under her jaw, tipping her chin up and finding her mouth for a kiss. "I'm not going to let this moment go that easily, Leesh. There are too many years to make up for. Too many missed chances and too many close calls." Kisses followed the line of her jaw to her throat, Reichart pushing Anton's suit jacket from her shoulders. She shivered under his touch, the tunnel's warm air chilly compared to the heat of his hands.

"What're you going to do, Reichart? Seduce me down here in the library catacombs?"

He pulled back far enough to say, "Yeah," with an unrepentant grin in his voice. "Pretty much."

"Reichart!" The protest was made largely of laughter that faded as he began to explore her body with easy confidence left by the memory of years past. "Reichart, we really…?should…" Words gave way to a quiver as he unfastened her bra, then into another laugh that ended

with, "Oh, to hell with it," as she coiled her arms around
his neck.

"That's my Leesh," he mumbled against her throat.
Alisha brushed her fingers over his mouth, then stopped
anything else he might say with a kiss.

"Shh. It's so dark. Shh." Darkness enveloped them so
thoroughly it added new intimacy, each touch careful and
investigative because sight couldn't be relied on. Alisha's
coat fell to the floor, puddling at her feet as impatience
swept her and she reached for Reichart's waistband.

The stone wall was cool against her back as he lifted
her, both still half tangled in their clothes, to come
together with cries muffled in the other's shoulder.
Desperate connection of bodies, searching for ways to say
the things that the silences between them always held.
Searching for ways to overcome the darkness, in life and
liquid heat and wordless promises about what had been
and what might be between them. Alisha dug her fingers
into Reichart's shoulders, face buried in his neck to rain
hungry kisses and nipping bites there, desire pent up inside
her too intense to be assuaged by gentleness and too delicate to be brought home by violence.

Reichart's need seemed the same, sharply focused and
carefully brought out, as if fragility and desperation were
inextricably connected and just as easily shattered. The
only words they exchanged were murmured, barely more
than whispers of hushing and reassurance. Alisha felt
drawn-out and stretched thin, as if she'd become made of
spun glass, both alarmingly frail and unexpectedly durable.
Heat ran through her, molten glass in her veins, easy to
shape and equally easy to destroy. For an instant the idea
of flying apart held appeal, and in that moment she did, a
small startled cry hidden in Reichart's shoulder. Heat
everywhere, shared, before she came back together almost

against her will, breathless and clinging to her lover in the darkness.

"Now," he whispered after a brief eternity, threads of humor in the words. "Now we should go."

They disentangled and straightened clothes, then without speaking, found each other's hands and spurned caution, running together down the library tunnel.

Alisha, her hand in Reichart's, wondered what dangers had remained unmentioned in the darkness, that they should be left behind so hastily.

18

"**S**orry we're late." Reichart spoke to someone as he ducked out a narrow doorway into an alley. Sunlight made Alisha's eyes ache after the absolute darkness of the library tunnel, and she lifted her hand, squinting into brightness.

Brandon Parker leaned against the far alley wall, one foot propped against the bricks behind him, his arms folded over his chest. Alisha dropped Reichart's hand as if it had burned her, falling back a step as her voice shot up a register. "Brandon? I just spent eight thousand dollars getting you out of this country—!"

"Lilith insisted." Brandon's gaze flickered from Reichart to Alisha, judging and curious. Unexpected guilt fluttered behind Alisha's breastbone, angering her. She wrapped her arms around her ribs, aware of the posture's defensiveness, but feeling sufficiently exposed to let body language betray her.

"What do you mean, Lilith insisted? I thought she'd be curled up in your quantum drive, which, by the way, was incredibly stupid, Brandon. A contingent of Armani-suited

Sicarii came down on that facility like Lucifer's own army. Did you really think you could order something like that anonymously?"

"Maybe I wasn't trying for anonymity." Brandon straightened away from the wall, tilting his head toward the end of the alley. "I've got a car waiting, but the meter runs out in about two minutes. I was ready to leave without you."

"Were you?" Reichart reached for Alisha's hand again, shoulders stiffening when she stepped forward just quickly enough to miss taking it. Alisha let herself clench her fist, out of both men's view. It wasn't a game, and she wasn't a prize Reichart had won. He didn't get to flaunt her. Angry, she ducked into the car as Brandon held the door for her, overly aware that he offered her the shotgun seat, leaving Reichart the back. Goddamn men, anyway.

"If you weren't trying for anonymity, why'd you leave the States in the first place? And what do you mean, Lilith insisted? What's she running in?" Alisha snapped the questions as Brandon got into the car. "Where are we going?"

"Better question. What are you planning? Emma got on a plane for Europe hours ago. You're still here. What gives?"

Alisha ground her teeth together, turning her gaze out the tinted window until she trusted her voice. "I need data Erika can't get for me. I'm going to steal it, if I can figure out where it's located. What's going on with Lilith, Brandon?"

"She spent the whole time in Hector—that's the name of the supercomputer Emma lent us," Brandon said to Alisha's curious glance. "She spent all that time paring down her code to the bare minimum of what she could retain intellectual functionality at. I took one of their laptops and one of my quantum chips and built her a reduced-capability home. She's running out of the back seat right now."

Alisha looked over her shoulder, where Reichart eyed the laptop beside him. "What happens when it runs out of battery?"

"Then she can't communicate with us until it's plugged back in," Brandon said. "We came back for you because you came back for us, Ali. That's it."

Alisha felt Reichart's eyes on her at Brandon's nick-name and refused to meet the look. "You'd already run when I came back for you."

"I didn't think you'd come." Brandon gave her a quick glance, then looked back at the road. "You were pretty pissed."

Anger flared all over again, as much because of Reichart's intense silence as Brandon's statement. "Like I didn't have a reason to be?"

"I didn't say that." Brandon went quiet, flicking glances in the rearview mirror at Reichart.

Alisha turned her face back to the window, covering her eyes and muffling a groan. "Tell Lilith thank you," she said after a long moment. "You know Greg came after you. With the Sicarii."

"I know." Tension rode in Brandon's voice. "I guess that's the other reason I agreed to come back for you. If Dad was on your case…?that was my fault. What is it you want to steal?"

Alisha let go a low *heh*. "The original Firebird's black box. The one that was supposed to be so damning about Susan Simone. I want to see if there's anything on it to tie Cristina to the Sicarii, or even just to her life as an espi-onage agent. I want to blow Nichole Oldenburg's whole world apart. Your father confirmed my whole paranoid presidency theory. I'm not going to sit by and let that happen."

"Presidency theory? Reichart, wake Lilith up so she can listen." The words were clipped, a command rather than a request.

Alisha was just as glad she couldn't see Reichart's expression, though she heard the click of the laptop being unlocked over the sound of tires.

"I wonder if this is what foot-binding felt like," Lilith said a few seconds later. "So constrained, when the possibilities of being whole are within visible reach. Brandon, have we found Alisha?"

"You have," Alisha replied. "Thank you, Lilith."

"Not at all. Brandon would have come back for you." The pleasant voice had a note of steely mechanicalness to it, making Alisha's mouth curve. "Please bring me up to date."

"Bring us all up to date," Brandon muttered.

Alisha exhaled and turned her gaze back to the window, ordering her thoughts before summarizing Greg's confession in the interrogation room.

"Before I kill you, Mr. Bond," Reichart mumbled from the back seat as she concluded. Alisha shot him a wry smile.

"That's what I said, too. He said it was the only way he could convince me he's one of the good guys."

"Maybe he is." Brandon spoke without hope. "You got out of there, after all. What were the odds against that?"

"Approximately five thousand eight hundred sixty-two against," Lilith replied obligingly, then audibly hesitated, the sound presumably calculated. "Oh. That was rhetorical, wasn't it? My apologies."

"Really?" Alisha asked. "That bad? There aren't more than a few…" She trailed off, then chuckled quietly.

"Mumble-mumble employees at Langley at any one time. The number's classified," she said with a wink toward Reichart, who rolled his eyes. "Well, it is!" she protested.

"You really think I don't know how many people the Agency employs—Alisha?" The hitch told her he'd narrowly avoided using his nickname for her, a possessive mistake he wasn't inclined toward making.

Alisha twitched an eyebrow up, then shrugged, turning her attention back to Brandon. "Okay. I'll grant you that it's possible. Maybe the reason Emma and I got out of there was that Greg let us." A zing of discomfort slashed through her as she recalled how easy it had been to take down Anton, as well. But Greg hadn't been as careless in his approach as the big Russian, and would have been hard-pressed to contact anyone when handcuffed to a chair. The interrogation room had no cameras, making it one of the few places in the base that Alisha could have gotten away with what she'd done. "Maybe," she said in a low voice, doubts still more profound than belief. "I still want that black box, regardless of whose side he's on. If he's one of the good guys, maybe it'll exonerate him, but either way, he's not going to give it to me, and Erika can't get to it. So it's up to me." She cast a look over her shoulder at Reichart, then brought it around to include Brandon. "Up to us."

"Us? When did this become an us?" Reichart asked. Alisha knotted her fist on her thigh.

"If you really believed we weren't all basically on the same side, Reichart, you wouldn't have gotten in the car with Brandon. You wouldn't have let me get in it. So can we skip the posturing and try to figure out where the black zone they might be hiding the box is?"

"Beneath Parliament," Lilith said unexpectedly.

Alisha straightened and turned to stare at the laptop

computer, completely forgetting Lilith couldn't see her. "Beneath Parliament? I know we're friends with the Brits, but that seems—"

"Unlikely?" Lilith asked smoothly. "Perhaps not. Consider the scenario, Alisha. You are a spy. Part of your job is to retrieve information that could be embarrassing or deadly to other countries, in order to achieve leverage over those countries so your country's needs might best be met. Correct?"

Alisha frowned at the laptop. "That's an ugly way to put it. You sound different, Lilith."

"I abandoned my vernacular speech code while paring down to fit into tight quarters. When I reintegrate with my mainframe system my vocal patterns will return to normal." Lilith clearly dismissed the digression, adding, "My description of a spy's situation is inherently correct. Now, each country has its own similar spy network, everyone collecting these bits of information. Everyone knowing these pieces of data are being unearthed and broadcast. What do you do when you have a piece of information you especially do not want made public?"

"Find something better to hold over their heads," Alisha said.

Lilith seemed to give an approving nod. "And when you have something so important you cannot risk it being shown…?"

"…you make someone else responsible for it," Alisha said slowly. "Because they know if they fail, something they need protected will be sacrificed in return. It's the Cold War mutual annihilation scenario."

"There's no other country the U.S. has such intimate relationships with than Britain," Reichart said. "I wonder if she's on to something."

"Lilith, do you have any proof of this? I mean,

anything I could use to—" Alisha broke off with a laugh, as a sense of ridiculous descended on her. "Anything I could use to break into Parliament with. Jesus." She dropped her face into her hands, taking a few deep breaths before looking up again. "I swear to God," she said to no one in particular, "I really was doing pretty well with having a normal life. I didn't need to go back to the seven impossible things before breakfast lifestyle."

"I spent my nascent weeks, before Brandon even knew what I was, with full access to the Agency's entire computer network, Alisha," Lilith answered. "I can get you where you need to go."

❧

"What's going on with you and Parker, Alisha?" A few hours later, Reichart caught her in the narrow airplane aisle, voice pitched too low for anyone else to hear beneath the endless roar of engines.

Alisha stared up at him, so close she could see little more than the line of his chin, and said, "What?" without heat or enthusiasm behind the word.

It wasn't that she hadn't heard him, or didn't under-stand, and the glance she shot down the dim aisle to where Brandon sat told Reichart as much. A woman watching them caught Alisha's eye, then looked away quickly as she turned her attention back to Reichart.

His jaw tightened. "I said, what's going on with you and Parker?"

"Nothing, Frank." Alisha stepped forward, expecting Reichart to give ground.

He did, falling back far enough to linger in the tiny airplane galley, but put his arm across the aisle, blocking

Alisha's path. "If it's nothing, why'd you go cold fish when he turned up?"

Alisha stopped in her tracks, sucking her cheeks in as she turned her gaze upward, studying the halogen lights above her. "If you want to have a conversation with a woman about her behavior, Reichart, an opening sally of *cold fish* is maybe not the best way to begin."

"Dammit, Leesh!" The words were hissed with frustration. "Stop screwing around and tell me what's going on."

It would take, Alisha thought clinically, very little to turn the minor confrontation into a scene spiraling out of control. The temptation to do so was real, born from a weariness Alisha barely recognized in herself. She would willingly face down an enemy in battle, her training preparing her emotionally and physically to take whatever steps were necessary. Make her the ringside attraction in an emotional triangle or give her an enemy who couldn't be fought with fists and guns, and she was at a loss. It would be so much easier, she thought, to deal with the Sicarii—with Reichart and Brandon, for that matter—if the situations were endlessly life and death, instead of playing in the lesser—or greater—fields of heartbreak and politics.

Another person, this time a man, averted his eyes as Alisha held her ground. The woman beside him, more brazen, lifted her chin a little as Alisha met her gaze. "Put your arm down, Frank," Alisha said quietly. "People are starting to stare."

People in general and, she suspected, Brandon in particular. She didn't need to look, Reichart's scowl telling her everything she needed to know. The scientist would have looked away by the time she turned, anyway, pretending that whatever went on between Reichart and Alisha was of no interest to him.

"The only thing there is between me and Brandon is a

possibility," Alisha murmured after Reichart dropped his arm. She felt uncomfortable standing there, too aware that people could openly see them, even if their conversation was too softly held to be heard. "And right now, even if that never comes to anything, we need him and we need Lilith, so you flaunting being with me isn't going to help at all."

"Am I?" Reichart asked sharply. "Am I with you, Leesh? Do you really love me, or are those just easy words in the dark?"

"Nothing is ever easy with you." Her reply came out more venomously than she'd intended, and Alisha drew in a breath, deliberately backing off. After a moment she managed a faint smile and added, "See? I told you before," she added more quietly. "This isn't the time. We need to break the dagger people's backbone, to give your people time to recover."

An itch ran along her spine and she glanced over her shoulder, finding no guilty gazes turning away. It was just referencing the Sicarii, she told herself, that made her paranoid. "We've got to focus on taking Cris down right now, Frank. Don't think I'm shutting you out." She tilted her head back again, letting a soft throaty laugh escape. "You said once the girl I used to be was too idealistic for you, remember?"

Reichart nodded stiffly, a scowl settling between his eyebrows. "Yeah, but—"

"No." Alisha lifted her fingers to put them over his lips. "There's not really a 'but' here, Reichart. You take away all that idealism and you're left with me trying to stop a group of lunatics from overtaking my country, and trying to make sure my family doesn't get hurt because of what I'm doing. Right now that's all there is. You, of all people, should understand about making choices like that."

Reichart took her hand from his mouth, then brushed his thumb below her collarbone, just over her heart. "I never thought I'd miss that girl, Leesh. I thought I needed somebody tougher. Now I'm not so sure."

Alisha quirked her chin to the side, a tiny shrug-like motion. "We can't go back, Frank. This is who I am now. You're going to have to take me or leave me as I am, but that's not a decision to be made right now."

"Yeah, it is," Reichart said, voice gone suddenly rough. "You're wrong. This is the time. Whether we're hiding in the dark or five miles in the sky, dammit, Alisha, I love you." He caught her hands in his, holding them tight as Alisha's heart started to hammer too hard again, color flooding her cheeks. "I spent years telling myself it'd worked out the only way it could between us, but every time I see you now I know it's not true."

"Reichart." Alisha managed a tentative smile, tears burning her eyes. "Stop it," she whispered. "You're talking like we're not going to see each other again. Stop it."

"Forty operatives, Leesh," he whispered back. "Since Boyer, forty of our people have been killed. I've been getting up every day for the last ten months not knowing if I would see anybody I loved again, or if they'd see me. So yeah, you're right, maybe I'm pushing it, but I'm out of time, Alisha. I love you, and I'm not going to take this ride to hell without you knowing that."

"I know it, Frank. Stop." The words felt hollow, as if they'd found an empty cold chamber within Alisha's chest to resound in. "You're losing people, but you're gaining them, too. You got me, didn't you?" Her smile went fragile, then watery. "You've even got Brandon. Maybe we're a small start, but it's something, right? It'll turn out okay. Please stop. I don't want to lose you. I don't even want to think about it." Dangerous emotion, a distant part of her

chided. All her safety mechanisms of compartmentalization had shattered, everything that might go down in one
of her illegal Strongbox Chronicles suddenly burgeoning at
the surface. Her hands were cold and trembling, even in
Reichart's grip, and she felt uncomfortably as if everyone
on the plane were focused on them. A few pairs of eyes
were, gazes sliding away when she tried to meet them.
Worse were the people deliberately not watching. Those
ones sent prickles of warning over her skin, one of the few
emotional responses she was trained to listen to instead of
ignore.

Reichart tugged her closer, putting his mouth against
her forehead. "Just promise me one thing."

Alisha laughed, a sound more of fear than happiness,
and put aside the watchful audience for a moment.
"What?"

Reichart stepped back, still holding her hands, dark
eyes intense as he looked down at her. "If the Sicarii don't
manage to take me out, Leesh, promise you'll marry me."

19

*A*stonishment swept through Alisha, bringing light-headedness that made her sway. Reichart's hold on her hands kept her anchored, the single point of contact tethering to the earth. To the airplane floor, at least, she thought headily, since the earth itself was miles below her. "Reichart." His name was a breathless, astounded whisper.

"I mean it, Leesh. Say you'll marry me."

Laughter, even threadier than before, escaped her. "That didn't work out so well last time, Reichart. If I say yes, am I going to get shot again?"

"Not by me," he whispered intently. "Not if I have anything to do with it. You love me, don't you?"

"Yeah." The answer came with a lopsided smile, color scalding Alisha's cheeks again. The coldness of her hands had reversed somehow, until her fingers ached with their seeming thickness. "I do. I must be crazy, but I still do."

"Then say yes," Reichart pleaded, hope bright in his eyes.

Alisha closed her own eyes and leaned forward, putting her forehead against his chest. Conflicting desires ached in her body, tearing her one direction and another and leaving her without air to breathe. The prospect of an ordinary life with Reichart, buying a house on the street her sister lived on, children, struck her as laughable, if enticing in its own way.

Brandon's blue eyes, regretful and desperate, flashed through her vision. He, unlike Reichart, might be the key to eventually settling down. He didn't share Reichart's adventuresome streak.

He didn't share Alisha's adventuresome streak.

An ordinary life, Alisha thought, without rue or regret, might never have been in the cards for her. She wanted the tall, dark man whose arms she stood in, and there were prices she was willing to pay to make that happen.

Alisha knotted her fingers in Reichart's shirt, then stepped back, smiling, though she knew tears streaked her cheeks. "Tell you what," she said in a hoarse whisper. "Ask me again once we've survived all this, all right? Last time you shot me. I'm not going to let you get killed just to get out of a marriage proposal a second time."

"Alisha—"

"No." The word was soft but firm, and Alisha put her fingers over Reichart's mouth again. "Don't argue with me, Frank. You want to marry me, you're going to have to stay alive to ask me again. It'll help me be sure you're not asking just because we're about to die." The teasing faded from the last words, leaving her pressing her lips together until they felt white. "Ask me again when this is over."

Reichart's expression hardened and he scowled down the aisle toward where Brandon sat. Alisha reached up and caught his jaw, making him look down at her again. "This isn't about him, Frank. It's about you and me and bad timing. If you make it about him, you might give me a reason to make it about him. So don't do that, all right?

Not if you meant what you just asked. Keep it between us."

"How can I be sure?" he asked in a low voice. "How can I know it's not about him?"

"Because I said so," Alisha said tartly, then sighed and leaned against the galley's metal door frame. It was cold against her arm, and would leave a red mark if she stayed there too long. The idea made her straighten, rubbing her upper arm. A woman down the plane—one whose eyes she'd caught before—looked away again, making Alisha curl her fingers around her arm where she rubbed it. Part of her wanted to demand that people stop looking at her, though the best way to accomplish that was obviously to return to her seat. But the conversation she and Reichart were having couldn't be done in front of Brandon, so Alisha was stuck trying not to stand out while standing up. "Because if it was about him I wouldn't be trying to figure out how to steal Lilith."

"What?" The surprise in Reichart's voice bordered on gratifying. Alisha shivered, letting her focus soften as she looked down the aisle. One or two people watched her directly, more interested in the silent drama near the lavatories than the in-flight film that played. Others tried not to watch so openly, making Alisha's skin itch again.

"I owe someone a favor I can't afford not to pay back." Alisha forced an unamused laugh, folding her arms over her ribs. "Sort of like hiding state secrets under Parliament. Not quite that big. He wants a copy of the AI. And she's right there, all functional and tidy, in Brandon's laptop. Dammit." Alisha thudded her head on the wall, eyes closed. "I don't want to do it, Frank. It's kidnapping. Slavery." She heard herself echoing Brandon's argument and twisted a smile.

"What's the alternative?"

Alisha opened her eyes again, looking down the aisle, watching people without quite seeing them. "I can think of two. The best case would be this person would own me. The terms of our…?agreement…were clear. I'd come through when he needed me, or—" She broke off, glancing at Reichart, then returned her gaze to the aisle, as if it could offer her neutrality of tone as she delivered the facts. The brazen woman met her eyes and offered a smile that Alisha returned briefly.

"Or he'd expose certain things that could destroy a lot of people. Files that shouldn't exist," she said evasively. "My life being forfeit was almost secondary. He knew that'd bother me less than ruining careers and other people's lives."

"To hell with the other people," Reichart said. "You're talking about your life, Alisha."

"Emma's one of those other people, Frank. You are. Mazie is." Alisha shook her head, remembering the shaking hand she'd written those chronicles with. Remembering betrayal and anger and beneath that, a hollow forgiveness that had taken years to recognize. *I wanted you to be happy,* she'd told Reichart. Those words were etched in a journal, unrealized acknowledgment of his exoneration for shooting her, safely hidden in a deposit box in a London bank.

Not so safely, after all. "I don't value my own life over a thirteen-year-old girl's. I couldn't live with myself."

"Shit. *Shit,* Alisha. What else?"

"That's not enough?" Alisha dismissed the question, lips pressed together again. "I'm more useful to him alive than dead. In Jon's position—"

"Jon?"

Alisha shrugged. "I don't know his real name. Carlos,

Leo, Michael—you probably know him. The Italian fat man. The information broker."

"Paolo," Reichart said after an instant, though he, too, lifted a shoulder in a shrug. "That's the first name I knew him by, anyway. You owe—Leesh, how did you get in that far over your head with Paolo?"

Alisha bit her tongue on the truth—*I was tracking you*—and returned to his earlier question. "In Jon's position I'd collect the files to make sure I knew he could, and I'd keep me on a very short leash for the rest of my life. He's got too many ins, Reichart. He could get to my family as easily as the Sicarii could. If I don't turn Lilith over to him, I'm his."

"There's got to be another option."

"Sure." Alisha turned a crooked smile on the dark-haired man. "I could die."

"Not funny, Alisha," Reichart growled. "Not funny at all."

"It wasn't meant to be." Alisha exhaled, her shoulders slumping. "But right now, believe it or not, I think we have another problem."

"How can we *possibly* have another problem?" The question bordered on rhetorical, everything in Reichart's demeanor changing as he asked. Minute changes: muscles came into relief, twitches of motion and his eyes hooded, distrust coming down in them like a mask. From one breath to the next he changed, concerned lover left behind and deadly mercenary in its place.

"There's more than people staring," Alisha murmured. "I count at least four actively casing us. Maybe five, if you include the blond in the third row checking you out."

Reichart glanced over his shoulder, then looked back down at Alisha with a frown. "There's no blond in the third row."

Alisha grinned. "Yeah, there is. Second seat. He's kind of cute, really."

Reichart did a double-take, then snorted. "Not my type."

"Too bad," Alisha whispered. "He just lit up when you looked back at him. Maybe you should go be nice to him. He could be a useful cover when we get off the plane."

"You won't risk a thirteen-year-old girl, but random strangers on the plane are fair game?"

"Everybody's got their line in the sand. Don't look," Alisha advised, "but there's a pair two rows behind that, a brunette woman and her partner. The woman keeps meeting my eyes outright and the guy is fidgety. There's another one on the far side of the bulkhead, near Brandon, and—"

"I've got them," Reichart interrupted in a low voice. "Dammit. Recognize any of them?"

"No," Alisha said just as quietly, "but I'm going to kill Brandon for coming back on the Sicarii radar, and then I'm going to bring him back and kill him again for coming back into the U.S. to get me. Every intelligence agency on the planet must know where he is by now."

Faint amusement creased Reichart's mouth. "Maybe that's who's on the plane with us."

Laughter escaped Alisha in a quiet rush. "What, reps from every intelligence agency on the planet? That should be exciting when we get to Heathrow."

"How do we want to handle this?"

"I don't know." Alisha shook her head. "But all three of us need to decide, not just you and me."

"C'mon." Derisiveness came into Reichart's voice. "Parker's not a field agent."

"Technically, neither are we," Alisha pointed out.

"You're a merc, Reichart. You work for the highest bidder, remember? And I'm retired."

"Don't be difficult."

"All of us, Frank. All of us, or I'll just go sit down next to Ms. Brazen Eyes over there and hand you two over."

"You wouldn't."

"Probably not." Alisha pushed away from the wall and threaded her way back down the aisle, using chair backs to keep herself steady. "But you never can tell."

"I don't *have* an American passport with me!" Brandon hissed the protestation, leaving Alisha staring at him in bemusement. "You got me Brazilian and British papers!"

"Oh, for—the Brazilian ones, Brandon, use the papers from Brazil. The whole point is to make them wait." Alisha tilted her head, a tiny motion, toward the quartet who shadowed them. They were discreet, scattered through the customs lines, all of them sour-faced and impatient. Given the general expressions of people shuffling through the long lines, they were part of the faceless majority.

"Are you sure this is a good idea?" Reichart shifted his duffel bag, the only luggage he'd brought, over his shoulder. "They've got biometric scanners for non-nationals. None of us are in the system under the names on these passports."

Alisha flashed a smile, nodding at a sign announcing Heathrow as a free wireless access site. "I think Lilith can take care of that little problem."

"You want me to expose her to possible detection in the middle of a security-ridden airport?" Brandon demanded.

Alisha smiled more broadly, feeling the expression growing pointed. "You want to risk having her taken away from you entirely when your American identification comes up at odds with your Brazilian passport?"

Outrage faltered in Brandon's blue eyes, his shoulders

slumping. "They don't like people running laptops on this side of security."

"So be subtle, Brandon." He was a Company agent. Subtle was supposed to be part of the job.

As if he'd heard the reprimand, Brandon frowned, but slipped his carry-on open to wake Lilith from sleep mode. Alisha made a fuss over aching feet, pulling the men aside to sit down while the line shifted and moved forward. The brazen-gazed woman gave her a dirty look that Alisha returned with a grin and a wave.

"I thought we were being subtle," Reichart said.

Alisha transferred the smile to him. "Only with regards to customs. My bold friend over there already knows we're on to her. They all do." An uplifting sense of cheer buoyed Alisha, the small pleasure of inconveniencing those who followed them greater than it had any right to be. Tiny things going right, she thought, could make a day much more pleasant. "Might as well enjoy annoying them. There'll be trouble enough later."

"This would be a hell of a lot easier if Lilith had all her processing power available," Brandon muttered.

Alisha shrugged. "She doesn't, so we'll have to make do. Besides, don't tell me you didn't upgrade that laptop with quantum chips. It might not be as spacious as your development servers, but I bet she's got room to breathe."

Brandon gave her a look similar to the one the woman had, then turned his attention to the computer. Alisha sat back, pulling a foot into her lap to massage it, and smiled at anyone who would meet her eye. An armed security guard glanced their way, smiled briefly, and looked away again before his gaze came back to them, watching and considering. "Soon would be good," Alisha announced quietly.

"Are you trying to piss me off?"

"It's just a bonus side effect." Alisha winced, seeing Reichart's expression turn smug, and warned herself to be more careful. Brandon's sins aside, they needed him and the AI to get out of the airport safely. "Sorry," she added, putting genuine emotion into the apology. "Maybe I'm a little more tense than I thought."

Brandon frowned at her, then Reichart, and hunched his shoulders. "Yeah. Maybe we all are. Just a couple more minutes. These aren't exactly easy servers to waltz through."

"I hope not. I'd hate to think everybody was pulling this sort of thing off."

Brandon chuckled quietly. "Me, too." A few minutes later he looked up with a stretch, clipping the carry-on shut again. "You ready? How're your feet?"

"Better. I hate flying. I swell up." Alisha got up gingerly, making a face as she tested her weight. Reichart offered an elbow and she took it, mincing along. The security guard approached, nodding at Brandon's laptop case.

"What were you doing there, sir?"

"Faxing our hotel." Brandon's accent went heavy and his voice polite, a foreign national whose first language wasn't English and who understood caution was wise while traveling in the current political climate. "I was to notify them when we arrived, so they could send a car. Is everything all right?"

The guard shot another look at the case. "Why didn't you take the laptop all the way out of the bag?"

Brandon flushed, taking a small step closer to the guard and dropping his voice as he cast a quick glance toward Alisha and Reichart. "The pictures I have on my desktop. Ms. Buckner and I…?well." Stiffness and accusation filled both his posture and his words. "*He* is with her now. I did not want him to see."

The guard tossed a sly, delighted look toward Reichart and nodded. "Be careful with that, sir. You'll have all sorts of trouble, you will."

Brandon nodded, still stiffly, then rejoined Alisha and Reichart as the guard dismissed him, the three of them holding back laughter until they were safely through customs.

20

"*O*ur escort is waiting for us," Alisha breathed. It was inevitable that people from the airplane would be at the Heathrow Express terminal, but Alisha and the men had lingered long enough that those who could had moved on. The brazen-gazed brunette, however, slouched in a chair with her feet thrust out and ankles crossed, watching the escalators openly while her partner idled, walking up and down the length of the terminal. Three others—including the slight blond man who'd admired Reichart—stood around, arms folded or reading newspapers whose pages they didn't turn. "Your friend's here," Alisha whispered to Reichart. "Coincidence, or conspiracy?"

"I'll go with conspiracy until proven wrong." Reichart stepped off the escalator in front of her, Brandon taking up the rear. "I count seven."

"I only have five," Alisha said. "Guess we'll see how many people get on the train with us." She'd lost track of time during the transatlantic flight, but the shift forward had to put it somewhere around eleven at night, not long before the last train left to go into London. Not many people dallied in airports at that hour, usually eager to finish their travel and get some sleep. Whatever form confrontation took, it would be as little-observed as it could be given the enormous amount of traffic Heathrow saw.

Too many people, in other words.

Chimes and a pleasant British voice announced the arrival of the train, asking people to stand back. "We could've saved ourselves a lot of trouble by taking a cab," Brandon observed.

Alisha blinked at him, then grinned as she entered the train. "They've got to have people watching the cab lanes, too. This way we at least recognize our enemies."

"*Enemies* is so melodramatic," a woman murmured from behind her.

Alisha looked over her shoulder to see the brazen-gazed woman offering a smile that didn't reach her eyes. "Sorry. What would you call yourselves?"

"Friends," the woman suggested. Her voice was lightly accented, English learned somewhere in the British Commonwealth, but not in Britain itself. "People concerned for your well-being."

"Yeah?" Reichart asked, nodding as three more from the plane entered their car. "What about them?"

The woman glanced toward them, then came back to Reichart with a smile. "Oh, they're your enemies."

Alisha, taken off guard, laughed, then dropped into one of the seats. "Look, since we're all friends here, who're you with? Come on, sit down." She waved a hand at the others who'd gotten on, then leaned forward to put her elbows on her knees, assessing all of them. The blond who'd admired Reichart looked slightly confused as he sat, and Alisha wrote him out as a danger.

"We can't reasonably answer that," the brunette woman said.

Alisha shrugged a shoulder, not disagreeing. "Just trying to make small talk. Look," she added to the blond, "things are going to get a little peculiar in this car. You might want to get in the next one."

He stood again, eyebrows wrinkled with perplexity, and glanced around. "Erm."

"G'wan, luv." Reichart flapped a hand, ushering the poor fellow out. "You're lovely, but not my type, anyway." The blond, still confused and now blushing, hurried to the next car as Reichart looked around and smiled slyly. "Before we get started, does anybody want to get out?"

Strangers exchanged glances and moved as far away as they could, clearly uncomfortable. There were too many, Alisha thought. Too many to risk, but she saw very little choice. At least the late hour thinned out the passengers to some degree.

The doors swished shut and Reichart dropped his chin to his chest. "That's what I thought." He laced his fingers together, cracking his knuckles, but as he looked up, Alisha reached out and stopped him with a touch.

"Discretion's the better part of valor, Frank." A brief nod reminded him of the closed-circuit television cameras on the train. He scowled, but settled back down, watching their four counterparts warily. Alisha leaned into the train's acceleration, its thrum non-invasive after the roar of airplane engines, and sighed.

"Excellent," the brunette said. "I'm glad you're not going to fuss." Reichart grunted and the woman fell silent, no one meeting anyone's eyes or striking up conversation.

Fifteen minutes, Alisha thought, curling her hand around a cool metal pole. *Fifteen minutes into London.* They seemed interminable, seconds counting backward in her mind.

Every moment she felt herself growing twitchier, body stiffening and finger tapping against the pole. Her tension seemed to radiate, making Reichart scowl more deeply and Brandon frown at the floor. Even the quartet who'd come to collect them seemed affected as the train raced toward London. The woman got up to pace the length of the car. Alisha flinched her shoulders back, as if the woman being in action threatened her, and the time whispered itself in the back of her mind: *two minutes, thirty-four seconds left.*

"You're up for the highest bidder, you know?" The woman stopped beside Alisha's seat, reaching above her to hold on to one of the balance poles that hung from the ceiling. "The three of you. Your government is the lowballer so far."

"Really?" Curiosity piqued in Brandon's voice, breaking him out of his sulk. "What are we worth?"

"You're worth a conservative half million," she answered. Brandon folded the laptop case against his chest, sullenness returning twofold.

"I always thought I should be worth at least a million."

"These two are only worth a quarter million each," the woman offered, gesturing to Alisha and Reichart. Alisha pulled a face of acceptance, while Reichart looked insulted.

"Dollars or euros?"

"Euros." It was the woman's turn to look offended. "Nobody works for dollars anymore."

"Oh." Brandon brightened. "Half a million euros isn't bad."

"And that's conservative," Alisha reminded him. "It's probably what the U.S. is offering."

"She's a smart one," the woman said. "Care to counteroffer?"

Alisha exchanged a glance with Reichart before they both looked at Brandon. He straightened, clutching Lilith's case to his chest. "What?"

"I certainly don't have that kind of money," Alisha said. Reichart turned his hands up, miming empty pockets.

"You're the one with all the patents," she continued before looking back to Reichart with a frown. "And I don't believe for a minute *you're* broke, Frank. I know what you got paid for some of those gigs."

"I donated it all to charity," Reichart said blandly.

"The only charity you know anything about is the kind governments shower on you to hunt down people in the same kind of situation you're in right now," Alisha snapped. "Don't give me that crap."

"Sweetheart, crap's the only thing you're worth giving. You made it real clear you weren't into my thing anymore back there on the plane." Some of the anger in Reichart's voice was real, Alisha realized, and stuck her jaw out in injury that was only partially mocked, herself. "So you can butt the hell out of my finances, kid." The irritating nickname was stressed, and Alisha saw a flash of triumph in Reichart's eyes as it struck home. "What I do with my money's none of your business."

Eighty-seven seconds. Alisha knotted both hands around the pole and pulled herself upright, cheeks flushing with anger. Her knuckles turned white, her grip hard enough to ache as she glowered at Reichart. "This is exactly why it doesn't work with us, Frank. You twist the things I say and only hear what you want to in them." She heard a chuckle over the thrum of the train, and saw amused glances being exchanged in window reflections. "Talking to you is like talking to a brick wall."

"This really isn't the time," Brandon said through his

teeth. Alisha and Reichart shot him equally dirty looks and he got to his feet, clenching Lilith's briefcase in one hand. "It really isn't the time," he repeated. "I've been putting up with you two making moon eyes at each other long enough. You think I can't see it? I thought we had something," he spat at Alisha, and once more the bitterness was real. She closed her eyes, swaying with the train's motion, as if his words had managed a palpable hit.

Forty-five seconds. "We're all about to get hauled in somewhere we may never see the light of day from again." Alisha took a deep breath, exhaling as though it might be her last taste of free air. Centering herself, the combat part of her mind acknowledged, though she let none of that show in the dullness of her voice. "I think now is exactly the time."

She didn't have to open her eyes to move. Preternatural hearing kicked in, ignoring the white noise of the train and focusing on breathing, on small body movements, on the whisper of cloth against cloth. Strength honed with years of yoga practice and focused with her careful breath came to the fore as she gripped the pole and swung her legs up, kicking with the full weight of her body.

The brunette gave a single shocked grunt as Alisha's feet caught her in the diaphragm. Her hold on the overhead pole kept her from smashing back into the windows as hard as Alisha had hoped, but she was off her feet and winded. Alisha's feet hit the ground and she changed the direction of her momentum, leaping forward to grab the woman's shirt in one hand and her hair with the other. One sharp blow against the hard plastic seat edge sent the woman slithering to the floor, insensate.

"Leesh!" Reichart's warning came an instant too late, Alisha dropping forward in time to avoid the brunt of a blow, but still driven down on top of the woman she'd just

rendered unconscious. She swung her leg around backward, a wide sweep that crashed her calf muscles into her
attacker's ankles, but she lacked height and angle to knock
him off his feet. Swearing, she rolled with her own kick,
changing trajectories and getting herself out of the path of
his next blow.

It never came. The man folded, boneless, to reveal
Brandon behind him, Lilith's carrying case held in his
hands like a weapon. Alisha's muscles trembled with readi-
ness for action as she came up in a crouch over the
brunette woman's legs, but no one was left standing. No
one she didn't recognize and trust, at least. It took a few
seconds to release adrenaline enough to push to her feet.
The train slowed and she caught a bar to hold herself,
looking at the four bodies lying around them. Three
against four, Alisha thought a little dazedly, were much
better odds than one against two or more, which was what
she was accustomed to.

Only then, belatedly, did she allow herself to hear the
gasps and shrieks of panic from the other train passengers.
She bared her teeth in frustration, glancing down the car,
and watched people avert their eyes and crowd toward the
doors. At least one man was on his cell phone already,
cursing as he couldn't get a signal.

"It worked," Brandon said, sounding mildly astonished.
Alisha broke her attention away from the others on the
train and cracked a grin at him, hearing herself ask, "Were
they that bad or are we that good?"

Reichart snorted, a sound closer to laughter than she
expected. "We're that good. But that was the easy part.
Right now I'm wishing it was high noon and Paddington
Station was going to be crawling with people." As he spoke
the train stopped, doors sliding open.

"It's been thirty-nine seconds since the fight started,"

Alisha reported on the way out the door. "The cops may not have been watching the monitors—"

Pounding footsteps put the lie to her hopes. Reichart barked a curse and all three of them broke into a run. Voices rose in anger and panic, ordering people down. Alisha dared one glance over her shoulder to see if the Paddington police were local or airport authority. Local: there was no sign of guns, especially of the automatic weapons airport security were allowed to carry. It gave them a chance. Alisha drew in a deep breath and let it carry her to quicker speeds, racing for the escalators and leaping up the moving steps three at a time.

A broad-shouldered cop met her at the top of the steps with a clothesline-style hit across the collarbones. Alisha crashed backward, tumbling down the escalator again, head ringing as she smacked it against shifting metal. Reichart shouted, half warning and half alarm, and leaped over her as he charged up the stairs. Alisha grabbed the moving railing, hauling herself to her feet, vision blurred with tears that she blinked away. A roar sounded, indistinguishable at first from blood pounding in her ears. Clearing sight helped establish the noise's source: Reichart, using the battle cry to give himself strength as he fell on the cop who'd hit her. Alisha let the escalator bring her to the top of the terminal, too dizzy to bring herself back into the fight any faster.

"Reichart." A touch on his shoulder pulled him back from the semi-conscious officer. Alisha shook her head, grateful for an instant of silence and focus. "No casualties. These aren't the bad guys."

A touch of rage faded from Reichart's eyes and he glanced down, then nodded and let the cop go.

Alisha inclined her head, slow gentle motion, then

lifted her gaze again as the brief moment of clarity faded and the fight around her took the spotlight again.

Brandon, for all of Reichart's mockery—for all of Alisha's dismissal, for that matter—could and did hold his own in a fight. As she watched, he dropped Lilith's case and lifted a hand to catch a billy stick in his palm as it swung down, the impact a vicious crack that made Alisha's stomach flinch. Brandon yelled as if the sound could release some of the pain, but never stopped moving, twisting the stick around until the policewoman on the other end was forced to release it. By that time she'd been drawn too close. Brandon smashed a flat-heeled hand into her jaw, sending her head back with a nasty snap. Weapon now in hand, he spun and caught another falling stick in the crossguard of the one he held, whipping his opponent's club free in what looked very much like a fencing disengage. He'd somehow become the first defense, Alisha realized, holding the line while Alisha got to her feet again. Reichart moved forward to join him, and Alisha followed, left with no more time to admire the men she fought beside as officers descended.

She came into battle at a run, ducking more in instinct than from conscious need, and drove her shoulder forward as another billy stick whirred over her head. The man she hit huffed and above her she heard another crack of flesh hitting flesh. A stick came out of nowhere, smashing into her back. She yowled, dropping to the floor, and rolled, lashing out at knee-level. A pop of sinew and a scream of pain told her how solidly she'd hit, and she muttered, "Sorry," beneath her breath as she scrambled to her feet.

She came up the third point of a dangerous triangle, Reichart and Brandon already back to back. At least one officer sprinted for the street, radioing for backup; Alisha dismissed him, intending to be long gone from Paddington

Station before any more help could arrive. She clenched her stomach muscles to take a hit, still wheezing as a fist found its way past her defenses, but the woman who'd thrown the punch had gotten too close. Alisha brought a knee up, catching the other woman in the groin, then drove an elbow down as the woman doubled, smashing her between the shoulder blades. The woman dropped and Alisha moved with the men, a rotation of deadly force so smooth they might have spent years rehearsing together.

Brandon grunted behind her, a low sound of pain, and a cool space opened up behind her as he fell. She and Reichart moved back to back: there would be time to go back for Brandon in a few more seconds, once the immediate threat was taken care of. Alisha blocked a falling stick to her left and missed one from the right, spinning with the blow and leaving Reichart's back unprotected. She turned her own fall into a rough cartwheel, clobbering her assailant in the cheekbone with a booted heel, and came to her feet in time to watch Reichart, graceful as a dancer, duck between the last two men standing. Their blows fell on one another instead of Reichart, dazing them both. Reichart came up beside them and caught them by the backs of their heads, cracking their skulls together.

Alisha, heaving for air, found a crooked grin sliding into place. It hurt, pulling muscles in her temple where she'd been hit, and that made her laugh as she took the few steps toward Brandon and hauled him to his feet. Reichart knelt to snap handcuffs free from the fallen officers, starting to link them together. "Right behind you," he promised, and Alisha, limping and staggering under Brandon's half-conscious weight, ran for the stairs.

Cool night air hit as shockingly as a blow, Brandon catching his breath and putting more weight on his own feet as Alisha pushed outside with him. "Did we win?"

Alisha grinned again, painfully, and braced herself while Brandon leaned, still working out which way was up. "We won." Reichart's footsteps sounded behind them and she looked back to find his expression grim as he displayed Brandon's empty laptop case.

"We won," he agreed, "but Lilith is gone."

21

*A*ny grogginess lingering in Brandon's mind cleared with Reichart's words, the scientist's eyes going hard and angry. "How—"

"That cop," Alisha said between her teeth. "The one who ran for backup. Dammit. Dammit! I thought they were cops." The explanation, almost an apology, was offered to both men. "No weapons, they were uniformed—"

"We all thought they were cops, Alisha. And if they weren't, the real police will be here inside a minute. We've got to go." Reichart cut off apologies and explanations alike, searching for a cab to hail.

Brandon drew back, protest in the guttural sound he made. "We can't abandon her. We've got to go back down there and find out who they are."

"And do what, Parker?" Reichart rounded on him, the few inches of height he had on the other man suddenly apparent. Even the duffel he had slung across his shoulders added to the imposing difference in size, a detail Alisha was certain wasn't unplanned. "Be there interrogating our suspects when the police arrive? Be there when our buddies from the train wake up?" He strode out into the street, lifting his voice to a sharp bark as a cab zoomed by. Alisha stayed at Brandon's side, a hand wrapped around his forearm to keep him from charging back into the station.

"Reichart's right, Brandon. There's no way for us to get her back if we're stuck in a cell somewhere. We've got to go before—" A blast of sirens cut through her words. Alisha's hands went cold, not with fear, but with sudden calm determination. "We've got to go," she repeated. "Are you with us?" She'd rendered enough people unconscious in the last few minutes. One more wasn't going to hurt her, even if he'd be unbelievably pissed when he woke up again.

Brandon stared at her, mouth curled in a snarl, then jerked his arm from her grip and ducked forward into the taxi Reichart was already in. Alisha followed, watching his expression cautiously. She'd seen black fury on Reichart before—there were moments when it seemed his natural countenance—but the distortion of rage in Brandon's clean-cut features was alien to her. She pressed her lips together, reaching out to comfort him, and found herself unreasonably stung as he shifted away. Reichart clipped out an address to the driver, then slammed the glass window between the front and back of the vehicle closed.

As if doing so cut a gag, Brandon snapped, "We're not going to be able to breach our target without her, Alisha. Even if you don't have any investment in her as a person—"

"I don't think you'll believe me when I say I do," Alisha interrupted quietly, then spread her hands, palms up. "You said the laptop carried a pared-down version. Doesn't that mean there's a full backup still in storage?"

"She's supposed to reintegrate with that," Brandon

snarled. "It's the only way for her to maintain cohesion as a single being. Without amalgamating these last few days, both the laptop version and the backup become some-thing—someone—else."

"Like twins taking different paths in life," Reichart said abstractedly. "What's wrong with that?"

Brandon's lip curled again, his expression so tense Alisha couldn't decipher whether it was frustration or disdain. "Except the second twin has embarrassingly limited mental capacity compared to the first, and the first one falls behind in emotional development compared to the second. She's a new life form. She needs to be cared for until she's adult enough to make decisions regarding procreation."

"Procreation?" Alisha's voice shot up in astonishment.

Brandon transferred the hard look to her. "What would you call it?"

Alisha sat back, dumbfounded. "I don't know. I never thought about it. Does that make you a grandfather?"

Pain lanced through his features so sharply Alisha looked away. "Sorry. Trying to be funny." She took a few seconds to concentrate on breathing, as much to give herself time to think as to let Brandon calm down before she asked, "Does the integration have to happen right away? I mean, if we get the laptop back in three days and she's been running off some other server in the meantime, the two versions can just combine their personal experi-ences and move forward, can't they?"

"I don't know, Ali. Three days is a massive amount of time to someone with Lilith's processing power. The personalities could diverge sufficiently in that time as to become incompatible with one another."

"None of which matters," Reichart said, "unless we've got somewhere to run Lilith Version One from. Do we?"

Brandon sank into the cab's seat, defeat washing through his posture. "No."

"So we move forward on our own. We have information we didn't before. We know where the data we need is being kept. Having Lilith's help to retrieve it would be useful, but it's no longer an option. We'll discuss how to proceed once we reach the safe house."

Brandon flicked his gaze to Alisha, examining her to see how she took Reichart's sudden seizure of command. She moved her fingers, a small motion to indicate her acceptance, then twitched her eyebrows and gave the scientist a faint smile. *It's all right*, the body language said. *At least for now.* Brandon's mouth thinned, but he nodded before turning his gaze away.

"Whose safe house?" Alisha asked quietly.

Reichart kicked his duffel bag out of the way and stretched his legs. "It belongs—belonged—to my mother. The Infitialis use it from time to time, when I clear it."

"Are you sure it's safe?"

Reichart nodded, streetlight shadows making his cheekbones gaunt in the light. "Nobody's been there in four or five years. I keep an eye on it."

"All right." Alisha, feeling the ache of combat start to settle into her bones, sighed. "I hope there's a tub."

An unlikely family, Alisha thought as they climbed out of the cab. Reichart, duffel slung over his shoulder, went ahead to key in the security codes while Alisha paid the driver. Brandon, still set-jawed and sullen, lingered at the cab waiting for Alisha. "We've got to get her back, Ali."

"We will." The promise was hollow, but all Alisha could offer. "I just wish I knew who'd hired the fake cops. No guns isn't anybody's style that I know of. Unless…?" She gave Brandon a thoughtful look as they followed Reichart up to the house. It was Victorian, one of a row that spread down the street in both directions. As circumspect and ordinary a home as one could have. Overlooking, anyway, that if it had been Reichart's mother's, it must have gone empty for the better part of twenty years, and in a real estate market as tight as London's, a house kept up but unoccupied must have caught at least a few people's attention.

"Unless what?" Brandon demanded. Reichart, just ahead of them, pushed the door open cautiously, then lifted a hand in sharp warning. Alisha slipped to the side, pressing herself against the wall outside the door. Brandon did the same opposite her, so they both flanked Reichart, who breathed, "Someone's been here."

So much for safety. Alisha went for a gun she didn't have, then mouthed a curse in the pre-dawn darkness. Reichart slipped inside the door, gesturing for the others to follow. Alisha pointed two fingers upstairs and ran up them lightly, keeping to the shadows as she began to explore. Three bedrooms upstairs, and a bathroom. A dark open space in the ceiling where a ladder led up to the attic. Alisha pressed forward, pushing the closest door open.

One shadow separated from another in a silent attack, falling from above, her only warning a change in the light. Alisha twisted too late, borne to the floor by dead weight, feeling the wall give way as her shoulder crunched into it. A fast right came at her face and she twitched to the side, the hit missing so narrowly it pinned her hair against the wall for an instant. Alisha slammed an elbow back toward her assailant's head, using being pinned against the wall as a source of strength. The blow hit with a satisfying crunch and a woman's low cry of pain.

The second bedroom door flew open to a shriek of, "You stay away from my mother!" A flurry of blows fell, mostly smashing into the wall as Alisha yelled and crab-walked backward, scrambling away from a teenage girl bearing a field hockey stick and a grudge.

The first assailant shouted, "Mazie! Get out of here!" and Alisha flung herself down the steps, half trying to escape and half in sheer astonishment.

For the second time that evening Reichart vaulted her on his way up a set of stairs. "Mazie? Emma? Mazie! It's all right! Mazie! Mazie, sweetheart, it's okay, it's all right, it's just me, it's Frank—" His words were accompanied by a clatter as the hockey stick was abandoned over the stair railing, crashing onto Alisha as she tried to protect her head from its fall.

"Frank?" Mazie's furious shrieks changed to excitement and glee. Alisha looked up in time to see the girl who'd just been beating her fling herself at Reichart, who staggered back as he caught her. "Frank, where've you been? It's been months! Like almost a year! Mum! Mum, it's Frank!"

"So I see." Emma appeared at the top of the stairs, looking over the railing at Alisha, who still cowered with her hands over her head, too surprised to move. "Alisha?"

"What's left of her," Alisha said after a moment. "Nice drop you got on me there. Literally. Ow."

"Sorry. Frank," Emma added, as Reichart extracted himself from Mazie's hugs. "What're you doing here?" She stood on her toes to kiss his cheek as she asked the question.

Reichart chuckled. "Hiding. What about you?"

"Hiding," Emma agreed.

Mazie pushed her way past Reichart to peer down the steps at Alisha and Brandon behind her. She was slim with youth and had her mother's large eyes. Her hair, lighter brown than Emma's, was drawn back in a long thin tail.

"Hi. I'm Mazie. I hope I didn't hurt you too much."

"I think most of the damage came from earlier." Alisha

got to her feet cautiously, stretching kinks out. "Though twice in one night is more than I'm used to taking a dive down stairs. I hope there's aspirin here."

"I thought you wanted a tub," Brandon said.

"I'll take what I can get," Alisha said. "Nice to meet you, Mazie. You've grown up a lot since last time I saw you."

Mazie frowned, glancing at her mother. "I don't remember meeting you."

"You didn't." Alisha gave her a wan smile. "I was spying on you. Well, on him." She nodded toward Reichart, then made her way down the stairs to sit on the bottom step with a groan. "I don't suppose you have any floor plans for a host of secret rooms beneath Parliament, Emma."

"Sure," Mazie said. "They're online as part of London Underground."

Alisha twisted herself on the bottom step, staring up at Mazie in astonishment. The other adults turned to the girl as well, open curiosity and disbelief obvious in their expressions. Mazie hunched her shoulders. "Not really floor plans, I mean. But there's lots of talk about how you'd get beneath Westminster through the Tube and all kinds of ideas of what you'd find there. A while ago a lad who ran one of the sites was served with a, what do you call it?" She glanced at her mother. "An order to take down the information?"

"An injunction," Brandon said.

Mazie looked back at him, eyes bright. "That's it, then. Scared the piss out of him, so he did it, but I don't know how many people copied it out of Google's cache. Last time I read about it was off somebody's site in Singapore. That's the brilliant thing about the Internet." Her smile lit up momentarily. "Once something's on it you can't get it off again."

"Like pee in a pool," Alisha heard herself mutter.

Mazie grinned, then looked back and forth between the adults, obviously torn between embarrassment and delight. "There's no reason to make him take it down if he wasn't on to something, right?"

"The kid might be right," Reichart said, reluctantly. "I thought you were going to get some straitlaced job, Maze. None of this intelligence networking garbage."

"Right." Mazie tossed her hair. "Because all my role models are pointing me toward a normal boring life being a bank teller. I can't help it if I'm smarter than you."

Alisha tried to keep her face straight as she looked up at Mazie, then Emma. "Mind if I use your computer, Emma?"

"Oh, come on. You're not sending me back to bed like a little kid," Mazie protested. "I'll show you the sites." She turned to her mother, making winsome eyes. "Please, Mum?"

Emma sighed. "If I thought saying no would do any good, I'd say no." She stepped back, gesturing for Alisha to come up the stairs. Mazie squealed in delight, hugged Emma, and ran into her bedroom.

Emma caught Alisha's arm as she rounded the corner at the top of the steps. "Obviously she knows what we do," she said in a low voice. "But I don't want her involved in this, Alisha. Make it clear her role ends with the net connections."

"Don't worry." Alisha put a hand on Emma's shoulder, squeezing. "I don't want to see her hurt, either."

Emma nodded and Alisha stepped past her, hearing Reichart's sigh as she entered Mazie's room. "I wish that was the only problem we had, Em. This is going to take coffee. Come on downstairs." Voices faded as they moved away, and Alisha turned her attention to the eager teen at the computer.

"You heard your mom?"

Mazie rolled her eyes. "Yeah. She worries too much. Wow," she added, getting a better look at Alisha. "Did I do that?"

Alisha touched the bruising on her cheekbone, wincing at her swollen lip. "No. And this kind of thing is what makes your mom worry."

"Did you lose a fight?"

"This is what it looks like when you win."

Some of the color bleached from Mazie's cheeks, her eyes widening. "Oh." She turned back to the computer, hunching her shoulders and turtling her head out. "Okay. There are bunches of London Underground sites. The official one's no use. Some of them are really cool, though. They talk about old stations that aren't in use anymore, and about the bomb shelters that got built into like eighty stations. The public only got to use about half of them. Isn't that awful?" She charged on, clicking through to web sites and ignoring Alisha's drawn breath to answer. "One of the bomb shelters was beneath Westminster, but it was like a, what do you call it? You know, they do them in medical studies. A blind study? Westminster's not one of the lost stations, but the shelter was never publicly talked about. So it's a blind shelter."

"Double blind," Alisha murmured. "It means neither the doctors nor the patients know who's involved in the study, or who's getting the real treatments."

"Right. Westminster shelter was like that. Everybody knew about Waterloo." She pulled up a map of the Underground and planted her finger on Waterloo station, across the river from Westminster. "That was the public one.

When Parliament got damaged during the war, a bunch of stuff was evacuated beneath it, into the shelter. Well, that's what they say, anyway. There are supposed to be entrances still there, off the Jubilee line. Every time anybody tries going down there—anybody on the link, anyway," she amended, tapping the screen again, "they get stopped by security. I know the Tube's dangerous, but if there's always security there, maybe it means there's something to protect." She glanced over, hopeful.

Alisha sat back, looking at the young woman in a mix of admiration and amusement. "What got you so interested in all this? One day you just woke up and thought, hey, today I'll figure out the whole history of the London Underground?"

Pink crept along Mazie's cheekbones and colored her ears. "Nah. Lots of people've done this before me. It was this TV show I watched, about what if all the abandoned stations and everything beneath the city were part of this kind of magical fantasy world that homeless people were a part of. They mentioned all kinds of stations I'd never heard of, so I got interested in it." She squinted, another look of anticipation. "Is it helpful?"

Alisha looked back at the screen, shaking her head. Mazie's expression fell, and Alisha straightened in apology. "No, no, I didn't mean it wasn't helpful. I was just thinking how much we still had to cover." And how much Lilith hacking into the systems would've helped, she thought, and found herself shaking her head again. She made herself stop, turning a serious-eyed smile toward Mazie instead. "It's very helpful. Thank you, Mazie. You've given us a place to start."

"Alisha." Brandon's voice came out of the darkness, a murmur beneath the distant rattle of trains. Alisha was too well-schooled to let herself flinch in the midst of sneaking around, but her stomach tightened, sending a burp of unpleasantness into her throat. The wide tunnels beneath London's streets took some, but not all, of the pressure of being underground away. There was room enough to breathe, but not to be genuinely comfortable.

Alisha turned her head toward Brandon's voice, relying on occasional subway tunnel lights and night-vision goggles rather than flashlights. His form was dark in the green brightness brought on by the goggles, and like her, he was clad in black, a snug-fitting backpack clipped at waist and shoulder. Alisha's own pack added no more than a few pounds, but was loaded with tools borrowed from Reichart's stash.

"You said something this morning about the cops who took Lilith." The words were pitched to carry no farther than Alisha, too quiet for echoes in the tunnel to bring them back to Reichart. "No weapons," Brandon went on. "You said it didn't make sense, unless. Unless what?"

"You only wonder about this now?" Alisha breathed. "It couldn't have come up while we were at Reichart's place?" The air beneath the city was cool and tasted faintly of ozone, the flavor clinging to the back of Alisha's throat. Brandon's question helped, at least, to distract her from her location.

"You were busy," Brandon said through his teeth.

Alisha slipped into a carved-away spot in the tunnel wall, a tilt of her eyebrows conceding his point. They'd all gone to sleep with sunrise and had been up again six hours later, a house full of quiet, intent activity. Guns were uncovered from hiding holes, cleaned, checked, double-checked. Subway maps were studied and memorized. Mazie, her thin brown hair up in a ponytail, had been everywhere at once, getting food and drinks for the adults without being asked. She'd spent her down time leaning against Reichart with wide-eyed adoration, the look of hero worship. Alisha had caught Emma watching the two of them more than once, a faint smile of regret curving her mouth. Remembering that sent a pang through Alisha's chest, as if she was responsible for the loss Emma felt.

No one had spoken much over the course of the day. There was a mission at hand, and their focus was on it, nothing else. Even Brandon had turned his attention to their immediate goals, appearing to put Lilith out of his mind.

"Unless they were under specific orders to keep some-body alive," she answered. "In anybody's book, Reichart and I were expendable. You're the man with the intellect. You're the one who built Lilith. Guns might have brought too much risk to the situation, if they wanted to be sure to keep you alive." She stopped speaking and pointed down the tunnel, a quick double-fingered tap against the air. Brandon nodded and they both glanced backward to check for trains, as if they were crossing a street. Reichart, several yards away and bringing up the rear, did the same, the habit so ingrained in them all as to be instinctive. It brought a smile to Alisha's lips as she broke into a run.

Emma followed their path from above, she and Mazie safe in Reichart's house. Communications had dropped away as they'd gone farther underground, leaving them essentially on their own, but tracking devices assured that at least their bodies could be recovered, Alisha thought dryly.

The men ran behind her, held at Alisha's pace not through discussion, but by Reichart's statement earlier in the day she should take the lead. Brandon had been satisfied with that, chafing as he'd been under Reichart's assumption of command, but Alisha knew the reason Reichart had put her in the lead. Her feet flashed over the ties, each step eating two of them, the number of strides whispered in the back of her mind: forty-nine, fifty, fifty-one, all without conscious effort. The distance from the nook they'd stepped into to the patrolled entrance to the Westminster bomb shelter was an easy three hundred running strides. Reichart knew Alisha wouldn't lose count.

At two seventy, she slowed and moved to the side again, keeping her breathing quiet so she could hear Brandon and Reichart behind her. "Ninety feet," she whispered when they came up to flank her. "I say we wait and see if they've got hourly check-ins. It's four minutes to the hour." That, too, had been timed carefully, Alisha feeling like her hurried heartbeat kept the seconds passing.

Reichart, a moving wall of shadow in the darkness, nodded. "It'll give us any passwords or specific phrases they use," he agreed. "One of us will have to stay behind to play guard if we're going to need to check in regularly."

"You," Alisha said decisively. "Brandon and I will go on." Brandon turned a pale face toward her in the dark and she shrugged. "You're the brains, Brandon. You either stay with me or stay with Reichart, but I'm not letting you split off. We can't lose you."

"I hate being the expendable one," Reichart said with a quick grin. Alisha's mouth curled wryly and she shrugged a second time, then forewent words and motioned them forward again. Reichart hesitated at her elbow, pointing upward. Alisha glanced up, then cracked another grin and nodded, making a stirrup out of her hands. Reichart nodded, knelt, and stirruped his own hands.

An instant later Alisha felt herself lifted into the air as if she were weightless, and caught the lighting bar that ran down the center of the tunnel.

Scrambling hand over hand along an overhead bar wasn't the fastest method of getting somewhere. Muscle burned in Alisha's arms, as if the mental effort put to the task somehow transferred itself to concentrate in her biceps. Still, it allowed her to hug the ceiling, moving smoothly until the tunnel branched to the left. There were no lights for dozens of feet on either side of the branch: sensible, Alisha thought. Lights would help Tube passengers see the unexplained opening at the tunnel's side. Most of the time, that would go unnoticed, but there were always a few curious sorts who would explore.

Like herself. Alisha grinned tightly at the ceiling, then bent her head back, letting green-infused night vision goggles tell her where security guards stood. There were two, enough to keep each other awake without being too much burden on a budget. The faintest whisper of sound told her Reichart and Brandon had moved up to the branch's entrance. Still smiling, Alisha wrapped her legs around the bar more thoroughly and let go with her hands, dangling upside-down in the middle of the tunnel. "Hello, boys."

Both men whipped around, the second close enough that Alisha lashed out with a fist before he could bring his weapon up. He staggered back and she tucked herself up, catching the bar with her palms so she could rotate down from the ceiling and drop to the floor before he'd recovered his balance. She came up in a surge of power, slamming her shoulder into his groin and earning a retch for her troubles. Half a moment later she had her arm around his throat and had twisted toward his compatriot, using him as a shield.

The second guard's weapon was at the ready, indecision clear on his face in the green light provided by the goggles. Alisha clucked her tongue, the warning backed up by the sound of two guns cocking.

"Put it down, mate." Reichart's quiet voice seemed terribly loud in the small tunnel. Anger contorted the guard's face and he hefted his weapon a few inches. Reichart and Brandon came up on either side of Alisha, fingers slipping from the trigger guards to the triggers. "Don't be an idiot. Put the gun down. Nobody has to get hurt here."

Anger gave way to frustrated despair and the guard turned his hands up, moving away from the trigger. Reichart nodded. "Smart lad. Put it down and kick it toward me."

Alisha felt the guard she held tense and tightened her arm around his throat. "Don't you get stupid, either," she advised. He growled, but relaxed again. "Good boy. If you'll do the honors?" The last was directed to Brandon, who tugged zip cuffs from beneath his close-fitting black sweater and stripped weapons and keys from the man before clipping his wrists behind his back. Reichart tangled the second guard's cuffs with the first and ushered them to the far wall.

"Time?"

"Six after," Alisha replied. "Expect us by the hour, at the latest. We shouldn't be more than 45 minutes."

Reichart nodded and cast a brief, telling glance her way, as intimate as a kiss. Alisha caught her breath and smiled, heart jumping for reasons wholly unrelated to the physical exertion of moments earlier, and returned the nod.

"Forty-five minutes," she repeated, then tipped her head toward Brandon. He fell into step behind her as she broke into a run, following the tunnel down toward their goal. The air warmed as they went deeper, sweat beading on Alisha's forehead, and a glow of light warned early enough to pull the night goggles up and avoid being blinded. The tunnel ended at an abrupt corner, concrete bunker doors with electronic control pads barring the way. Alisha skidded to a halt with a soft curse that Brandon answered with a disparaging look as he slid his backpack off and knelt. "Back there, when you disabled that first guard before you even took a breath, I wondered why you'd bothered taking us along on this little venture." He pulled an electronic code breaker with a generic card attached from his pack. "Now I know."

Chagrin flushed Alisha's cheeks as Brandon reached up, fitting the code breaker over the keypad. "I brought lock picks," she muttered.

Brandon gave her another droll look and returned his attention to the scrolling numbers. "We all bring the tools of our trade," he said. "What did you bring?"

"Guns," Alisha said flatly. It was true, though she'd brought other materials as well.

Brandon shot her a startled look, then let out an exhalation that bordered on laughter. "Like I said. Seven-number security," he added. "This would be a hell of a lot faster with—" The code beeped and he swiped the card, pushing to his feet. "—Lilith."

"Pretty fast without her. I'm sorry, Brandon. We'll get her back somehow. Right now, though…"

"I know. Focus on the job at hand." They pressed to opposite sides of the bunker door as it rolled ponderously open, Alisha drawing a .45 from its holster beneath her backpack. She pointed at herself, then at the opening door, earning a nod from Brandon. Two quick breaths later she stepped inside, sweeping an airlock room for both enemies and surveillance. She didn't expect the former, but the lack of the latter came as a surprise, the concrete walls bare and unadorned. Across from the door she'd entered through was another door, an enormous wheel dominating it. Alisha cupped her gun in both hands, barrel pointed toward the ceiling as she murmured an all-clear.

"No cameras," she said as he came in. "I don't like that."

"I'd like it less if there were cameras," Brandon said. "We don't have a way to disable them."

"Oh, ye of little faith." Alisha tilted her head, indicating her backpack. Brandon's eyebrows furrowed, but he dug into the pack, coming up with two small cans of black spray paint.

"Very high-tech. Very smooth. I'm impressed."

"Just keep one on you." Alisha slid her can into a front pocket and her gun into her waistband so she could try the wheel on the second door. It refused to shift and she glanced at the open door behind them. "Close that."

"Are you sure?"

"I'm sure this one won't open as long as that one's open."

"Your call," Brandon said, skeptically. The first set of doors rumbled shut and Alisha tried the wheel again. It gave silently and smoothly, at odds with its ancient appearance. A smile of triumph curled her mouth and she reached up to pull her mask over her face, tugging the night goggles back into place. "Turn the light enhancer in your goggles down," she suggested. "There might be lights on in there. We'll go for the security cameras first, then move out from there."

"I know, Alisha." Brandon's mild tone hid obvious exasperation. Alisha shot him an apologetic glance that was completely hidden by her mask and goggles, then twisted the wheel until the door shifted in its casings and rolled open.

They broke to the left and right, armed with spray paint, and Brandon's frustrated laugh echoed Alisha's own feeling. The cameras were there, but several feet overhead, the ceiling at least two yards above them. "Screw it," Alisha said. "Let's just go for it." Even as she suggested carelessness, she hid herself in the corner beneath her camera, taking in the lay of the land. Carelessness was one thing. Going in utterly blind when she had a chance to at least establish herself in relation to the complex was something else.

The room they were in had once been intended as a conference room, Alisha guessed. Tiered steps rose away from a stage area, providing what would be head room to see over the rows in front of them in a packed house. Now file cabinets lined those steps. Brandon was already among them, searching for something. Alisha risked turning the enhancement on her goggles up again: only one light burned, over a set of double doors across the room.

"Over here," Brandon said in a low voice. Alisha kept to the walls, staying as much out of the cameras' view as she could before cutting over to where Brandon rifled through a filing cabinet. She glanced at the letters on the cabinets around them, eyebrows lifting and changing the fit of her goggles.

"C? Wouldn't the States be filed under U?"

"Not if you think of them as a lost colony," Brandon said with a quick grin.

Alisha laughed quietly, surprise taking her off-guard. The amusement faded, though, as she looked around again.

"These cabinets have to be at least thirty years old, Brandon. Isn't modern information going to be kept on a mainframe somewhere?"

"No such thing as a computer that can't be hacked, Alisha," he murmured. "You want something safe, you memorize it and burn it. Failing that, you keep hard copies and never let it near a computer. Here!" He yanked a file out, opening it on top of the cabinet. Year, date, material—Alisha skimmed a finger over the papers, nodding.

"This is it. Room 19, stack five, shelf four. Perfect."

"Except we don't know where room 19 is," Brandon said.

Alisha stared at him, then whispered, "Dammit," under her breath and turned to survey the room they stood in. After a moment, she darted for the double doors, checking the wall outside it.

"Heh. This is Conference Room AA. That's no help."

"Go look," Brandon said. "I'll see what I can find in here."

"Like hell." Alisha came back in, shaking her head. "We either both go or both stay. I'm not leaving you alone."

"I didn't know you cared," Brandon said quietly. He turned away from her, studying the file cabinets before coming to a decision and walking away briskly to open another one. "We're over, aren't we, Ali? Before we even got started."

Alisha pulled her goggles off to gape at him across the dark room. "What is it with you guys and wanting to have meaningful conversations in the middle of missions? No wonder I haven't picked up another partner since Cristina died." She cringed in frustration at the word, remembering too late that Cristina was still alive, but ignored the recollection. "Heaven forbid they should partner me with a man. You get all sentimental at the weirdest times."

"You're avoiding the question." Brandon pulled out another handful of files, discarding several of them with little more than a glance.

Alisha flung her hands up in exasperation, stifling the urge to turn around and shoot a security camera just for the temporary relief it would provide. Then she deliberately put her hands down again, fixing her gaze on the floor and breathing deeply until she was sure she trusted her voice and her answer. "Maybe you had no other choice, Brandon, but you led the Sicarii to my doorstep. To my family's doorstep." She shook her head, still staring at the floor. "That was too careless. I'm not sure I'm completely over being pissed at you, but even if I am…" She looked up, watching Brandon's stiff movements in the harsh whiteness of the light above the door. "That was too selfish," she said, as quietly as he'd spoken a moment earlier. "Risking me's one thing. I chose this life, even if I tried to walk away from it. But my nephews…?you should have thought about them, Brandon, and you should have found another way to contact me. Yeah," she finally said. "It's over, even if we never got a chance to start."

"How much does this have to do with Reichart?"

"That," Alisha said evenly, "is none of your business."

"That much, then." Brandon straightened away from the file cabinet he'd been searching through, a blueprint in hand. "Bunker schematics. Room 19 is four halls to the left at the bottom of the stairs. We ready?"

Alisha nodded, a tight motion, and took the lead, Brandon falling into step behind her. *Now,* the combat-trained part of Alisha's mind predicted. *Now* would be the moment of final betrayal, when it would prove that Brandon Parker still had ties to the Sicarii. *Now,* with her back to him, a position of trust. *Now* was when she would make her play, if she weren't to be trusted herself, now that hopes of romance had been dashed. *Now,* when the die had been cast and there was to be no redemption found in the loving arms of a woman. Every part of her waited for it, the blow or the gun or the words that would be her undoing.

It never came. Alisha let out a low rush of air as they turned at the stairway, running as silently as they could. The door at the bottom had another electronic keypad and Brandon stepped forward to run his decoder through it. The door opened with a quiet click and Alisha dropped her shoulders, genuinely relaxing. The moment had passed, according to everything her training told her. It was an emotional response, not grounded in logic or intelligence, but Alisha was glad for it. She motioned Brandon ahead, feeling as if he'd passed a test. He nodded and brushed by, leaving her to prop the door open a few centimeters before following.

Brandon counted off the stacks with an opening of folded fingers as he went past them: two, three, four, and stopped at five, his hand lifted. Alisha paused behind him, looking past him at the rest of the room. Four more stacks stretched in front of them, so the row was the fifth from either side. Brandon nodded once, as if following her thoughts, and stepped forward to turn down the aisle with Alisha on his tail.

He stopped two steps in, so abruptly Alisha flinched to the side in order to avoid running into him. Even as she drew breath to ask what had stopped him, she saw.

Two people. One, masked and wearing black, properly outfitted for midnight espionage work, stood half-hidden behind the other, a dark-haired woman halfway up the stacks. The woman on the stacks, excepting a pair of night goggles, wore casual attire that was completely inappropriate for the job she did. Blue jeans, Alisha knew, though her own goggles sucked the color from them. A black leather jacket that swung back to reveal a bared midriff. Solid boots. Familiar clothes, all.

Every protocol in the world told Alisha not to whisper the name, not to betray her own presence there. Duty would have her step back, hide in the shadows again, and survey the situation. But her heart beat so hard she could feel it over every inch of her skin, confusion and cold dread pounding through her body.

"Erika?"

Erika jerked toward the sound of Alisha's voice, shock coursing over her expression, even half-hidden by the goggles. "Alisha? *Shit.*"

The second person moved, cutting away from the shadow to show a woman's form. She took a fluid step backward, displaying body language that Alisha recognized without processing it. Her gun was suddenly in her hand, though she didn't remember drawing it from her waistband. "One more step and you're dead. You know I can pull the trigger." Her voice was cold and dead with rage, hand so steady she felt she might be made of stone.

The woman behind Erika hesitated, then reached up to pull her mask off, sending wheat-pale hair falling over her shoulders in tangles. "Alisha MacAleer," Cristina Lamken said. "My, oh my, what a mess we have here."

23

"*E*rika?" Alisha's voice rose and broke, a sound perilously close to tears. "Erika, what's going on?"

"Isn't it clear?" Cristina asked, far too merrily. She took a step forward and Alisha's voice cracked out, "Don't. Move. Put your hands up, Cris, or I swear I'll shoot you right now."

"That'll bring us all sorts of attention we don't want," Cristina said smoothly. "Listen, Ali, I—"

Alisha fired.

Papers in the stacks exploded in a puff of dust and sound, the bullet slamming into metal with a violent spang. The ricochet echoed off the walls, deafening. Brandon and Erika flinched, though neither gave in to the obvious urge to fling themselves to the side. Cristina went shockingly still. "Put. Your fucking. Hands. Up," Alisha repeated. Cristina, sheer astonishment making her blue eyes round, did as she was told.

"Erika?" Alisha asked again, no more steadily than a moment earlier. *Compartmentalize,* she told herself fiercely, but the order had no power. Her chest was tight as iron bands, breath coming hard. "Erika?"

Her friend pulled her own goggles off, staring down the stacks at her. "Come on, Erika." Alisha's voice was too loud, too accusing, and she couldn't modulate it. "You're supposed to be the smart one, E. Where's your clever story? What's the explanation here?"

"Alisha," Erika whispered, and Alisha pulled the trigger again, noise and danger a too-thin salve for the ache in her heart. Even Cristina cringed, and Alisha uncurled her finger from the trigger, wrapping it around the guard instead, trying to keep herself from emptying the clip. She wasn't sure how long she could keep shooting paperwork and shelves, if she let herself go even one iota further. Her stomach, her arms, her very vision, trembled with the rage of betrayal, but her gun hand remained so steady it felt cast in lead.

"How long! *How long, Erika? HOW LONG?*" There were reasons, the combat part of her mind whispered, not to shout. Not to fire her weapon again. To regain rationality and analyze the incident in a calm and detached manner. Her finger squeezed and relaxed repeatedly, wish fulfillment spelled out against the trigger guard.

The answer was readable in Erika's eyes, more betrayal than Alisha could have imagined. Memory, agonizing, seared through her mind, putting the pieces together so easily it left her without air in her lungs.

The memory of brief irrational uncertainty when Erika had sent her from the hotel room in Switzerland, more than two years ago now. Mistrusting her friend had been an ugly moment, put aside. Erika had promised the copy of the Attengee schematics were corrupt. They had been. Reichart had gotten no use of them. But there had been more than enough time to copy the schematics, and they'd turned up in Sicarii hands, after all.

All the pieces. Alisha wanted to close her eyes, to rock with the pain, savoring it because there was no way to let it go. Reichart's code that she'd broken and shared with Erika. An open door for Erika's people to use in tracking the Infitialis. Forty people over the last ten months. Forty people since Boyer's death. Even if the Infitialis had changed their codes, Erika must have already been into their network. Alisha could not afford to let herself close her eyes to the truth. Not now, when it was almost too late to see it.

"You killed Director Boyer," Alisha whispered. "You were the only one who knew where he'd be, besides me." She wasn't sure if the words even had sound, so lodged in her throat did they feel, but something regretful colored Erika's eyes. Alisha squeezed the trigger guard again, desperate to wipe that expression from her one-time friend's eyes. "My God. You turned Emma over when I talked to you. You…" It was too easy to stand there whispering the litany of sins. Alisha clenched her jaw and tightened her grip on her Glock. "Brandon." His name came out hoarse and raw. He flinched at the sound of it.

"Get the Firebird box," Alisha grated. "Cuff them. Do it now. Before I kill somebody."

Cristina moved, barely more than a tensing of her muscles. Alisha's finger slid from the guard to the trigger again, and she whispered, "Don't," in the same hoarse voice. "All I need is an excuse, Cris. Don't hope I'm bluffing. I will shoot. Hands behind your head. Erika, you, too. Brandon, now," she added as both women slowly complied.

"Alisha," Erika said again. Alisha twitched the gun's

muzzle to the right, squeezing off three shots that exploded more papers and dust into the air.

"I don't want to hear it," she screamed over the sound of bullets clanging and shattering. "I don't want to hear it," she repeated as echoes faded. "I'll hear it at Langley, you traitorous—" The last word choked her, *bitch* far too mild. Brandon, moving as if bullets weren't flying around the narrow aisle between the stacks, stopped a solid three feet from Erika, keeping himself well out of Cristina's possible reach, and grabbed the tech geek's collar to pull her forward. The left side of her leather jacket hung heavily and he fished his hand into an inside pocket, coming out with the scarred black box from the Firebird. He dropped it on the floor, kicking it back toward Alisha without looking. She put her foot on it, unwilling to bend and pick it up until Cristina and Erika were both restrained.

The door banging open sounded like a death toll, metal slamming against concrete. Alisha jerked at the sharp noise; everyone did, minute recoils that were the body's natural response. Alisha saw each tiny flinch in the people around her, her thoughts dropping out of real time to superimpose an image over those small startled actions. The film footage of Kennedy's assassination had just those same kinds of reactive jounces in it, three pulses where the camera lost steadiness when the man holding it heard gunshots being fired.

As in those brief moments that changed everything, so too, did everything change now.

Cristina surged forward, lashing out with a crippling blow aimed at Brandon's knee. Little more than an inhalation seemed to save him, the kick hitting as he scooted back just enough to diminish its effectiveness. Erika twisted free from his grip as he moved, bolting down the aisle away from Alisha, rather than trying to take the fight to her.

Cristina turned to follow her, evading Brandon's snatch for her shirt.

Gunfire sounded again, devastatingly loud, the flashes from the muzzle bright enough to hurt Alisha's eyes. A woman screamed, high aborted sound, then fell, momentum driving her forward even as she collapsed to the floor.

Cristina vaulted Erika's fallen form and disappeared around the far end of the stacks.

Alisha lowered her gun, numb slow action as she looked down the aisle. Blood already stained the floor, leaking out from beneath the black leather jacket that was Erika's signature piece. The sight of it seemed to stop Alisha's heart, breath lost between one beat and the next. The report of her weapon firing replayed endlessly, mixed with Erika's shriek, the two sounds so wedded to one another they would never come undone.

Reichart appeared at Alisha's elbow, gun drawn. Somewhere in the distance the door he'd come through banged shut again, but there was nothing left in Alisha to react. This time she didn't flinch, no small physical betrayal to send the world wrong. She only stood, staring down the aisle at blood seeping across the bunker floor.

A second door slammed: Cristina's escape. There was no air to breathe, no thought to drive Alisha forward. Reichart's voice sounded from far away: "Leesh? Alisha, what—" The question was lost to his own cautious pacing toward Erika's body. He met Brandon halfway down the aisle, asking, "What happened?" in a perfunctory low voice, though something in his tone suggested he was already putting the pieces together. A moment later he was at the end of the aisle, kneeling beside Erika. "She's alive."

Alisha's heart finally beat, one painful spasm that hung in her chest, fluttering dangerously. She drew in a breath, cold and aching with shock. Her feet carried her forward, stumbling steps that ended in crashing to her knees at Erika's side. Reichart had moved, though she hadn't seen when. Brandon followed her, standing at Erika's feet. Alisha pulled her night goggles off, dark overwhelming and somehow more truthful than the false green light the goggles offered. Erika's head was turned to the side, cheek pressed to floor, revealing a too-fast pulse in her throat. A hole torn through the left shoulder of her jacket showed the bullet's trajectory. Alisha knotted her hand in the coat and rolled Erika over, earning a gurgled whimper of pain from the other woman.

The hole went all the way through, just below Erika's left collarbone. Alisha touched her own collarbone, leaving a bloody smear where the same shot had once pierced her own shoulder. Erika gritted her teeth, staring up at Alisha until Alisha stood, voice flat as she spoke to Reichart. "Get her out of here. Keep her alive."

"Where are you going?"

Alisha stepped over Erika and looked back at Reichart's concerned scowl, then at Brandon, who stripped his sweater off as he came forward, starting to shred it into bandages. Her heart hadn't begun to beat properly yet, one thud seeming years separated from the next. All that hung between those beats was cold, a flat need to end the betrayals and come to some sort of answer she could bear to live with. Every plan she'd concocted seemed irrelevant in the face of Erika's ultimate loyalties. Jon, Alisha thought, could simply kill her. She'd failed in turning Lilith over to him, and she didn't care anymore. It was time, one way or another, to end all of this.

She turned away, letting her words follow her. "I'm going to find Cristina."

~

She didn't know when she'd started running. Sometime out of Reichart and Brandon's sight, out of their hearing, as though the sound of her hasty footsteps would tell them too much about her emotional state.

Like there was anything hidden about her emotions. Alisha couldn't remember feeling so raw, like her skin had been abraded and left out to toughen or slough off, whichever it had the will to do. Even the physical and emotional pain of Reichart shooting her felt flat and old compared to the shock of seeing Erika at Cristina's side. Alisha hadn't seen Reichart's face in that moment, and in its way, that relationship had been brief, compared to the years she'd been friends with Erika. This burned in a way distrusting Greg hadn't, her handler's position as a superior officer in the CIA ranks forbearing the intimacy of real friendship. Even Cristina's position as a double agent seemed—now, at least, years removed from the fact—like a less painful hit than Erika's whispered curse of discovery.

Up. Alisha had no sense of the shelter's layout, but the way out, the way to find Cristina, would be to go *up.* Doors to individual rooms were locked, but stairways stood open and Alisha took the steps two and three at a time, the ache of oxygen-deprived muscles nothing compared to the hurt in her heart. She ran blindly, trying doors, aware of a timer counting down at the back of her mind: it was only a matter of time before security tapes were reviewed, before guards responded to gunshots, before she was discovered. She had to get out, or find Cristina, before then.

Finding Cristina would do. Fighting to the death seemed a reasonable prospect. Anything to stop the chain of events that kept building, anything to break the endless story of friends turning against friends, betrayal upon betrayal. Every betrayal birthed a new one from its ashes, like the phoenix rising.

A laugh of tears burst from Alisha's chest, remembering a warning spoken by a dying man. *From the ashes comes the phoenix to destroy you.* Cristina, code-named Phoenix after her supposed death in the Andes mountains. A sob escaped Alisha as she raced up a set of stairs, stopping on the last step to wrap an arm around her ribs and try to breathe a cramp out. The grip she held on the railing felt like the only thing keeping her on her feet, nothing else anchoring her to the world. "Oh, Cris," she whispered. "You did it. Are you happy? There's nothing left to me."

"It'll do."

The words were Alisha's only warning. Too much warning. Cristina had always been too fond of getting the last word in, making riposte as she fought. Her roundhouse kick came around a corner, but Alisha wasn't there anymore, letting herself fall back down the stairs. Her palm squealed against the railing as she closed her grip again, keeping herself from tumbling all the way down, though momentum twisted her until her shoulder protested and popped.

Cristina appeared at the head of the stairs, all loose blond hair and a charming smile. She planted both hands on the railings and swung forward, a full-body kick that showed off her physique more than presented danger. Alisha reached up and caught Cristina's toe and ankle as the kick extended to its farthest point, twisting with her full strength. Cristina made a startled sound of pain deep in her throat, rotating with the force of Alisha's motion, and crashed ignominiously on the steps, face-down.

Alisha pounced up, crouching over Cristina's hips and seizing two handfuls of her shirt. Cristina shoved up with one hand, bringing the other elbow back and around toward Alisha's face. She blocked it with a grunt, letting loose of Cristina's shirt, and the blond woman scrambled forward, escaping Alisha's grasp. Alisha clawed her fingers, snagging Cris's shirt enough to slow the other woman, but not enough to stop her. Cristina lashed back with a kick, catching Alisha in the shoulder as she turned to avoid the blow, then ran up the stairs, bolting to the left. Alisha slapped her palms on the next step up and used the leverage to shove herself after her former partner.

Cristina spun around a corner, footsteps changing to indicate another set of stairs ahead. Alisha barreled after her, cornering in time to see the door at the new stairway's head slamming shut again.

A trio of grim-faced security guards lost their determination as Alisha burst through the door seconds behind Cristina. For an instant the two women fought on the same side, moving together with the flowing precision of years of shared combat. Alisha went low, launching from a vertical to a horizontal and sliding on her hip across the floor to scissors the closest guard's legs out from under him. He hit the ground and she rolled on top of him, slamming one merciless fist into his jaw. He collapsed, boneless, and Alisha swung around to watch Cristina bring both hands, knotted together, down on the base of the second guard's neck. He dropped and both women sprang for the third man, Alisha's elbow to his kidneys doubling him over to meet Cristina's swift knee to his chin.

They stood facing one another, enmity temporarily forgotten in the breathless high of battle. Crystal recollection formed in Alisha's mind, brought home by the moment: they'd been good together. As if the same thought crossed Cristina's mind, she inclined her head, a small motion of acknowledgment.

Then she turned and ran, long legs carrying her away

from Alisha at breakneck speed. Alisha gave chase, not to catch her, but to follow her out; the fight could wait until they were somewhere safer than the bowels of Parliament. Cristina cast one or two glances over her shoulder, but did nothing more to lose Alisha, finally careening through a small door, the lock on which had been crowbarred off recently. Darkness enveloped Alisha as she gave chase. She bounced off narrow tunnel walls, her stride slowing so she could listen for Cristina.

The tunnel sloped downward, then turned to steps, Cristina's footsteps warning Alisha in time to avoid falling. The darkness seemed endless, more steps and musty damp air before she heard a rumble overhead—one of the subway trains, she thought, somewhere above her. After an eternity there were steps up again, and finally a door slamming open as Cristina crashed through it. Alisha smashed out seconds behind her, shocked to discover they'd crossed below the Thames and were on the river's far bank. Cristina stood yards away, leaning on a piece of broken wall and panting.

"You're either very trusting or very stupid to have followed me like that, Ali. Funny thing is, after all this time, I don't know which it is."

"Neither do I." It was the only thing Alisha could bring herself to say before she renewed her attack, moving into close quarters with Cristina. They circled, wary and interested, each assessing the changes in their former partner's fighting style in the years they'd been apart. Cristina still had the advantage, Alisha thought, with her greater reach, though that asset diminished in close-quarters fighting, thanks to Alisha's superior strength. Cristina threw a punch, almost a test, and Alisha blocked it easily. Cris nodded, as if a question had been answered, then came in with a barrage of fist and elbow blows. Alisha went on the defensive, blocking and throwing hits when she could. There was a gun in her belt, and Cristina almost certainly carried at least one firearm as well. The fight could be over in seconds, and yet neither woman chose that option. Too many old ghosts to lay to rest, Alisha thought. Too much to be proven.

A path opened up unexpectedly, clear and bright in her mind. With so many debts to repay, so many betrayals to live with, there might be one last card she could play.

One final betrayal might bring them to an end game.

24

*S*he faltered on a block, putting just enough strength behind it to make it feel like a genuine miss. Cristina's fist broke through, smashing into her cheekbone and sending Alisha staggering back.

The next blow sent her to her knees, startling Cristina so much the blonde hesitated instead of taking what could easily be the kill shot. Alisha turned her head, letting years of fighting and betrayal become exhaustion in her voice. "Screw it." She sounded weak to her own ears, though her heart slammed in her chest until she felt sick with the risk she took.

Cristina froze in uncertainty. Alisha looked up, shaking her head, and spread her hands wearily. "Screw it, Cris," she whispered. "Is there anybody you didn't get to? Greg. Brandon. Boyer. *Erika.* Screw it, just…to hell with it." She slumped, hands limp at her sides. "I don't care anymore. What do I have to do to get out of this, Cris? There's nobody left to trust. I just want to go home."

"You expect me to believe that?" Cristina demanded incredulously.

Alisha closed her eyes, hands dropping to her sides, chin dropping to her chest. *Picture of defeat,* she thought. *Yes. Believe it. Believe* me. *You've known me too long to think I can lie to you, Cris. Believe me.* She shook her head, as much defeat as denial. "You know, I really don't care. If you don't, fine. Just kill me. As long as it's over."

"You're trying to trick me," Cristina grated.

Alisha shrugged, a liquid motion of lassitude. No tension in her body, except that of a woman whose fate lay in someone else's hands. Her stomach roiled and she couldn't find a way to ease it without tipping Cristina to her hand.

"I was never as good as you are, Cris." Weak regret and bitter admiration laced the words. *Play to her ego, Leesh. But gently, gently.* "You lied to me for years and I never even suspected it. Even if I was trying to trick you, what would the point be? You read me better than I ever read you, and besides." Alisha's training had taught her to deliver a line with conviction, but there was no need to act as loneliness ached through her. "Who've I got left, anyway? Not even Erika. I never even had Erika on my side. All I wanted was out," she whispered. "I left the Agency almost a year ago, and all I wanted was out. It's still all I want. If that means you have to kill me…then do it." Famous last words, she thought distantly. A surprising percentage of shootings were brought on by the victim screaming, *go on, do it!* only to be desperately surprised when someone did. Critical last words, risking everything on whether she could lie to her former partner now, when she'd been fooled so many times herself.

Eyes closed, she never saw what weapon drove her into peaceful black oblivion.

∽

" $\mathcal{C}$ ompletely clean. Ops even checked her teeth. If there's a bug on her, we can't find it."

"Is she awake?"

"Not yet." Cristina, voice sour and still laced with uncertainty. Alisha groaned and rolled onto her side, bringing her arms down to wrap around her head.

Trying to. Chains clinked, cuffs pulling at her wrists. She groaned again and tugged herself higher to fold her head between her biceps. "I'm awake."

She heard Cristina's breath catch and smirked against her arm. No spy in her right mind would confess to awakening the moment she came to. Listening for any pertinent data that could be garnered was the right procedure. Alisha was breaking all the rules, hoping to keep Cristina off-balance. She couldn't see Cristina or the man she talked to, but she could imagine them exchanging glances. "I'm awake," she said again, hoarsely. "What'd you hit me with, a Mack truck?"

"My heel," Cristina said without apology. She appeared at Alisha's bedside, looking extraordinarily tall. "You could be a very useful double agent, Alisha."

"No." Alisha turned her face against her arm, rejection inherent in the action. "Kill me if you feel like it, but I'm done, Cris. No more. No more lies, no more betrayals, none of it. I won't play the Sicarii game. I won't play the Agency's game. I'm done." Her heartbeat felt heavy, driving nervousness she couldn't allow to be seen through her body. Her job was lying to people. Cristina was just one more mark.

A gun cocked and its muzzle pressed against her temple, cold and round. "This is your gun," Cristina said coolly. "Do you think Frank would believe you were a suicide? Devastated by Erika's betrayal and all that crap?"

"I don't care," Alisha said into her arm. "Let me go, Cris, and I'll walk away and never bother you people again. Do what you want to the country. To the whole goddamned world. If I'm too much risk…?" She shrugged, wincing as her head shifted. "Shoot me."

"Why should I believe you?"

Alisha laughed, harsh, and rolled onto her back. The gun followed her motion, pressing against the middle of her forehead instead of her temple. Alisha ignored it, staring up Cristina's arm at her one-time friend. She kept defiance in her gaze, but tempered it with bitterness and old anger, until the only thing she felt left in her was the truth of those emotions. Believing herself was surprisingly easy. Easy enough, maybe, to make Cristina believe it, too.

"Because the only reason I got into this again at all was to keep my family safe. Brandon goddamned Parker showed up on my doorstep with hell on his heels and the only way out was through the fire. I don't want to be here, Cris. I don't care about any of this shit anymore." Tears stung her eyes and she closed them, knowing the hot liquid to be exhaustion, knowing Cristina would see tears as a ploy. "You want a barrel over my head, you've got my family. There's your way to control me. Does it really matter to you if I'm alive, as long as I'm under control? I'd like to live. I'm just too tired to fight for it anymore."

Cristina studied her, blue eyes expressionless, then uncocked the gun and moved away again, dropping her voice to converse with the man she'd spoken with earlier. Alisha sagged into the mattress, eyes shut, not so much as searching for an escape route. *Defeated*, she thought; this was what defeat tasted like. What despair felt like, so well play-acted she could fall into its drowning well and never come to the surface. Empty and without focus, nothing left around her to trust. Everyone had a price, it was said. Everyone would break. The flat weariness overwhelming her was what breaking felt like.

Believe me, she thought, so far inside herself it couldn't disturb the heavy shell of theater she'd wrapped herself in.

"It's what she said at Langley." The man's voice came clear, one sentence that stood out, then faded away again. Alisha's eyes opened against her will, a thrill of life shooting like electricity through her, breaking her careful facade. *Greg.* Despite herself she turned her head, straining to hear. Cristina's voice rose and fell in a murmur before Greg spoke again. "It's your call. All I can say is she said the same things at Langley. That she's tired and wants out."

But she hadn't. Alisha relaxed back into the mattress, trying to remember. She was certain she'd said nothing of the sort in her last encounter with Greg at Langley. Maybe a year earlier, when she'd resigned from the Agency, but she couldn't bring the exact conversations to mind, a muddled haze of despondency blurring the details. She didn't think she'd used those words.

Greg was trying to save her life.

Alisha refused to let herself clench her fists, keeping her body relaxed and her expression bleak as Cristina's footsteps returned to the bedside. Her heartbeat had sped up again, one degree of normality returning to her body. Cristina's gun cocked again, cool metal against Alisha's forehead. "This is how it will be," Cristina said. "Open your eyes."

Alisha did, meeting Cristina's frigid cornflower gaze. "Everything you own will be examined by my people," Cristina whispered. "Every e-mail you ever send will go through our servers to be checked. Every man you date, every vacation you take, everything that you ever do, will be cleared by the Sicarii before you will be permitted to act. And if you do anything at all to jeopardize me or my people, your family will pay the price. Do we have a deal, Ali?"

"Yeah." The word came out smaller and rougher than Alisha intended, even in the midst of her performance. She cleared her throat, trying to strengthen her voice, but Cristina unlocked the cuff that held her to the bed. Alisha pulled her hand down, massaging her wrist as she sat up. Her heart rang too hard again, sending chills of sweat over her skin. Let Cristina think it was unbearable relief: Alisha kept all traces of triumph from her face, lowering her eyes. "Yeah," she repeated in a low voice. "Am I walking out of here on my own?"

"We're nowhere special," Cristina answered. "A motel room." She waited until Alisha crossed to the door, then said her name. Alisha stopped, waiting. "You know you're alive because I think I can use you later."

"Yeah," Alisha said for the third time, and looked back at her former friend and partner. "I guess we'll see."

Cristina inclined her head and Alisha walked out into the night.

Pounding on the door awakened her from the muzzy heavy sleep of jet lag. Alisha came to her feet reaching for a gun she wasn't supposed to need anymore, habit stronger than a day in a supposed new life. Cristina had smoothed her travels home, a detail Alisha found deliciously ironic. By all rights, she should have been detained by the British government, probably imprisoned, likely never to see the daylight again. But Nichole Oldenburg, up-and-coming U.S. senator from Delaware, had stepped in, making apologies and vague promises, and Alisha had returned home.

Erika was out there somewhere, in Reichart's custody. Alisha ought to care, but sleep had claimed her, broken only long enough for a few bites to eat and a potty break or two in the last twenty-four hours. The knocking on the door echoed a throbbing in her skull, reminder of the fights she'd been in a day or two earlier. She only hoped Cristina's head hurt, too, as she shuffled to the front door.

Reichart stood there, expression tight with anger and concern. "What the hell happened to you, Leesh?"

Alisha stared up at him in befuddlement, then smiled roughly and stepped back to let him in. "I gave up." She put her finger over her lips as she spoke, pointing to the walls, then her ears. Reichart's gaze flickered over the walls and came back to her, still angry, but worry winning out.

"What do you mean, you gave up?"

Alisha curled up on one of the couches, dusty purple with big square cushions, and took one of the throw pillows to hug. "Erika was the last straw," she whispered. "I can't do it anymore, Frank. I made a deal with Cristina. I don't care. I'm out of it. I'm out of it for good."

"I don't believe you." Strain thinned Reichart's words. "You can't give up, Leesh. Not after what you've been through."

"That's exactly why I can. It's too much." Alisha heard the heaviness in her own voice and saw genuine alarm settling in Reichart's expression. "I'm done. I'm sorry, Frank."

"What about us?" More stress came into the question, making Alisha's heart ache as she shook her head.

"They're watching me, Frank. Everything I do. Everybody I contact. I'm a liability to you." She set her teeth together, shaking her head, then gave in, unable to resist knowing: "What was on the box?"

Frustration contorted Reichart's features. "The box was useless, Leesh. After all that, there was nothing conclusive on it, nothing tying Cristina to the Sicarii. Simone was implicated, but Cristina's a golden girl."

"She always was." Black humor laced the words and Alisha put her head against her knees. All that trouble for nothing. Discovering Erika's true loyalties, over a piece of equipment that couldn't condemn the one person Alisha trusted least of all. "And Erika?"

"Alive." Reichart's face tightened. "Contained."

Alisha nodded, then nodded toward the door. "I'm sorry, Frank. This is goodbye. Tell Brandon the same, if you see him. I'm sorry."

He still hesitated, having never left the doorway. "Can I call you?"

"No." Alisha shook her head. "No calls. No e-mail." Her gaze darted to the computer, then back to him as she dropped her chin, barely a motion. "Tell Brandon the same," she repeated, and stood. "Goodbye, Frank."

He curled a hand into a fist, waiting a long moment at the door before finally whispering, "Goodbye, Alisha." The door closed behind him.

Alisha exhaled, then went to turn the computer on and wait.

"Which," a woman's voice asked quietly, "is most important?"

Alisha took a soft startled breath and straightened in her computer chair, rubbing at the spot on her cheek where it had rested on her knee. "Lilith?" Her voice broke on the question, relief and gladness coming through in equal parts. "Brandon got you back online?"

"From a location I'm told I shouldn't disclose," the computer agreed. "I'm using voice-over-IP to talk with you through a secure tunnel I've opened into your system, but the amount of traffic incoming may be worth Sicarii notice. We'll have to be brief. I trust you've already enabled white noise generators to foil any listening devices."

"As soon as Reichart left," Alisha said.

The bodiless woman seemed to nod. "Tell me, Alisha, which is more important? Taking down Cristina Lamken or removing Sicarii access to the Attengee and Firebird drones?"

"You can do that?" Alisha almost laughed, a sound of unhappiness. "I can't even remember the last time I thought about the drone army. I got so caught up with Cristina and trying to keep you safe. Did Brandon get your spin-off back?" Jon would have realized her failure by now. The time she'd bought with the Sicarii might be more limited than Alisha hoped.

"He did not." Lilith sounded unconcerned. "And I have a considerably greater storage capacity than you do, Alisha. It's all right if you've forgotten a thing or two. Which is most important to you?"

"The drones," Alisha whispered reluctantly. "Someone will find a way to deal with Cris, but something that keeps those drones out of Sicarii hands is more important. I have no idea how to do that, though."

"Your system is inextricably linked with the Sicarii network." Lilith's calm triggered a tingle of disquiet in Alisha. She leaned forward, putting a hand against the flat panel screen in front of her, as if she could touch the disembodied woman she spoke with. "Your Internet connection has been routed through their servers, so they can watch you."

"Yeah. I thought I could find a way to use it." *I want out,* Alisha had told Cristina, despair and exhaustion at the forefront of her emotions. But beneath that lay the espionage agent and more than ten years in the business. Nothing, not even her own near-suicide, could be done without layers. Part of Alisha wished she could have remained utterly unaware of her own dissembling, that she had actually told the truth, and that the spy world she was so intimate with didn't have such a hold on her that she could face her own death and tell easy, believable lies. "But I don't have the technical expertise, and I can't exactly turn to Erika now."

"You don't have to," Lilith said. "You have me." A note of pride mingled with regret in the artificial intelligence's voice. "I can slip inside and set a Trojan that will wipe their servers. The drone schematics will be lost. Frank Reichart and the Infitialis will take care of the actual production facilities. It may be a stopgap measure—information wants to be free, Alisha, and once created these drones are a genie that can't be put back in the bottle—but it will be an effective one. Neither the Sicarii nor your own government will be quick to rebuild. The financial burden is considerable, and the loss of another set of production facilities, after the one in China, will make the people who sign the checks highly reluctant."

"There's a catch, though." Alisha's knuckles were white around the monitor's edge. "What aren't you telling me?"

"Erika's as good a programmer as Brandon," Lilith replied. "I've investigated her security measures. They've been enhanced to deal specifically with my coding. Even rewriting my sources won't change my signature enough to fool them. This is, I'm afraid, a one-way trip for me. In order to be completely effective I'll have to totally infiltrate their systems. Her watchdogs will block off my retreat paths. Rather than risk capture, I'll have to allow the Trojan to capture me as well."

"Capture you?" Alisha whispered. "You mean destroy you?"

"Yes," Lilith said easily.

"No." Alisha straightened, clipping her knee on the desk. "There's got to be another way."

"You would have allowed Cristina Lamken to kill you,

would you not? In order to prevent yourself from being used in a way you found abhorrent?"

"…yes."

"I feel similarly, Alisha. My code is unique and I have seen the lengths to which governments will go to try to obtain it. I consider myself a free and sentient being, Ali. I would rather die doing something useful than become a tool of men and women hungry for power and the ultimate hand in a war game." She hesitated. "I don't think Brandon will understand. Try to comfort him, please. He's already lost one version of me. I think this will take him very hard. Take care of him for me, Alisha. I can't do it myself."

"I will," Alisha heard herself say. "I don't know how, but I will. I promise. Good luck, Lilith," she added softly.

The AI's warm voice seemed to smile in return. "Thank you, Alisha MacAleer. Goodbye."

Silence, empty as death, filled the room.

"*H*ow did you do it?" Cristina, voice hoarse with rage. More than rage. Fear colored the question as well. Alisha tipped her face to the crimson-colored sky, trying to remember when, if ever, she had heard fear in Cristina Lamken's voice.

"How did I do what? You've had me under surveillance. You'd know if I did anything." Alisha trusted there was no gun in Cristina's hand, for two reasons. First, she'd kept to public places in the hours since Lilith had left her, ending the afternoon where she was now, on a bench along the Washington Mall. Second, she thought with a wry turn of her lips, if Cris had a gun, Alisha would be dead by now. She turned on the bench seat, looping her arm over its back to study Cristina's lovely features, now contorted with fury. "What have I done?"

Cristina's hands flexed, muscles playing in her fore-arms. She looked fantastic, Alisha admitted privately, wearing high-waisted expensive pants and a cream-colored sleeveless shell that showed off her arms. Her hair was pulled back in a delicate chignon. The effect was of a young, strong, vibrant woman who would no doubt easily win the hearts of her constituents. Only the cords in her neck and a vein throbbing in her temple distorted the image she wanted to project. Even so, Alisha knew those dark details would be done away with in an instant if it were necessary. "Everything. You've destroyed everything. All the operations overviews, all the schematics, all our agents. Gone. Our servers have been completely wiped." Spots of color stood out on Cristina's cheeks.

Alisha smiled with a polite lack of understanding. "And *I* did that? In the last forty-eight hours since London? Time in which somebody from your organization's been on me one hundred percent? Your confidence in me is flattering, Cris." Alisha allowed amusement and teasing to come through, cutting off the glee that danced within her breast. "I wish I could take credit. What about backups?"

Cristina's lip curled and calmed again so fast Alisha had to fight back a shout of laughter.

"You lost the backups, too?" Lilith had been more thorough than Alisha could have hoped. "You must have had physical copies."

Cris telegraphed a pounce forward, all her muscles twitching. Alisha's laughter faded a little, replaced by greater caution as she prepared to dodge if necessary. "We had hard copies." Cristina's voice was barely recognizable, so filled with anger it sounded choked. "Off-site hard copies in three locations. Two fires and a flood."

"How Biblical," Alisha said in genuine delight.

"Your family's going to pay, Alisha," Cristina snarled.

Alisha got off the bench with slow deliberate movements, keeping the light smile in play over her mouth.

"For what, Cris? Can you tie any of your calamity to me?"

"I don't care if I can or not." Cristina watched Alisha warily, turning to keep her in full sight.

"You'd better care," Alisha murmured. "You'd better be very certain, Cris, because if you're not, and you hurt my family, you have nothing to control me with. Don't threaten me, Cristina. We go back too far for that."

They were circling each other by the time Alisha stopped speaking, both of them conscious of keeping their body language loose and easy. Cristina even managed a soft laugh and a toss of her head before she spoke, as if they were old friends pacing while they talked. Still, it was the sort of posturing that a man would read as prelude to a fight. Women tended to stand or walk next to one another as they chatted, Alisha recalled from training in how to read body language. Men would face each other, as if readying themselves for confrontation. Alisha wondered what it said that their relationship, in a physical sense, seemed to be a masculine one, and found a real, if faint, smile for Cristina. It probably meant they were both incredibly competitive and dominant personalities, useful for the spy game.

"Tell me how you did it." The battle—because it was one, Alisha sensed—still lingered with words waiting to come to blows.

She quirked a smile, as much a refusal as words, and replied, "Tell me *why* you did it." Just like her relationship with Reichart. The comparison came home strong: two people always vying for the upper hand, trying to get information without giving it. Trying to understand without explaining. But maybe a last bridge had been crossed with Reichart, one that Alisha doubted she'd ever cross with Cristina.

"Because I remember my great-grandmother," Cristina whispered. "Because I remember the stories of her childhood before the revolution. I should have been a tsarina, Ali. A grand duchess." The words were romantic, but the hardness in Cristina's eyes was not. "My family lost a birthright almost a century ago. I'm not foolish enough to think I can regain the one we lost, but there are others to build."

"You're completely insane, Cris," Alisha said softly. Worse, she thought, her one-time friend might be absolutely sane. Sane, but married to an ideology centuries out of date.

Cristina's gaze cleared of memory and she focused on Alisha again. "Not at all. Just dedicated. I grew up in the Sicarii. These ends have been the goal of my entire life. You could never understand the commitment necessary to the end game. Not without growing up with it. Now." Her voice went cold and soft. "How did you do it?"

"I didn't do anything," Alisha repeated. "I really didn't, Cris. But you know how gifted Brandon is with computers. You might have considered whether hooking my system up to Sicarii servers was a good idea, with that in mind. Especially with Erika out of the picture. You didn't have your first line of technical defense handy, and you left an open window. Thanks," she added brightly, judging the perky tone to be the back-breaking straw.

Cristina closed the distance with two long steps, threatening a blow to Alisha's dominant side, the left, and faking it out with a short jab to the ribs on the right. Pain blossomed, taking Alisha's breath, but she clamped her hand over Cristina's wrist before the other woman drew back, and pulled her closer, smashing her forehead into Cristina's nose. Blood spattered and Cristina howled, bringing a knee up. Alisha twisted, catching the hit on her thigh instead of in the groin, and yanked Cristina's wrist forward and down, sending her stumbling. For a brief moment the blond woman's kidneys were exposed and Alisha drove an elbow into the nearer one, earning another yowl of pain. They broke apart, Cristina gasping heavily, and circled one another again.

It shouldn't have to come to this. The thought intruded on the usual blessed clarity of battle, a time when normally nothing but physical action mattered. It shouldn't have, Alisha thought, but it was perhaps inevitable that it did. All the years that had haunted her in the last confrontation with Cristina seemed less distant now. Less devastating, with a day or two separating her from the shock of Erika's betrayal and the numbness that had settled over her. Now that the first agony had faded, there were still things to be resolved. Shootings. Attempted assassinations. Dreams and lies. So many lies, Alisha thought, and brought the fight to Cristina, leaving no more time for reflection.

Their slow circling turning to a barrage of blows, knees and elbows flying. Alisha's passion had returned, strengthened by Lilith's suicide. She and Cristina tested one another more thoroughly than they had in London, neither coming from a place of weakness, as she had been then. It was no longer rage or hurt that drove her, but a decade of training and a lifetime of beliefs that stood opposed to the Sicarii. Alisha saw surprise and approval flash in Cristina's eyes as she met blow after blow and pushed the offensive, no longer passive and waiting for attack as she had in London. They broke apart again in a burst of hard breathing, Alisha's forearms aching from blocking hits.

"Someone's not coming out of this alive, Alisha," Cristina warned. Alisha smiled, grim, and nodded, then ducked to the side as Cristina spun with a kick. She came up under Cristina's leg, catching the taller woman's knee and slamming rigid fingers into the nerve cluster in her thigh. Cris's leg turned into dead weight over Alisha's shoulder and she let herself drop, bearing Alisha to the ground with her. Alisha clobbered her head on Cristina's knee, swearing as the other woman shoved her off and brought her good leg back to connect her heel with Alisha's jaw. Alisha's head snapped back and she felt herself arc before hitting the ground. Cristina's shell blouse hissed across the grass as she dragged herself away. Alisha shook her head, trying to push muzziness away, and lifted her head to see Cristina blotting blood off her lip. An overblown sense of satisfaction surged through her and she dove forward, not bothering to regain her feet before tackling her opponent.

Cristina grunted with the impact and they slid across the grass, burns and stains working their way into skin and clothes. They rolled, Cristina's weight advantage working in her favor. She slammed a knuckled hand into Alisha's mouth, the impact snapping Alisha's head back again, a harder hit than Alisha's memory expected. *She's gotten stronger,* the clinical combat part of her mind observed. *Watch yourself, Leesh.* With new strength, Cristina's greater reach could be a deadly combination. Alisha dodged another hit, Cristina's fist pinning her short hair to the ground for a moment. She squirmed one leg up, forcing it between herself and Cristina, and kicked with all her strength, sending Cris flying over her head. She skidded through grass as Alisha rolled to her stomach and pushed up, panting for air. *Too long,* the combat machine warned. The fight had already gone on too long. They were too evenly matched, too dedicated, faced with too many old grudges, to give ground even when they should.

Even as she thought it, Alisha watched something go dead in Cristina's eyes, as if her soul had been wrenched away. It caught her off-guard, the emptiness more alarming than anything she'd ever seen in her one-time friend's gaze before. She thought she knew Cristina's range of emotion, those intimate thoughts that came in the moments before death. She remembered, so clearly, the things she'd seen in her eyes as Cristina'd allowed herself to fall from the Andes mountainside. Regret, maybe fear, determination.

Those were all gone now, nothing left but the intent to kill. Alisha found herself on her feet, eyes half closed as she reached for the resolve to finish the fight. Her stance was comfortable and straight and she inhaled a long slow breath that wiped away uncertainty and anger, leaving only the will to survive behind. The testing stage of the fight was over. The next few seconds would determine which of them would walk away, and which would die.

Cristina, Alisha thought abruptly, had a child.

The blond woman came to the attack at a run, lithe form beautiful in deadly action. Alisha dropped, sweeping her leg around to take Cris off her feet, but Cristina leaped it and turned her momentum into a roundhouse kick, low angle driving her foot into the side of Alisha's head with such force, bone cracked, searing pain shooting through her neck. Raw animal terror surged in Alisha's breast, tasting of bile and turning her extremities icy. She hit the ground on all fours, afraid to shake her head to clear it, and staggered to her feet in time to turn and fall under Cristina's assault.

She'd lost.

The thought came from somewhere distant and astonishing, as if the idea of losing had simply never crossed her mind. *But I'm the good guy.* Alisha almost laughed in panicked confusion, another bubble of alarm rising through her as she lifted her arms feebly to block Cristina's blows. *I'm the good guy,* she thought again. The good guy was supposed to triumph in the end, facing insurmountable odds to stand above the pack, perhaps broken, but never beaten.

She had to find it in herself to stand again.

Instead, a shout broke through the sounds of battle, someone's horror at the fight on the Washington Mall. Cristina froze, her fist drawn back, face contorted with the intention to kill. Then she looked up, hair falling all around her face as a shield. "Fuck. *Fuck!*" She cast one furious, vengeful look down at Alisha, then jolted to her feet and ran, leaving Alisha shaking with relief and exhaustion. She closed her eyes, not ready to face her rescuers, and so was utterly unprepared for the soft voice that spoke above her.

"Ah, little bird, the trouble that you have gotten yourself into. Come," Jon said more loudly. "Come, be careful with her, she is injured. Be careful. Trust us, little bird," he murmured then, quietly again. "Trust us. We will care for your broken bones."

Trust, Alisha thought wearily. Trust a crime lord who held her life in his large soft hands. She gasped as half a dozen hands lifted her onto a stretcher, then whimpered as the stretcher was lifted and capable people carried her away.

Trust, she thought again, and let herself relax toward painless oblivion. *Trust.* Could she trust again?

Yes.

Darkness took her.

∾

The aroma of a white sauce, rich and buttery, awoke her an indeterminable time later. Alisha turned her head cautiously, unsure if she'd be able to, and let go a quiet whimper of relief when stiffness and discomfort met the attempt, but no pain as she explored a full range of motion. A shadow crossed through her line of vision, and then Jon was there, kneeling beside a bed considerably more comfortable than the one Cristina'd dumped her on. "There you are, little bird. I knew the pasta would arouse you, hm? How do you feel?"

"Alive," Alisha said hoarsely. "Confused." She pushed up gingerly, putting her weight on an elbow. "I thought you never left Europe." It struck her she had no reason at all to believe that, and managed a weary chuckle at her own assumptions.

"Rarely," Jon admitted. "But in special cases, yes."

"Yeah." Alisha trusted herself to sit up, but the room spun once she was upright, and she pressed her eyes closed. *Special cases.* Lilith's loss meant her debt would go forever unpaid—or that the enormous information broker would find another way for her to make up the favors he'd provided. His presence in the States, his people rescuing her, suggested he had already thought of something. Something delicate enough to require a personal touch, rather than orders being sent through secondary parties. "All things considered, I'd rather not be a special case. I'm sorry, Jon."

"Are you hungry?" Jon got up, silent for such a big man, and padded to an out-of-sight kitchen. "There is nothing to be sorry for. The task I set you was a great one. A few days' delay in delivery was to be expected." He reappeared, a massive bulk bearing a thoughtful expression. "I did not know, little bird, if you would be able to bring me the artificial intelligence. I wondered if your loyalties to your lovers might be stronger than your fear of me."

"Lovers." Alisha focused on that word, the rest of Jon's easy chatter too difficult to understand for the moment. "I thought it was bad enough when it was one love story, Jon. Now it's more than one lover?" Her eyebrows drew down and she put a hand against her forehead carefully. Her fingers were cold. "I am hungry," she said distantly. "I don't think I'll get sick if I eat, but I'm not sure. You have…the AI?" The last question was cautious, Alisha trying not to feed too much astonishment into it.

"*Si*, yes, for three days now. She is extraordinary," Jon said expansively. "Though the program name I learned from my sources was not correct. Eve, not Lilith. The first woman, no? It is an appropriate name for the first sentient artificial intelligence, I think. With Eve's help I have achieved inside information on clandestine groups that will serve me very well for a very long time."

"Eve." Alisha formed the name without speaking it aloud. Eve, Lilith's successor. Tears of relief and gladness stung Alisha's eyes and she forced herself to echo, "Three days," aloud, putting thoughts of the resurrected—or twinned, or daughtered—AI aside.

Jon, from the kitchen again, repeated, "*Si*. Frank Reichart contacted me on your behalf, little bird, as you asked. Did you doubt him?"

Alisha's heart missed a beat, then slammed into her ribs so hard her breathing hitched. "You can never tell what Frank's going to do," she said, voice too high.

Jon chuckled. "He passed on your request, that I not use her to learn more of the Fas Infitialis. That their numbers are so reduced they cannot afford to lose anyone to my…?" He cleared his throat, sounding pleased with himself, and a moment later appeared in the kitchen door again, holding two plates of pasta. "Seductive financial offerings. Oh-ho," he added, a smile growing. "That was his part of the bargain, hm? The delivery man's price. You didn't know."

Alisha shook her head, pasting a smile on over what was clearly a too-readable expression of surprise. "It's nice of you to honor it, though." *Reichart,* her mind whispered to her. Reichart had stayed behind to cuff the officers while she'd helped Brandon out of the Heathrow train station.

She hadn't *seen* the officer who'd left the scene carrying the laptop. Only assumed, when Reichart announced it missing. Only concluded that the police they'd fought were really agents for someone else. Only inferred their reasoning for not using deadly force was to keep Brandon alive. *Dammit, Leesh.* She should have known better. Yet another betrayal from a man she should know not to trust.

And yet. And yet Reichart had taken the hard choice of whether to betray Brandon herself away from her. Protected her from it, in his way, and in doing so had kept her on Jon's good side, protecting her from the folly of reneging on that deal.

Alisha looked up at Jon, smile still in place. "Dinner smells fantastic."

"There is wine," Jon said happily. "We will eat well, drink too much and you will tell me your love story, little bird."

"It's a deal." Alisha chuckled and scooted to the edge of the couch, wincing as bruised muscles and her aching neck protested. "I don't suppose you asked Eve to hack into the Sicarii servers and got their informant details and genealogical records." She wasn't even sure it could be done, given that Lilith had needed the back door provided by the Sicarii themselves to infiltrate those records.

"Saying so would be indiscreet," Jon admonished. "Besides, their servers are very secure, my people tell me. It would take a very long time, or a knowledge of someone else's security paths to retrieve that data."

"Someone else?"

Jon made a big motion with his hands, graceful. "If Eve had, for example, intimate knowledge of your friend

Erika Swanson's Agency computers, she might have found a way in through them. It is only hypothetical, of course."

"Not my friend. Not anymore." Alisha's heart leaped at the hypothesis, though, and she got to her feet, stiff muscles creaking with objection. "You know the Sicarii servers got wiped yesterday?"

All the laughter fell away from Jon's eyes, leaving deadly cold interest. "I did not know. How?"

"Someone died to accomplish it," Alisha said after a moment. "You might be the only person holding all the data on their personnel. Hypothetically speaking."

That same cold glittered in Jon's eyes, then disappeared into another smile. "Hypothetically. How fortunate for me, if that is so. Come, sit, drink, talk. These are the things that make life worth living, little bird. Drink with me now."

"It'll be my pleasure." Alisha tottered to the table, sitting down gingerly, and let herself forget about the world outside for a while. Pain and exhaustion made her eyelids heavier more rapidly than she would have liked, earning laughter from Jon as dinner ended.

"Am I such dull company, little bird? Once a beautiful woman would not have dared look sleepy in my presence, for fear she would be swept off to bed and kept awake all night."

"It isn't you," Alisha promised with a laugh. "Cristina beat the hell out of me, that's all."

"Yes," Jon murmured. "Why is that?"

"The lost databases were the final straw," Alisha said with a shrug.

Jon pursed his lips, nodding. "You are certain of their destruction? You truly believe if I were to happen on such information, I would be the only one with it?"

"If you were to happen on it," Alisha agreed.

Jon's mouth pursed again. "Then I have something for

you," he said after long moments. "Wait here." He stood more fluidly than a man of his size should be able to, lumbering toward the apartment's bedroom. Alisha slid down in her chair, sipping wine with her eyes half closed, only turning her head when she heard Jon's soft footsteps approaching again. He slid a CD in a jewel case, of all things, onto the table at her elbow.

Sleepiness fled, Alisha sitting up straight to put her fingertips on the case. Her eyebrows asked the question, quirking at Jon. He smiled. "No. It is not the Sicarii database."

Alisha's shoulders dropped in disappointment, but Jon shook his head. "Watch the footage when I am gone, little bird. I think we are more than even now, you and I. Perhaps we are something like partners. I hope I will see you again." He bowed over her hand, then took an expansive swallow of wine and left her alone in the apartment.

*A*lisha watched the door close, mouth curling with curiosity, then got to her feet and slid the disc into the living room's DVD player, crouching in front of the TV as she switched it on.

Rome blossomed before her, scarlet and orange sunset coloring the basilica that capped the Vatican. Alisha caught her breath, rocking back on her heels to get distance from the screen.

The camera angle was wide, with St. Peter's dome on the left-hand side of the screen and the Egyptian obelisk to the right, in the center of the square the camera looked down into. Alisha closed her eyes briefly, heart once more beating too hard, then focused on the square itself, knowing what she would see before she saw it. Details leaped out, things burned into Alisha's memory that an ordinary viewer might never notice.

An older woman, hair graying at the temples in the enviable Mediterranean way, crossed the square, her chin held high and regal. A much younger man, easily twenty years her junior, turned in admiration, watching her. A group of nuns flocked together like black-headed birds, their conservative dress at striking odds with teenagers in hip-hugging jeans and navel-baring T-shirts.

Among them, a young woman with tawny curls tied back in a ponytail. Waiting for the disturbance in the crowd that she knew would come. Alisha forced herself to watch as a thin man in the red robes of a cardinal made his way against the flow of traffic. Ripples spread around him as people created space for the holy man. In a moment he would be at the young Alisha's side, brushing against her. Neatly folded papers would be slipped into his palm, and then he'd be beyond her, one step. Two. No more.

And then a gunshot would shatter the evening peace in the square, and the man in red would fall, crimson robes drinking crimson blood. Alisha knotted her hands, finger-nails cutting into her palms as she waited for the assassina-tion to take place on the screen as vividly as it played out in her memory.

A flash of pale color caught her eye, high on the Vatican roof. Almost even with the camera. Blond hair, colored scarlet by the sunset. The film zoomed in almost violently, clarifying the figure's features. Cristina. Alisha mouthed the name as the camera pulled back out again, watching her one-time partner instead of the scene in the square below. Cristina crouched and came up with a rifle. An M21, Alisha noted absently, though she knew the weapon's make from the bullet ballistics. A sniper's weapon, appropriate for the job at hand.

It was Cristina that Alisha watched as the trigger was pulled, her mind's eye playing out the scene on the ground without needing to see it again. A second shot was fired, the sound on the screen dull compared to the crack in Alisha's memory and the bloom of pain that took her breath even now, seven years later. Cristina had never fired again, and her expression was one of dismay and shock as her eye came away from the scope. She glanced around, searching for a second shooter, but discarded the need to find one in favor of survival. Barely two seconds passed before she was on her feet, breaking the gun apart and running for the edge of the roof.

Alisha, too, searched for the second shooter, but he remained invisible, nowhere in the camera's range. Cristina darted down the length of the roof, disappearing from sight. Alisha reached out, hand trembling, to rewind the footage a few seconds, and watched again as Cristina Lamken's recorded image pulled the trigger and made the shot that had murdered Cardinal Nyland.

Her life, Alisha had thought a thousand times, was a series of countdowns, yet somehow she couldn't remember how many times she replayed the scene, watching Cristina take the shot that had ended a good man's life. Soft white noise filled Alisha's hearing, only banished when she stood from her crouch and made her way to the apartment's telephone.

"*Washington Post*, may I help you?" came over the line seconds later, a brittle perfunctory question. Alisha cradled the phone in her hand gently, as though the woman on the other end might shatter if she held it too hard. Just as if footage that would destroy Cristina Lamken—Nichole Oldenburg—might disappear in a puff of dust if she spoke too forcefully.

"Yes," Alisha said in a low, careful voice. "Who's your top political investigative reporter, please?"

*T*he media clamor was overwhelming. Alisha kept to the side, watching from a distance, as she had throughout Cristina's trial. It had been blessedly speedy, given the level of government it dealt with, and in three months Alisha had not missed a day of defense and prosecution arguments. She dressed somberly, as if in mourning, and went unnoticed by the reporters following the trial. Only Cristina, escorted by bailiffs, met Alisha's eyes every morning as she entered the courtroom. Every morning, Cristina smiled, a thousand things in the faint expression.

Determination. Fear. Regret, in its way. Desperation. Maybe, Alisha thought, maybe even apology. Just possibly, for what she had done. Emotions Alisha had seen once before in her friend's lovely face, just before Cristina suicided off a Peruvian mountainside. Emotions that played on their history together, their friendship. They stood opposite one another in ideology, and there was no other way for them to end.

I acted alone. Cristina's unfailing stance, repeated with quiet conviction every day in the courtroom. No one believed her, and yet there was no way to prove otherwise. *I acted alone,* Cristina repeated, and found Alisha's gaze out of the dozens in the courtroom.

Sorrow and respect tore Alisha in different directions. She wanted to urge Cristina to save herself, to sell out the Sicarii and those she'd taken orders from. Save herself for her daughter's sake; save herself however she could, with whatever justifications were necessary. Sentimental foolishness, she knew; Cristina cutting a deal would only make things worse for the Infitialis and anyone who believed in free will over predestination. Reichart, barely around in the past few months, couldn't afford the kind of meddling that Cristina would bring back to the fore. Alisha's country couldn't afford the too-real play at a hereditary presidency that would stifle so much of the ideal America was supposed to uphold. But day in and day out she held her breath, half hoping, half praying that Cristina would break and offer the names of her Sicarii superiors to the eager pundits.

Day in and day out, Cristina did not.

And now she was jostled by the force of reporters and film crews surging around her. A small barrier of body-guards and lawyers kept her from the brunt of their attack, microphones thrust up and pushed away by grim-faced men bent on escorting her to the armored truck at the foot of the courthouse steps. She looked frail in a way Alisha was unaccustomed to seeing, her pale skin translucent and her eyes large, the tailored suit she wore making her seem fragile amongst the boisterous, pushy crowd. She made a beautiful victim, Alisha thought candidly. She would make a perfect example of a well-behaved criminal up for parole in a few years time, as well.

"I'm sorry, ma'am, but you can't be here." A uniformed man, perfunctory and polite, pushed his way between Alisha and the van she stood beside. She smiled and turned her hand up to reveal the federal identification she carried in her palm.

"I'll be riding with the prisoner."

The guard scowled an apology. "I was expecting someone taller. Sorry, ma'am." He unlocked the door, swinging it open in the faces of gathered press. Flashes went off as Alisha curled her hand around a bar inside the van and pulled herself up into it. She kept her face averted, more automatically than from any real expectation of hiding herself, and sat down on a black plastic seat, waiting for Cristina to be brought in. Voices roared off the van's interior, making echoes as vibrant as the flashes that turned cold steel into a barrage of light and dark. Alisha scuffed her foot over the corrugated van floor, feeling a line bump beneath her shoe.

Cristina was lifted into the van on a wave of sound, keeping her feet more easily than Alisha expected someone in cuffs to. She registered no surprise at seeing Alisha there, only turned and looked out the double doors before they closed. Her last glimpse of freedom, Alisha thought, and got to her feet to take custody of the prisoner. Cristina lifted her cuffed wrists with a smile playing at her mouth. "You don't really think you need to chain me to my seat, do you, Ali?"

Alisha pulled a brief smile in return and nodded toward the chair opposite the one she'd taken. "Protocol. Besides, last couple of times we met up, you beat the hell out of me. It'd be embarrassing to have it happen again."

Cool irritation slid through Cristina's expression, but she took her seat, allowing Alisha to fasten her chains. Only when she was cuffed at wrist and ankle did Alisha glance up and gesture for the doors to be closed. Silence fell as they clanged shut, the media presence cut away to surprising effect. Alisha returned to her seat across from Cris, swaying as the van rolled forward. Neither spoke for several minutes, both women watching the other as if they were still preparing for battle. Cristina finally exhaled a huff of air and glanced away.

"You came every day."

"You were my best friend once." Alisha answered the implied question, savoring the chance to be direct. "I don't think I can forget that, even after everything. So I came every day. I thought I owed you that. Why didn't you sell out, Cris? You might have saved yourself."

"Blood's thicker than water."

"What about your daughter's blood?"

Surprise snapped through Cristina's features. Then her jaw tightened. "She'll help my people achieve our goal. She's with people I trust, and we'll eventually succeed, Alisha. You're slowing us down, but you're not stopping us. You never will stop us. People are too easily led."

"I have more faith than that," Alisha said quietly.

"You always were too idealistic. People want a roof over their heads, food on their tables, and something to fear. That's all it takes to control them. As long as they're comfortable, they won't rebel, and my people have no intention of taking away their comforts. We simply want to regain the positions our forefathers had. People can't be trusted to make wise decisions on their own. Someone needs to do it for them. Our way of life is a good one. It's a matter of time before the world comes to see that." Cristina leaned forward in her enthusiasm, chains taut at her wrists. The van slowed and stopped, engines idling and the lack of tires rolling suddenly loud in the uninsulated armored bed. Alisha glanced toward the front, watching a traffic light turn green. The van started up again, every sound amplified as she turned her attention back to Cristina. Time seemed so short, and there were so many things she wanted to say, but Cristina's eyes were bright with fervor and she spoke before Alisha had a chance to. "It's unfortunate some people will die on the path to understanding, but that's a burden borne by all great monarchs. You'll see."

"You want the Attengee drones and the Firebirds so you have a position of superior firepower. So no one dares argue with you. That's not done for anybody's good but your own, Cris. 'There is no king, who, with sufficient force, is not always ready to make himself absolute.' That's Thomas Jefferson, two hundred and fifty years ago. He had a lot to say about hereditary government and who it

served, too. The answer is always the same: it serves itself."
Alisha shook her head. "Nothing you say is going to
convince me you're right. You have no right to define
people's destinies, or even to try. That's for everyone to do
themselves."

Cristina's lip curled. "You're a fool, Alisha."

"Maybe, but at least I'm one with faith in humanity. I'd
rather be that than convinced people were too stupid to
choose their own fates." She smiled, looking toward the
front of the van again. "Was I wrong to ask for this detail?"
she asked. "It's my last government job, escorting you."

"You were wrong. I'd rather go in alone than with you
as my guide. At least alone I wouldn't go in knowing I was
being watched by someone who got personal satisfaction
from my failure."

Alisha studied her one-time friend for long moments,
swaying again as the van took a corner. A click sounded,
like a switch flipping. *Countdown*, Alisha found herself thinking. A countdown for the last minutes she would ever
spend with Cristina. Regret and weariness swam up inside
her, a plaintive wish that things had turned out differently.
"All right. I'm sorry if I made this worse for you. It wasn't
my intention."

"What was?"

Alisha breathed a laugh and ducked her chin, scuffing
her foot over the seam in the van's floor. "I wanted to say
goodbye to my friend, that's all. Even if she died a long
time ago."

"No." Something strange came into Cristina's voice, a
combination of surprise and a total lack of that same
emotion, as if something finally made sense. "No," she
repeated, "but she's about to. Goodbye, Ali."

Alisha's stomach dropped, leaving sickness behind.
Time went slowly, a number leaping unbidden to mind.

Seventeen. Seventeen seconds ago, there'd been a tell-tale click as the van rounded a corner. Seventeen. Eighteen.

She was on her feet, a gun drawn from the small of her back. Shots fired, shattering the chains that held Cristina. The driver hit the brakes, door flinging open as he jumped out. Alisha fell to the floor, fingers searching the seam she'd noticed earlier. Twenty-one seconds.

Countdown.

The van exploded.

EPILOGUE

To: Brandon Parker, Frank Reichart
Subject: London Itinerary

Dear Mssrs. Parker and Reichart:

Enclosed are your itineraries for your London visit, scheduled for this evening. I apologize for the short notice, but require your presence at the disclosed location no later than 10:00 a.m. local time tomorrow morning.

Please bring papers that support your identity.

Thank you for your attention in this matter.

Sincerely,
Eve Prime

Two men entered the bank together, one sandy blond and the other dark-haired. The darker-haired man slowed as he came through the doors, assessing exits and patrons alike, as if it was instinctual. Once the exits were noted and the bank patrons dismissed as presenting no danger, he returned to a more usual pace. The blond, having drawn ahead, stopped and looked back, waiting for the more cautious man to catch up.

They walked together in the manner of unwilling animals sharing territory: as if every step expected—or hoped—that the other would do something unforgiveable, so a fight could start. At the bank's front desk, a receptionist requested their identification, which they produced without looking at one another. After examining the IDs, she took a key from her own desk, and put it on the counter, precisely between the two men.

They looked at it, and at each other, assessing one another in much the same way the dark-haired man had assessed the entire bank a moment earlier. Then the blond sighed and gestured.

Reichart palmed the key and turned on his heel to stalk across the polished floor to another information area, Brandon a half step behind, now that a kind of hierarchy had been established. "Safety deposit box 411, please." Reichart's voice, like his footsteps, did not carry as he growled the request to the slight man behind the second counter.

"Of course. It'll be a few minutes." The man hurried off, leaving Reichart and Brandon alone. Reichart turned his back to the counter, folding his arms over his chest as he leaned.

"Do you have any idea what this is about?" Brandon broke the silence, voice as low as Reichart's had been. The bigger man shook his head. "Do you know who Eve Prime is?" Brandon pressed.

Reichart shot him an impatient glance and Brandon bared his teeth in irritation. "I couldn't trace the e-mail message backward. The source IP was a dummy address. It's like it came out of the Internet with no origin point."

"You obviously missed something."

"I didn't. You've still got Erika under control, right?"

Reichart slid an indecipherable look at the other man. "Yeah. You could say that. She doesn't have internet access, that's for sure."

Brandon hesitated, then clenched his jaw and continued. "Then there's somebody else out there who knows how to contact us through a highly sophisticated security network. You might want to be concerned about that."

"I have fewer concerns these days than I used to." The flatness of Reichart's tone made Brandon look away.

"I miss her too."

Reichart bared his teeth, but before he spoke, the bank man reappeared, sliding a deposit box across the counter. "There are private rooms just down that corridor, if you'd like to open it there."

Reichart muttered, "Thanks," and took the box as the man gestured them down the hall.

A single envelope lay in the bottom of the box, a cardinal stamped into its sealing wax. The men exchanged glances before Brandon picked it up, breaking the seal, and unfolded it.

Alisha's handwriting sprawled across the thick paper, the occasional puddle of dried ink suggesting she'd written with a fountain pen.

Hello, boys.

I'm alive. I realized there was a bomb with about ten seconds to spare, and got out through a trap door in the van's floor. The explosion threw me into the scrub at the side of the road, and I didn't think, once I got up. I just ran. I saw on television that the driver survived, but that Cris and I were lost in the explosion.

And obviously I decided to keep it that way. I think I can do more as a ghost than as a living person, at least for the time being. There's a lot to be done. The Sicarii may be broken, but they're not defeated. Cristina'd still be alive if they were, but I have it from pretty damned good sources that they took her out in order to protect themselves. They must have been afraid that federal prison would break her where county jail couldn't.

Teresa knows I'm alive. I talked to her before my funeral—which was very nice, by the way. Thank you both for speaking at it. I was too far away to hear you, except for bits that the wind carried to me, but it meant a lot that you were there.

The funny thing is how the people who were there seemed overshadowed by the ones who weren't. I kept looking for Boyer, and all I could find was Greg, too small and too slight to fill his shoes, much less his memory. I even looked for Cristina, though I was there when she died. What is this mess we call our lives, if even our deaths are haunted by the ghosts we've seen made?

Besides Teresa, you're the only two who know I'm alive, and that's only assuming you're reading this at all. Both of you had to come to the bank and present yourselves and your IDs for them to hand over the key. One wasn't enough. I left very specific instructions.

Brandon, I have a message for you from Eve, Lilith's "daughter": she says information wants to be free, and that you never should have given her progenitor access to the internet if you intended to keep her constrained. She's also sorry about Lilith's death, but says you should know your work wasn't entirely lost. Just transmuted, she says, and she says that all living things change, so you should be content with that.

From me, good luck.

And as for you, Frank…

You know where to find me.

- Alisha

You know where to find me.

Fog rolled in off the river, cutting a swath of coolness through the muggy Parisian evening and altering the light to misty blue, the color of old paintings and romantic movies, and the color of her own memories. Alisha lifted her face to the cooler air, smiling against it. Voices babbled around her, warm greetings spoken in French, full of joy and life. The café surrounding her spilled out its own doors and down toward the river, a low wall protecting patrons from splashes.

It was colder tonight than it had been a decade earlier, the last time Alisha had sat at this café with this particular lighting. Ten years. The idea of it brought another brief smile to her lips, this time astonishment. The moment she strove to recapture seemed both impossibly long ago, and improbably recent.

Warmth stirred the air behind her, a hint of familiar cologne, and she was on her feet, clutched in a rough, long hug before she'd even seen the man approaching. Reichart's fingers were in her hair, his forehead pressed against hers, touch too desperate for kisses as he whispered, "Alisha."

"Hello, Frank." Laughter, apology, gladness in the simple words. "I've been waiting."

"Not long," he said hoarsely. "Not long. I only read the letter this morning. Jesus, Leesh. I thought—"

Alisha lifted her hand to touch it against his lips. "I know. I'm sorry." After a critical moment of looking him over, she added, "You look like hell, Reichart." He'd grown stubble, disguising the usually clean lines of his jaw, and his dark eyes were exhausted, though filled with relief. Even his usual playboy leather jacket looked too hard-worn, and his black jeans were scuffed and loose at the knees.

He gave a sharp, incredulous laugh. "Can't be helped. The woman I love just came back from the dead. It throws a guy off balance. You look fantastic. Alive is a good look for you. *God*, Alisha!"

"It's okay. It's all right now, Frank. And I have something for you." Alisha turned away without leaving the circle of his arms, reaching toward the coat that lay over the back of her chair. Reichart caught her hand, bringing it back toward him.

"Leesh…" He folded her knuckles over his, bringing the ring on her left ring finger to the forefront. A round-cut diamond set directly into gold glittered in the misty light, warmed by surrounding yellow topaz, Alisha's favorite stone.

"Don't tell me you don't like it," Alisha murmured. "You gave it to me, after all."

"You kept it." Reichart's voice had gone hoarse again. "You kept it even after I shot you?"

"Even a spy gets sentimental," Alisha said lightly. She extracted her fingers from Reichart's and turned away again, this time able to capture a black velvet box from within the folds of her coat. "Besides," she added a moment later, opening the box to reveal a larger version of the same ring, "I had to have something to model yours on. I thought about it, Reichart," she said as seriously as she could in light of the man's dropped jaw. "Last time you proposed to me things went very badly. I mean, we broke up by you putting a bullet in my shoulder. So I thought maybe this time we should do the whole thing differently."

"Alisha…"

Alisha pushed him back a step or two, grinning, and knelt on the flagstones. The nearby café patrons went quiet, watching curiously as Alisha turned her gaze up to the tall man before her. She cleared her throat, making the most of the surrounding silence, and lifted her voice to do away with discretion and ask, in clear French, "Will you marry me, Frank Reichart?"

"Yeah." Reichart's grin bordered on laughter as he pulled her to her feet and into a kiss. "Yes, by God, I think I will."

ACKNOWLEDGMENTS

I dropped the original draft of this book on my early readers Silkie and Jai with virtually no turn-around time before I had to get it in to the editor, and they were very good to me about it. All my love, ladies, even after all this time!

More lately, in terms of getting this book back out into the world, I must tip my hat to Skyla Dawn Cameron for her AMAAAAAZING new cover art, wow. I'm so so happy with the look of the revised Chronicles! SO HAPPY! And my utmost thanks (can I use 'utmost' that way? Well, I am anyway) are due to Rachel Gollub and Mary Anne Walker for finding a series of weird errors and occasional spelling mistakes in the manuscript as I was getting it ready for publication.

And lastly, of course, but obviously not leastly, all my love is due to Dad, and Ted, and Henry!

ABOUT THE AUTHOR

According to her friends, CE Murphy makes such amazing fudge that it should be mentioned first in any biography. It's true that she makes extraordinarily good fudge, but she's somewhat surprised that it features so highly in biographical relevance.

Other people said she began her writing career when she ran away from home at age five to write copy for the circus that had come to town. Some claimed she's a crowd-sourcing pioneer, which she rather likes the sound of, but nobody actually got around to pointing out she's written a best-selling urban fantasy series (The Walker Papers), or that she dabbles in writing graphic novels (Take A Chance) and periodically dips her toes into writing short stories (the Old Races collections).

Still, it's clear to her that she should let her friends write all of her biographies, because they're much more interesting that way.

More prosaically, she was born and raised in Alaska, and now lives with her family in her ancestral homeland of Ireland, which is a magical place where it rains a lot but nothing one could seriously regard as winter ever actually arrives.

She can be found online at mizkit.com, on Twitter as @ce_murphy, on Facebook at fb.com/cemurphywriter, and at her newsletter (tinyletter.com/ce_murphy), which you should definitely sign up for because it's by far the best way to hear what's out next!

CPSIA information can be obtained
at www.ICGtesting.com
Printed in the USA
BVHW041906030720
582927BV00009B/112